"She's mine, isn't she?"

Lila could hear the hope in his question. Her throat closed. Katie had been hers alone for eight years. She'd been the one to cuddle her, feed her, nurse her and play with her. She'd been the one to tuck her in at night with a hundred kisses. And now she'd be the one to introduce her to her father.

"Yes." One word whispered on a thin breath of air. She gave Jason the word that would change everything for both of them. She said it again—louder this time—and watched his smile emerge. The smile that could melt her like rich chocolate on a hot summer day. His grin widened, a dimple appeared....

And, God help her, she was eighteen again....

Dear Reader,

After his twin brother died on the night of their senior prom, Jason Parker disappeared from Pilgrim Cove. Nine years later he returns in order to make peace with his family... with Lila Sullivan, the woman he can't forget...and with himself. But nothing and no one is the same as he remembers. Certainly not his family. Not Lila, with her fiancé and a child. Not even his old house. Can a wanderer ever find home again? Do second chances really exist?

Bart Quinn and the ROMEOS say *yes*. All Jason needs is a quiet place on the beach to do some catching up, and Sea View House is the perfect place for that. Little do the good-hearted seniors know that for Jason, Sea View House holds explosive memories. Exciting memories. Memories of Lila.

Pilgrim Cove. I'd like to extend my deep appreciation to each and every reader for joining me on my visits there. Special thanks to those who wrote to me. It seems we'd all like to live in Pilgrim Cove! Also, a sincere thank-you to my editors for believing in the idea and for giving me a chance to make that idea a reality. I have truly loved writing these stories.

Enjoy!

Linda Barrett

P.S. I'd love to hear from you! Please e-mail to linda@linda-barrett.com or write to P.O. Box 1934, Houston, TX 77284-1934. Visit me on the Web and enter a contest: www.linda-barrett.com.

THE DAUGHTER
HE NEVER KNEW

Linda Barrett

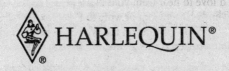

HARLEQUIN®

TORONTO • NEW YORK • LONDON
AMSTERDAM • PARIS • SYDNEY • HAMBURG
STOCKHOLM • ATHENS • TOKYO • MILAN • MADRID
PRAGUE • WARSAW • BUDAPEST • AUCKLAND

ISBN 0-373-71289-8

THE DAUGHTER HE NEVER KNEW

Copyright © 2005 by Linda Barrett.

CAST OF CHARACTERS

Lila Sullivan	Bart Quinn's granddaughter and partner
Jason Parker	Twin son of Sam Parker
Katie Sullivan Parker	Lila and Jason's eight-year-old daughter
Maggie Quinn Sullivan	Bart's daughter, Lila's mother Partner in The Lobster Pot Married to Tom Sullivan, Lila's father
Adam Fielding	Veterinarian, Lila's fiancé
Bart Quinn	Realtor for Sea View House Father of Maggie Sullivan and Thea Cavelli Grandfather of Lila Quinn Sullivan Great-grandfather of Katie Sullivan
Thea Quinn Cavelli	Bart's daughter, Maggie's sister Partner in The Lobster Pot Married to Charlie Cavelli

THE ROMEOS (RETIRED OLD MEN EATING OUT)

Bart Quinn	Unofficial leader of the ROMEOS
Sam Parker	Jason's dad, works part-time with older son Matt
Joe Cavelli	Thea's father-in-law
Rick "Chief" O'Brien	Retired police chief; married to Dee Barnes
Lou Goodman	Retired high school librarian; Rachel's father; married to Pearl
Max "Doc" Rosen	Retired physician
Ralph Bigelow	Retired electrician
Mike Lyons	Retired engineer

To Sandy and Rick

Sometimes a love is so right....
When I think of you together, I smile inside and out,
and can't wait to dance at the wedding!

Books by Linda Barrett

HARLEQUIN SUPERROMANCE

PROLOGUE

Los Angeles, CA

WAS THIS THE BEGINNING of his life or the end?

Jason Parker removed his headset and stared into the glass booth at the Latin heartthrob whose voice had captivated millions of listeners in recent years. The singer had just finished recording and looked like he was in another world. A good sign, thought Jason as he waited for the vocalist to emerge. Luis Torres would spin Jason's words and music into gold…or platinum…as he'd done several times before.

This particular lyric, however, had come at a high price. With every word Jason had written, pain had traveled from his hand to his heart. But he'd kept on writing. About Jared. About Lila. About loneliness. About home.

However, he'd finished the damn song without Jack Daniel's to keep him company! And that felt good.

"J.J.," called the singer, coming toward Jason,

then slapping him on the back. "We have a winner! When this song hits the air, every woman in the world is Lila. Or wants to be. Yes? No? You agree?"

Jason inhaled hard. Lila! For nine years, he'd carried her image with him. Hearing her name in conversation jarred him. He didn't care about every woman in the world! He cared only about Lila and her reaction to the song. But he nodded and thanked Luis, and tried to focus on the man's next words as he waved over the conductor and technicians.

"The chorus would be richer with harmony," said Luis. With features set, he stared at Jason. "And your voice will blend very well, my friend. Let's do it."

Jason took another deep breath, then turned around and walked a few steps before facing the singer again. "We've discussed this before, and the answer's still no. You're the voice. I'm the writer. If you want harmony, we can cut another track, and you can sing with yourself."

But Luis was shaking his head, his dark eyes intense. "Ahh, *mi amigo,* trust me to know. Do what I say, and the music will be complete. And maybe you will be, too."

Jason stood rigid, and Luis continued. "We'll take a vote when we're done if you don't like the sound. In the true American way." He looked at all the musicians in the studio and swept his arm toward them. "We have very qualified voters, no?"

Glaring at the vocalist, Jason knew he'd been outmaneuvered. Luis was the one with the real clout. It was his voice and style that sold records. Jason sighed, took his headset and walked into the recording booth. New beginnings were always difficult. A little more pain wouldn't kill him.

CHAPTER ONE

Three months later
Pilgrim Cove, Massachusetts

ON THE FIRST TUESDAY MORNING in May, Bartholomew Quinn, dapper in bow tie and suspenders under a lightweight sport jacket, tugged open the glass door of the Diner on the Dunes and made his way to the reserved booth at the back. He glanced at the round table, but none of his pals had shown up yet. He was alone, on purpose, with some special reading material he wanted to enjoy.

He chose a seat facing the front of the diner and made himself comfortable. From his inside jacket pocket, he withdrew a white business envelope, removed a thick sheaf of papers and flattened them out on the table. Although it was still in draft form, he was eager to get started on what would be the newest entry to the *Sea View House Journal*. The courtship of Rachel Goodman and Jack Levine would be the most exciting chapter yet.

Of course, he'd felt the same way when he'd read

Shelley Anderson and Daniel Stone's tale, and before that, Laura McCloud and Matt Parker's. He chuckled softly. Where would all those young people be without him? Hadn't he thrown each couple together at Sea View House? He'd done some mighty good deeds lately in the name of love. His Rosemary was probably having a good laugh up there in heaven watching his antics.

He glanced at the sunny day through the picture window on the opposite side of the aisle, and listened with half an ear to the rich voice coming in over the speaker system... Beautiful song...whatever it was.

Suddenly, he sat straighter and listened harder. What was the man singing about?

"In my dreams, I am racing there,
To my Lila at the water's edge."

Lila? Which Lila? Who was racing? Where was the water's edge? His heart picked up speed, and his important papers were forgotten. Only one Lila mattered—his precious granddaughter—his only granddaughter.

Bart took a calming breath, then banged his fist on the table, annoyed with himself. He was jumping to conclusions. The song could be about a hundred other Lilas. He listened again.

"A broken pledge
Is all that's left,
In my hometown at the water's edge…oh,
Lila…my Lila…"

The words repeated and faded. *My Lila*. Bart sat perfectly still. Could it be…Jason Parker? Jason certainly had the talent to write a song about the girl he'd loved and abandoned in a hometown near the water's edge. Jason Parker, the boy who'd broken the hearts of so many people.

Bart had known this day would come, and in the beginning, he'd prayed for it to happen as soon as possible. But now, after nine years, he'd been blindsided. Like all of them would be. Especially Lila.

WITH HIS CAR RADIO tuned to his favorite soft-rock station, Sam Parker headed toward the Diner after dropping off his daughter-in-law at the harbor in time to make the 7:30 ferry. Tuesday was one of Laura's Boston days, and she'd get to the city in thirty minutes flat. Sam couldn't help but smile at how wonderfully his son Matt's new marriage was working out.

Nothing was more important than family. At sixty-six, Sam had lived long enough to have learned that. The joy made up for the pain. At least, most of the time.

"Two boys glance in the mirror,
One face is all they see,

Along the shore, they are no more,
What's left of them is me."

What was that? What was Luis Torres singing
about? The words pinched Sam's heart. His hands
broke into a sweat, and the steering wheel slipped
through his fingers, the car lurching to the side of
the road. "Easy, easy, old man," he whispered,
clenching the wheel again. But those words! Two
boys with one face. Like his boys. His twin sons.
Identical twin sons. Jason and Jared.

Sam forced himself to concentrate on his driving.
Straighten the car, watch for cross traffic at the in-
tersection. Accelerate to the next corner. Red light.
Thankfully, he could pause.

He'd missed some of the lyrics, but now he at-
tended to the words once more.

"…in my dreams, I am running there,
With my brother to the water's edge."

The water's edge. Sam's heart thudded again.
The words echoed his sons' childhoods at the beach.
Sam couldn't count the number of times his twin
bundles of energy had run ahead of him to the ocean.
"Only to the water's edge," he'd call after them.
"Those are the rules until I get there." And they'd lis-
tened to their dad. They'd been good boys.

Could the lyrics really be Jason's? Jason, the son

who'd survived the car wreck on the night of the senior prom. Jason, still in pain. Still blaming himself.

Sam listened hard. And unbelievably heard Jason's voice join Luis Torres's. For the first time in nine years, he heard his son's voice! And knew he was alive.

"COME ON, KATIE! We'll be late for school." Lila Sullivan continued to unload the dishwasher as she called to her eight-year-old daughter, but most of her attention was on the music that filled the kitchen with glorious warmth. What a voice! She stood quietly for a moment and closed her eyes, savoring the richness, the yearning. Torres felt the music. Made her feel it, too. She reached for a dinner plate, then paused. Had he said, Lila? She listened again, but only caught the last two lines:

"A broken pledge is all that's left,
In my hometown at the water's edge...oh,
Lila...my Lila..."

Now she focused on the announcer's voice. "That was Luis Torres singing the title cut from his brand new album *At The Water's Edge.* The song was written by J. J. Parks. They've collaborated on others, but I'm predicting platinum for this CD after it's released for sale next week...."

It wasn't the dunes, the sand or the water's edge that pointed to Jason Parker. It wasn't even her name. Not really. Not until he combined it with the broken pledge.

Lila's legs didn't work. She couldn't breathe, couldn't think. But inside, she screamed one word: *Jason.*

Like a tightrope walker balancing on a frayed cord, she made her way slowly across the room. With shaking hands, she placed the dish she held on the counter.

"…The phones have been lighting up," continued the DJ. "One listener said it could be a love song to Pilgrim Cove with our wonderful beach and dunes. But is there a Lila out there in our listening area?"

The announcer's words faded away. The room darkened, and once again Lila walked carefully across the floor, this time allowing herself to collapse into a chair. She took a deep breath. Exhaled. Took another one.

The DJ had given her all the information she needed. J. J. Parks *was* Jason Parker. She didn't have to be Einstein to figure that one out. The two *J*s stood for Jason and Jared.

"Mommy! I'm ready now."

Lila raised her head to look at her excited daughter—who was also Jason's daughter. Katie stood in the doorway with a loaded backpack weighing almost as much as she did. Her grin had gaps where baby teeth used to be, but she looked adorable with her bangs peeking out from under the baseball cap she insisted on wearing.

• "It's sports day at school…and we're gonna play with the teachers and I gotta have my own glove and bat and ball…and…and… Whatsa matter, Mom?"

Lila forced a smile. "Just waiting for you, sweetheart." *And wondering what other surprises Jason might spring after all this time.*

But maybe there wouldn't be anything more. Perhaps he'd written the song simply to earn money. He seemed to have caught a lucky break with Luis Torres, and maybe he just wanted to make the most of it.

Lila clenched her teeth. Money was no excuse. Jason's disappearance had affected so many people who loved him. Including herself. For a long time after he'd left, she wouldn't allow another man in her life.

But nine years was…nine years. She was a woman now, with another life. And another man. She looked at the sparkling engagement ring on her finger. One of Jason's lyrics had hit on the truth. "Too late…" It really was too late.

Strength returned to her limbs, and she jumped from her chair, caught Katie and swung her around the kitchen. "I love you, Katie girl."

"I love you, too, Mommy. For ever and ever and ever."

By the time Lila dropped Katie off at school, she knew she had to make one stop before going to work, even though she and her granddad were in the midst of their busiest season of the year. The phone had been ringing constantly for weeks at Quinn Real Estate and Property Management with people looking to rent for the summer or to buy.

She headed north on Main Street and turned into the Diner's parking lot, checking out the other cars. She saw Bart's Lincoln Town Car and Lou Goodman's Plymouth. She scanned up and down the rows. Yup, there was the chief's Ford. Doc Rosen's Buick. Sam Parker's van. It seemed the regulars had already arrived.

When she reached the entrance, she glanced briefly at the red-and-white sign on the door that proclaimed: Home of the ROMEOs. Despite the unnerving morning she'd already had, a grin emerged as she thought of those *R*etired *O*ld *M*en *E*ating *O*ut. And not a one of them truly retired yet. She doubted they understood what the word meant. And she knew for certain that they'd never retire from what they loved doing: keeping tabs on Pilgrim Cove.

She waved to Dee O'Brien, the chief's wife and the manager of the Diner, ignored her concerned expression, and continued to walk toward the ROMEOs' table.

The table was crowded. Lila studied the men she'd known all her life. Bart spotted her first and poked Sam, who shushed Lou, who motioned to Doc Rosen, who jabbed Chief O'Brien, who tapped his glass of water for attention. Which shut up Mike Lyons, Ralph Bigelow and Joe Cavelli. For the first time in the history of the ROMEOs, their table was fully occupied but silent. Eerily silent.

Lila put her hands on her hips and looked at her granddad's friends, men who'd watched her grow up, men who cared about her not only for Bart's sake and not only because she was part of Pilgrim Cove. She knew they loved her for her own sake, too. She focused immediately on Sam's worried expression.

"Relax, everybody. I heard the song. I'm not falling to pieces. I'm a big girl, and you don't have to protect me. In fact, you can't."

She walked around the table to where Sam Parker sat and took his hand. "I think J.J. Parks is Jason, too, Sam. I...I hope you hear from him. He owes you that much. And more."

The man's hand trembled in hers, and she blinked quickly and cleared her throat. "What does Matt say?" she asked, referring to Jason's older brother, whom she considered a good friend.

Sam shook his head. "Haven't spoken to him yet. Heard the song in the car on the way over from the harbor." His eyes locked on hers. "Did you hear him sing, Lila? I—I heard his voice today."

Concern pierced her. "No, Sam," she replied

gently. "You're confused. That was Luis Torres. Jason wrote the song, he didn't sing it."

But Sam was shaking his head. "Listen to the harmony in the chorus. It's Jason." He sounded confident.

Lila studied the man with the salt-and-pepper hair. A piano man who'd passed his strong musical genes down to each of his sons. If he said Jason provided harmony, she didn't doubt him. But she looked around the table at the other ROMEOs for confirmation. Some shrugged, some nodded, but they all looked as concerned as she felt. Except for her grandfather.

"My money's on Sam," said Bart, his blue eyes fierce. "He's always had perfect pitch, so his ears aren't getting older like mine."

Sam laughed. "No logic there, Bartholomew, but I like the thought." He raised his coffee cup in the air. "To my son, Jason. May he find his way home."

Eight men saluted with their mugs. Lila had none and was glad, eager now to get away. But when she turned to leave, Sam stopped her.

"You think he owes me," said Sam, "but how much does he owe you and our little Katie?"

"He owes me nothing," she replied softly. "And as for Katie—well, Katie will soon have a new dad in her life."

He sighed, and she hugged him. "But you'll always be her grandpa. Nothing will change that." She kissed him on the cheek and raced to the door.

When she walked into her office only a block and a half from the Diner, her phone was ringing. The sound hurt her ears, which was a rare occurrence. Usually she welcomed every phone call with eagerness, each one an opportunity to build the business. But today, she wasn't in the mood to handle normal business.

She took a moment to refocus before picking up the receiver. And then wished she hadn't as her mother's voice accosted her.

"Your engagement to Adam Fielding is the best thing that's happened to you in years. Don't let anything ruin it. Or anyone!"

"So tell me how you *really* feel," murmured Lila under her breath.

"What, honey? I didn't hear you."

"Adam's a wonderful man," said Lila. "I'm fine. Now, go cook something."

"Tonight's special is potato-encrusted red snapper. You love it. Why don't you invite Adam and Sara to join you and Katie at the restaurant. Dinner's on me."

Her mom sounded desperate, and Lila almost felt sorry for her. Almost. Strong-minded Maggie Sullivan always thought she knew what was best for everyone and had a habit of taking over everybody's life—or trying to—and Lila wasn't buying. Not that she didn't love her mother. She did. But as her granddad had said after Lila had given birth to Katie,

"Two bossy women don't belong in one house. Lila and the baby will live with me." Then he'd turned to Lila and winked. The arrangement had worked beautifully for eight years.

"Thanks, Mom, but I'm showing some houses to a Boston couple tonight. They're coming here about half-past six. But I'll send Granddad and Katie to you."

"Of course," said Maggie, more quietly. "My family always has a table at the Lobster Pot. I just want what's best for you, honey. You know that."

Yeah. That was the hard part. Maggie wanted the best for her daughter because she loved her. "Mom…I'm an adult. How about letting me decide what's best?"

Silence on the other end. Then Maggie said, "Do I have a choice?"

"He wrote a song. Maybe it's the first successful song and the first money he's earned in nine years. Who knows what happened? I won't begrudge him a way to earn a living."

"As long as he earns it far away from here!"

"Oh, God, Mom! Listen to yourself. What about Sam? And Matt? And the boys?"

"They can go visit him—far away."

Lila shook her head. Her mom had made up her mind and would never change it. "Hang on a second," said Lila, booting up her computer and typing in Luis Torres's name. "You're safe, Mom. Torres lives in California, so Jason's probably there, too. Is that far enough for you?"

"Not Hawaii?"

"California is the best I can do."

"I'll take it." Maggie laughed, and Lila sighed, content for the moment. "There's really nothing to worry about, Mom. Take it easy."

"Sure. But if you hear from him…"

"What?"

"I have a feeling about this…."

"And I've got a business to run. So do you. Bye." Lila hung up the phone and shook her head. Her mother's imagination had taken flight.

She reached for a client's file, and then paused. Hearing the song at any point during the first five years of Jason's absence would have sent her into an ecstasy of anticipation. She'd believed in their love and devotion to each other. Remembering how it felt to be in his arms, she'd had no reason not to.

When he'd left town a month after the tragedy and asked her to wait for him, her "yes" had been expelled in her next breath. She and Jason had been part of each other and after the accident, she'd understood his pain. She'd known how close the twins had been, how bereft Jason had felt. And how full of self-reproach.

Lila had been with the boys on prom night. They'd shared a keg, and Jared's good time had gotten out of control. Lila had said so then. She'd say it again now if asked. But Jason had wrapped himself in a cloak of blame. She hated thinking about that night and mostly didn't. Too awful to dwell on.

Then four years ago, Matt Parker had visited and shown her Jason's annual Christmas card. Instead of holiday greetings, the card said, "If she's still waiting, tell Lila to forget about me. To have a nice life."

In her office, she cringed in remembered pain. Nothing since Jared's death had caused her as much agony as those two brief sentences. When the shock wore off, she'd worked harder with Bart, volunteered more and helped out in her mom's restaurant whenever she could—all in addition to taking care of Katie. She'd left herself no time to think. This method of survival had worked for her.

And then last year, she'd met Adam Fielding, the new veterinarian in town. Lila glanced at her ring and rubbed the stone gently. A good man, with a sweet little girl who was best friends with Katie. A perfect arrangement for everyone.

CHAPTER TWO

JASON PARKER GLANCED at his watch as the wheels of his plane touched ground at Boston's Logan Airport. The hands pointed to seven-thirty. He'd taken the red-eye from Los Angeles, and now it was Tuesday morning, May 1st. A date he'd remember forever as a date of "firsts." The first time he'd been back to Massachusetts in nine years. The first time he'd used his own name when making a plane reservation. The first time one of his songs was being released as the title of an album. And it was the first time in his life that he felt as nervous as he did now.

Leaving home, even under those terrible circumstances, was a hell of a lot easier than coming back. Especially when he didn't have a definitive plan other than to rent a car and check into a motel outside of Pilgrim Cove. But he'd come up with something. He always did. Keeping a low profile and thinking on his feet had ensured his survival for the first few years, and he hadn't broken the habit. Back then, he'd traveled light and often. Always covering his tracks. Now he was twenty-seven years old and felt like fifty. He was tired of playing.

After the plane landed, he went directly to a car-rental company and requested an unspectacular four-door sedan, the type that could be found in driveways across the country. In a pair of faded jeans, an old Red Sox baseball cap and a navy T-shirt, Jason aimed to blend into his surroundings, as well.

He reached for his driver's license on the rental counter and chuckled to himself. He still got a kick out of using his real ID. He'd established a life and a career and was finally ready to face the past. He had no reason to hide anymore—and many reasons to visit his hometown.

He glanced at the picture on his new license. He'd grown to man-size since the last Jason Parker DMV ID shot was taken. He and Jared had been lanky teenagers when they'd passed their driving tests. In the old days, he and Jared could clean out their mom's overstocked fridge and not gain weight. He shook his head and sighed. Jared. Jared…his brother still nested in the back of his mind. He'd sit there until Jason finally made peace with him, with the rest of the family, with himself—and with Lila. If Jared was constantly in his mind, then Lila was in his heart.

He'd seen, listened and learned a lot since he'd left—or, more accurately, since he'd run away. But most important of all, he'd learned that the demons would chase him until he confronted them. His first stop after finding a motel would be the cemetery.

Two hours later, after fighting traffic that was worse than he remembered, after listening to "At the Water's Edge" on the car radio more times than he wanted to count, and after speaking on his cell phone to Luis Torres who'd called with excellent reports on their targeted test markets, Jason finally pulled into the driveway of a motel several miles outside of Pilgrim Cove. He was hungry, tired and annoyed at being both.

"I'll take the room for a week," he said to the man behind the desk. "As long as it's got a comfortable bed. A big bed."

The clerk grinned and winked. "You got it."

Jason's mouth tightened but he didn't bother to correct the guy's interpretation. Maybe he wouldn't stay here for the whole week. Maybe, if all went well in the next few days, he'd move into the Wayside Inn in Pilgrim Cove. He drove around to the back of the courtyard and carried his suitcase into his room. A bare-bones room, but clean. No extras. Fine with him. He'd slept in worse.

He yawned and tested the bed. Forget food. He hadn't slept in…he tried to recall…at least thirty-six hours, and now the whole trip was catching up with him. But at least he was here.

He opened his window, inhaled the tang of ocean air and walked back to the bed. He had no energy to fight and fell asleep on top of the spread.

"HE'S STAYING at the Sea and Sand Motel a few miles east of town."

From behind the counter at Parker Plumbing and Hardware, Sam Parker looked at the retired police chief, grateful for the news, but not surprised that Rick O'Brien would be on top of the information. Not that Sam had asked him. He didn't have to. Rick's friendship went back for so many years, Sam had lost track. All he knew was that Rick's contacts in the police department seemed endless, not just in Pilgrim Cove but also in the county and farther.

"How about us taking a ride when Matt gets back?" asked the chief, looking at his watch. "It's almost dinnertime. We could grab a hamburger at the diner and be at the motel fifteen minutes later."

But Sam shook his head. "No. We're not hunting him down. He's here, and he's not going to run." He clasped his friend on the arm. "He needs to take the last steps. He needs to come home on his own."

The cop said nothing. "What do you think Matt will say?"

Strength flowed through Sam's body. He lifted his chin. "It doesn't matter what Matt says. I'm still their father. My hair may be graying, and I may have failed Jason in the past, but I'm still the dad. Matt will do as I say."

Rick stared and nodded. "I don't know if I'd have your patience or courage."

"Courage? No such thing. Surprising Jason will

only create more problems, and I'm not willing to take that chance." Sam began to pace as he spoke. "Don't want to spoil anything. No matter how much I want to put my arms around him right now."

Sam looked hard at his friend. "You won't say a word to Matthew when he gets here." It was a statement, not a question.

"He's closing up tonight?"

Sam nodded.

"Just as well. Nothing he can do, anyway. I won't say a thing." Rick paused a moment. "You're a damn good father, Sam. Your boys are lucky to have you."

Sam replied with a grunt. The chief was wrong. If Sam had been a better father, maybe Jason wouldn't have run away in the first place.

The bell rang and Matt walked in. A happy Matt. Full of joy since Laura had come into his life. Just the way it should be, thought Sam, his heart swelling with love for his oldest son. His boy couldn't have made a better choice. Laura spoiled them all, including Sam.

"Laura and the kids are holding their dessert until you join them at the diner," said Matt to his dad, before turning to Rick. "And Dee said she's waiting for you to have dinner with her. So get on out of here, the two of you. I can handle the customers."

"Dee's the boss," said Rick with a wink. "I've got to run."

Sam and Matt both burst out laughing. Rick

would run all right…because he was crazy in love with his wife of…

"Holy Toledo, Rick!" said Sam. "You and Dee are coming up to your first anniversary. Memorial Day. I remember clearly."

He turned to his son. "Which means that yours and Laura's isn't far behind. Middle of June."

"The year is flying by," said Matt with a grin.

"It sure is," agreed Rick.

"That's because you're happy," said Sam. "It's as simple as that."

He thought of Jason and Lila Sullivan, the girl Jason had loved as soon as he'd realized that girls and boys were different. Then he sighed. Jason had disappeared, and Lila had found her happiness with Adam Fielding. The young veterinarian was a good man, and Sam couldn't quarrel with that situation at all. If Jason still had Lila on his mind, he was too late. He'd have to find happiness somewhere else.

JASON PARKER SAT UP in bed and looked toward the window. Night had fallen, and he knew he'd have to change plans and visit the cemetery in the morning. No problem. He'd needed to sleep, but now he needed a meal. He immediately thought of the Lobster Pot, the best restaurant in New England according to Lila's mother, Maggie, who owned the place with her sister. Maggie and Thea. He hadn't thought of them in a long time. But he'd have to postpone sampling their wares for a little while. No way was he walking into their restaurant tonight.

He took a quick shower and changed into a dark sports shirt and chinos. Worth the effort to get a good steak instead of fast food. He drove to the only steakhouse he remembered near Pilgrim Cove, took a corner booth and faced the wall. He ordered without looking at the menu. He wanted to eat and run. For the first time since his songwriting career had taken off, he understood Luis's desire to travel incognito and the lengths the star went to in order to do so. Jason wasn't fighting professional recognition; he was fighting personal recognition.

He took out a pad of paper and a pencil from his breast pocket and kept his eyes on his work. No glancing around the room, no looking for the waitress. The steak was good, the baked potato with all the toppings, too. He paid the bill with his credit card, and walked down the aisle toward the door.

Then Lila walked in, and he forgot to breathe.

She was more beautiful than he remembered. Her blond hair was still long, this time brushed behind her ears where gold hoops reflected the light. She'd grown up. In all the right places. Lila had become a woman while he'd been gone. A woman who was laughing into the face of another man. They walked arm in arm toward a table on the opposite side of the room.

Jason headed for the door. Held his breath until

he sat behind the wheel of his rental. Then all his good intentions went to hell.

"You're an idiot for thinking you could handle seeing her with someone else."

He threw the car into reverse, and made his way to the exit. A left turn would take him straight into Pilgrim Cove. He pushed the indicator down. He'd ride through town, check out the store, Matt's house, his parents' house, just to see if he remembered everything, just to see his boyhood home once more, and then he'd disappear. Again. Maybe nine years wasn't enough. Maybe a hundred wouldn't be. If an accidental sighting of Lila could make his heart burst, what would a reunion with everyone he loved do? What was the point, anyway? He was probably no more than a fleeting thought to them these days. They'd all gone on with their lives. Certainly, Lila had. And Jason's showing up now would disrupt everything.

He passed the Welcome to Pilgrim Cove sign— not that he could read it in the dark—but he knew what it said. Population: Winter: 5000. Summer: A Lot Higher. Everyone who visited chuckled about the town with a sense of humor. Jason's mouth tightened. Nothing funny about *his* visit.

The state road turned into Main Street when he got to the neck of the peninsula. "A finger in the ocean is our Pilgrim Cove," Lila's granddad used to say. Ahh. Bart Quinn. Finally, a corner of Jason's mouth inched into a smile. Quite a character, Lila's grandfather, and his own dad's good friend.

When he hit the neck, he took a left onto Bay Road, past the intersections of Sloop and Oyster streets, and then headed west toward his brother Matt's house. Matt and Valerie's son, Brian, would be about eleven or twelve by now. If Jason were lucky, maybe the boy would be outside riding a bike or shooting hoops in the driveway. Maybe he'd gotten a little sister or brother by now. Jason passed the intersection of Outlook Drive and continued on the winding road that hugged Pilgrim Bay. Until he saw the warmly lit home on the corner of Neptune Street.

Jason slowed his rental to a crawl and dimmed his headlights, looking for a convenient place to park—a minute or two would be enough. Finally, a piece of luck. He slipped the car into a spot near the house, but on the side street. He could see the driveway.

And his luck was holding! The front door opened almost as soon as Jason lowered his window and cut the engine. A woman emerged—tall, short dark hair—then twirled and faced inside.

"Jack," she called, "it's a gorgeous night! Want to take a walk after we put out the trash?"

The woman was familiar, but she wasn't Valerie. And Jack? Where was Matt? Jason craned his neck to check the street sign. What the heck was going on?

A big man joined the woman on the front porch and closed the door behind him. He dipped his head, kissed her on the mouth. Said something too low for Jason to hear, but the woman giggled. She lifted her head, and in the moonlight, Jason recognized the beautiful smile of Rachel Goodman.

In Matt's house? And what was she doing in Pilgrim Cove? The last time Jason had seen her was on a Mississippi gambling boat a couple of years after they'd both left town. A lifetime ago. He idly wondered if she'd kept their promise not to tell anyone about that accidental meeting.

He watched for a few moments more, and when the couple walked up their driveway toward the garage, he turned his key and drove quietly away.

On automatic pilot, he headed west toward his parents' house. They lived in an older residential neighborhood toward the center of the peninsula. The third house on Poseidon Street off the corner of Sloop. A Lexus 400 stood in the driveway, and Jason jammed on his brakes.

Impossible! Unless they'd won the lottery. But even if they had won—the car didn't match his practical, down-to-earth dad. A man who'd known how to run a business, manage income and expenses and provide for his family. They'd had luxuries in moderation—a vacation to Disney World, tickets to the Boston Symphony and the Boston Pops—although in their family, those tickets weren't luxuries; they were necessities. A house of musicians needed to hear music.

Jason shook his head as memories rolled through his mind one after the other. He'd had a damn good childhood in Pilgrim Cove until that May night nine years ago. And now this. This Lexus in his dad's driveway. What was that all about?

He drove past the house, made a U-turn in the next intersection and drove slowly back again. Trash cans stood at the curb at some of the other homes. Seemed like Pilgrim Cove had a trash pickup in the morning. If he were lucky, his folks would remember to put theirs out soon.

It took five minutes before the garage door lifted. A man, much younger than his dad, emerged wheeling his trash to the curb.

"Dad-dy," came a high voice through the clear night air, "reading time…"

The man turned toward the house. "Be right there, sweetheart."

Who were these people in his parents' home? Which seemed not to be his parents' home anymore. A knot grew in Jason's stomach. Where was everyone? Had his whole family moved away? Away from Pilgrim Cove?

HE STARTED THE CAR and headed for Main Street. Parker Plumbing and Hardware would provide the answer. People could move around more easily than businesses. Coming from the west, he passed Quinn Real Estate and Property Management, then the

Diner on the Dunes, the bank and after Conch Street on his left...should be...should be...and it was. Parker Plumbing and Hardware, just as he remembered.

Jason sagged with relief. Man, he'd really been stressed. He wiped the sweat from his forehead with his sleeve wishing he had a towel. And for the third time in the last half hour, he found a shadowed parking spot, lowered his window and shut the car's engine.

He glanced at his watch. Nine o'clock, and the lights inside the store were still on. A pickup truck and a passenger car were the only vehicles in the lot. A young couple appeared with a box and a bag of something, got into the car and drove off. Last customers of the evening.

"Come on, Matt," Jason whispered, hands clenched on the wheel. "Let me see you." Minutes passed, long, long minutes when Jason realized his brother still had to ring out the registers, check the building, set the alarm and follow whatever routines he normally did at the end of the day. He also realized that Parker Plumbing was the only store on the block open late that night. Spring was the start of their busiest season, and Jason wasn't surprised Matt kept the store open.

He waited until finally, one by one, the lights inside went out and only a single fixture remained shining in the entrance area. Matt Parker was clearly visible as he opened the door, and Jason felt a big grin cross his face.

Matt looked great. Jason barely blinked as he stared at his brother. In the quiet of the night, he could hear Matt singing softly as he searched for the correct key on his big key ring. Beautiful voice, but…"Home on the Range"? Jason almost shouted with laughter.

Jason watched as his brother turned his back toward the street in order to lock the door. Then, without warning, Matt stopped midnote. He cocked his head and froze in place, not moving a muscle. He stood as still as the breath Jason now held. Nothing moved outside, not a branch, not a leaf. No people, no cars. Then another song came from Matt's mouth:

"In my dreams I am running there,
With my brothers to the water's edge."

His big brother knew he was out here. Could he have seen Jason reflected in the window? Or was their intuitive ESP working again? Although Matt hadn't turned around, nor had he called Jason's name, he *had* changed the lyric by making "brother" plural. A simple error? A rebuke for focusing only on Jared? Or a reminder that there were still two living siblings?

Maybe one day, he'd ask. But not now. Jason started the car and saw Matt stiffen, then rattle his key in the door. They'd communicated well.

A vehicle turned onto Main Street, came toward them, then turned into the store's lot. An American sedan. A woman emerged. Young. Wavy light hair, nice figure.

"Thanks, Sam. We'll be home in a little while." She closed the door and walked right into Matt's open arms. Their kiss could have ignited the town.

What the hell was going on now? That woman was certainly not Matt's wife.

Jason pulled out of his spot. When the car straightened out, he glanced into the rearview mirror. His brother's gaze followed him as he drove away.

THE MORNING SUN STABBED his eyelids, and Jason winced. His own fault for not drawing the curtain the night before. Man, he was tired. After all the surprises last night, he hadn't been able to sleep. Instead, he'd driven around searching for some upscale club where he could commandeer a piano. He'd gotten lucky some thirty miles out of Pilgrim Cove. By the end of the night, he'd had enough money in the tip jar for the manager's daughter to have piano lessons for a few months. He chuckled remembering the expression on the guy's face when Jason gave him the cash. Returning his earnings was the least he could do. The instrument had been well tuned recently, something Jason had learned to appreciate over the years when he'd worked a different lounge every night or two.

Of course, the nightclubs had almost killed him. The liquor had flowed—his glass was always full, watered down by the bartenders so he'd be able to continue into the wee hours. And he had. The owners had recognized a good piano man. So had the customers. But no one understood that he was playing because Jared couldn't. That he couldn't stay in one place too long. That he had to keep moving. Running. Until he finally learned that he couldn't outrun his memories. Not even with Jack Daniel's to keep him company. But that lesson had come later.

He yawned, rolled over for another moment, then headed for the shower. A half hour later, feeling more human, he drove to a florist shop and went inside. So many choices—bright bouquets, wreaths, simple flowers and green plants. Too many choices. A wreath would be the easiest and appropriate, but…he wanted something special for Jared. Nine years was a long time between visits.

And then he spotted the selection of roses behind the glass doors of a temperature-controlled cabinet. "Nine yellow ones," he said to the proprietor. "In a box, please. No wrappings."

Yellow for loyalty. Perfect. How could an identical twin be anything else? He handed over his credit card and in five minutes, walked out the door.

When he arrived at the cemetery's parklike grounds, he slowed to a crawl, trying to get his bearings. His memory fogged when he tried to recall his last visit, the day of Jared's funeral, the worst day of his life. Or was the accident the worst day? Or maybe the worst had been a month later, the day before he'd left Pilgrim Cove. He squeezed his eyes tight for a moment and wiped the scene with his mother out of his mind. Hopefully, he'd make peace with her later. Now, only Jared was important.

New Hope Cemetery covered a lot of ground. He turned into the driveway of the administration building to get directions. No point in wasting time.

It took ten minutes to get the information and drive slowly down the narrow paths to the correct area. On this beautiful weekday morning, he wasn't alone in the park. He'd passed a woman planting flowers, and an old man sitting on a stone bench drinking a cup of coffee. Peaceful scenes. A vehicle stood near the section he was looking for, but Jason barely gave it a glance as he climbed out of his car, now intent on identifying Jared's grave. He saw the headstone and made a beeline for it…and spotted a second headstone. And next to that…a third.

He took a step closer. Then blinked quickly, shook his head in denial. He couldn't absorb it. Margaret Parker. His mother. His eyes burned as he forced himself to read. Two years after Jared.

"No!" The roses dropped to the ground.

He'd imagined a thousand variations of his reunion with his mother—what he'd say, what she'd say—a thousand different dialogues, but never once had he imagined this.

"Her last words were 'Tell Jason I'm sorry. I was wrong. And I still love him and miss him so much.'"

The voice came from behind him, a deep familiar voice, but sounding a bit raspy now. "I'm glad I can finally deliver the message."

Jason stiffened for a moment. Then he turned around.

"Dad?"

Sam Parker held out a trembling hand. "And I'm sorry, too. I shouldn't have made excuses for her." He paused and stared at Jason. "Welcome home, son." And somehow the handshake became a hug.

"I pictured everything the same… I thought nothing would change."

"More snow on the mountaintop," replied Sam, pointing to his head.

Jason chuckled and felt himself begin to relax. His dad looked great. "I'm an idiot," he said. "How can anything stay the same after all this time, even in Pilgrim Cove?" He bent down to retrieve the flowers.

"I'll wait in the car," said Sam, nodding at a green van. "You do what you intended when you arrived."

Jason nodded. As he straightened, his glance fell on the third stone. Suddenly, he couldn't swallow. "What happened to Valerie?" he whispered, gazing at his sister-in-law's grave. "Poor Matt. Poor Brian."

"And poor Casey," offered Sam. "That's when he started to stutter."

Jason held up his hand. Casey? "What happened?" he asked again.

"Cancer," said Sam. "Both Mom and Valerie. Different types, but in the end, it didn't matter. We lost them." His eyes focused first on one, then on the other grave. "Hard years," he muttered. "Very hard years."

Guilt pierced Jason. He'd caused his share of pain merely by being absent. One less pair of shoulders to lean on; one less person to share with. "I'm so sorry, Dad." Such mundane words, but he couldn't think of any others.

"I know, Jason. I know," Sam said. "You have a good heart. Always did. But loving hearts can get bruised mighty bad sometimes. And that's what happened when Mom lashed out at you. She was in such pain herself, she didn't know what she was saying. Jared's death was not your fault, Jason. She knew it, and I know it."

"I had to hit bottom to figure it out," Jason said, as he stepped away to lay three roses on Valerie's grave. Then three roses on his mother's. Until finally, he knelt near his brother's and carefully placed his yellow roses in front of the stone.

"I need to talk to Jared," he said without looking up at his father.

"Take all the time you want. I'll be at the car."

Jason nodded, then heard Sam step away.

"I'm here, Jared," he began, "and as long as I'm alive, you're alive. We're J.J. Parks. We make some mighty nice music. You're in my head every time I'm at the keyboard… I hear you harmonizing with me…."

SAM PARKER LEANED against the side of his SUV, listening to his son's memories and stories of the last nine years.

"I left town with five hundred dollars that I'd withdrawn from the bank. I hitched rides on the interstates. But where the hell was I going? I had no idea. One night, I'm in a bar in Hannibal, Missouri. I pay for my booze, finish it and go outside…and get my ass kicked. I woke up lying in the gutter. Wallet gone. That was about ten days after I'd left town…. God, I was so green. Living in Pilgrim Cove doesn't prepare you for life on the streets."

Jason was quiet for a minute, and Sam almost called to him. But then more words spilled out.

"I actually went to a homeless shelter. I needed a shower. Bad. And I needed a job. So I washed dishes on the riverboats…gambling boats. Me and Huck Finn, huh? But you know what? I liked it. People kept coming and going. I was simply a faceless worker, and that suited me just fine back then. Mind-numbing work. And God knew, I didn't want to think!

"And that's how my life began away from home.

You can see I survived," said Jason. "But the lone-liness…that's what got to me. That's when I started writing…and drinking. And didn't want to stop either of them."

Sam examined Jason closely. The boy looked good. Eyes clear. Muscles tight, no puffiness. Skin unblemished. He tuned in again to Jason's ramblings.

"I just kept thinking about you, and Ma and… Lila… It always came back to her…and the pain would be so bad…and I'd go to the piano and compose, trying to make sense of it all."

Sam's breath caught. He loved his son, but Jason had forfeited his claim to Lila years ago. She deserved her newfound happiness with Adam Fielding, and Sam was not going to allow Jason to make trouble there. Not even for Katie's sake.

Katie. His heart pounded at the thought of his beautiful granddaughter. Jason's daughter.

He eyed his boy. Jason would have been a great dad had life been normal. But life hadn't been. And now Katie was thrilled at her mom's upcoming marriage. Thrilled with becoming her best friend Sara's sister.

Sam curled his hands into fists. Jason had made choices. So had Lila. Everyone's life was running smoothly now, and he would not interfere. How and when Jason learned about Katie would be totally up to Lila. Sam could do that much for his granddaughter's lovely and loving mother.

CHAPTER THREE

LILA RACED DOWN THE HALL toward her grandfather's office. Calls for summer rentals had been nonstop all day. Jane Fisher, their secretary cum office manager, had taken a dozen messages in the last hour while Lila had been out of the office with a client. It was already three o'clock, and both she and Bart had work to do. A lot of work. Thank goodness.

She heard the music before she reached Bart's door. "Must you play that bloody song?"

Her words accompanied her across the threshold, but she regretted them when she saw her granddad's shocked expression. When his shock changed to determination, however, she knew she had to hold her ground. Although she loved Granddad dearly, she knew he was not easily thwarted when acting "for her own good."

"I thought you liked Luis Torres," said Bart, leaning back in his chair, his expression changing to one of pure innocence. "You've got his other CDs in your collection."

She walked to his desk. "Granddad, this is not about Luis Torres, and you know it."

She didn't like the gleam in his eye or the smile that inched across his face. "Bull's eye!" he said, sitting upright again. "I'm glad you brought this up, lass, because it's awfully hard to tiptoe around here when you've got feet the size of mine."

He could always make her laugh, but she didn't want to laugh now. "We're talking about Jason Parker," she said, running the two names together as fast as she could.

Her grandfather nodded. "Sam called me a little while ago." His voice trailed off.

Lila's legs trembled, and pinpoints of sweat dotted her arms. She said nothing, but walked to the chair in front of Bart's desk and sat down. If Sam Parker had called Bart, then Jason was really involved in that song. Her wishful thinking had been in vain, but at least she'd been warned.

She took a deep breath and met Bart's pointed gaze. "I'm listening."

"Jason's here in Pilgrim Cove," Bart said quietly. Then he paused, one eyebrow raised as though waiting for permission to continue. Giving her time to adjust.

She lifted her chin. "A little late, wouldn't you say?"

Bart sighed. "He's in shock himself, Lila. Didn't know about his mom or Valerie…and still doesn't know about Katie."

She collapsed against the chair, relief turning her muscles to rubber bands. But she did wince as she pictured his reaction to the losses in his family. A moment later, she rallied. "The shock is his own fault, you know. He could have kept in touch… called…."

Bart nodded. "Well, you can ask him about all that…"

"Not I," said Lila, shaking her head. "Not interested. Like Mom said, 'I'm finally moving on with my life.'" She glanced at the ring she wore on her fourth finger, and heard her grandfather sigh.

"And what about Katie?" he asked.

"What about her?" she retorted. "I work hard so I can support her without anyone's help. I don't need Jason's money. And besides, how long will he stay? Two days? Three? No," she said, conviction in her voice. "Katie doesn't need that. She's crazy about Adam, chatting about how she's going to have a real daddy, not merely uncles and grandpas."

"She's got it all figured out, eh?" said Bart. "Just like her mother?"

Lila nodded. "Yes," she replied. "Katie's got it all figured out and likes the plan very much." And why not? Adam Fielding was a wonderful father to Sara, who'd raised her all alone after losing his wife. As young as she was, Katie understood that.

Bart clutched his empty pipe, pointed the stem at her. "You know what they say about the 'best laid plans,' don't you?"

"These plans are carved in concrete," Lila replied. "And unless Sam or Matt says anything about Katie…" She stared at Bart, then sighed in relief when he shook his head.

"There's no man more honorable than Sam Parker," said Bart. "He won't say anything."

Finally, Lila felt a genuine smile appear. Her grandfather was right. Sam was one in a million. She glanced at Bart and grinned. A little too much leprechaun in him, but she'd keep him. She placed a list of names in front of him and stood up to leave. "You've got calls to make."

"Any special ones?" asked Bart.

Lila frowned. "What do you mean… Oh! Possible candidates for Sea View House?" She placed her hands on her hips and forced herself to tease him. "Don't you think you've already used up the quota for good luck in that house? What was it? Three marriages within a year? You can't do better than that. You'd better give it a rest before the luck dries up."

For a second he looked concerned, and she couldn't restrain a giggle.

"So you're thinking I'm a bit daffy, are you?" Bart shook his head slowly. "No, lassie. The luck is there for all with open hearts…and especially for those with hearts that need healing."

Her laughter vanished. She thought of Matt Parker and Laura, who'd dealt with breast cancer, then rented the first floor of Sea View House. She thought of the young widower, Daniel Stone, and his Sea View House neighbor, Shelley Anderson, who'd fought like a tiger for custody of her kids. And then there was Rachel Goodman who'd come back to town and wound up sharing Sea View House with Jack Levine. They'd gotten married last month during spring break, bought Matt Parker's old house and remained in Pilgrim Cove.

Lost in thought, Lila absently tapped her lip. Her granddad was right about one thing. Everyone who'd lived in Sea View House had needed healing. And had received it.

Everyone…except her. The big house on the beach had been her house, too. Once upon a time. She knew it well. She and Jason had made love there. Conceived Katie there. Listened to the music of the ocean there. It had been a special place to her in the past, and had remained special as long as Jason's promise to return had kept her going. But Lila had received his message loud and clear. And she'd moved forward with her life.

Now she avoided Sea View House as much as possible, thankful that Bart enjoyed handling the leases. He was the one who selected the tenant and decided how much rent to charge on the sliding scale established by the Adams Family Trust, owner of the property.

She felt her grandfather studying her. The Quinn prided himself on his gut instinct for people, and she could hide nothing from his discerning gaze. For the very first time since Katie had been born, she regretted sharing a home with him.

AT LEAST the Diner on the Dunes hadn't changed much. A one-story white clapboard structure with an upper row of small round windows like portholes, reflected the nautical theme. Below the portholes were big picture windows before the walls continued to the ground.

Jason pulled his car into the spot next to the Parker Plumbing van the morning after his visit to the cemetery and his family reunion at Matt and Laura's new house, which was his dad's house, too. He'd had a wonderful evening, considering all he'd absorbed during the day. Laura was a great woman, and anyone could see how crazy Matt was about her. And Brian! He shook his head in remembered awe, regretful that he hadn't been around to watch the boy grow up.

Of all the surprises, however, perhaps eight-year-old Casey was the most fun. "Uncle Ja-Ja-son looks a lot like you, Dad," he'd said to Matt. "But I-I-I don't think he's as smart as you."

"No?" replied Matt. "How come?"

"'Cause you *never* get l-l-ost. And Uncle Ja-Jason almost never got f-found."

A poignant silence had followed, though Casey hadn't noticed. The boy kept on chatting away, directing his remarks at his uncle. "But now you know where we are, don't you? You won't forget?"

"I won't forget," Jason had promised, picking up the little guy and swinging him around. And he couldn't forget to attend the baseball practice his nephew had that afternoon. It seemed he was expected to make up for lost time by attending every activity his family was involved with while he was in town.

Right now, the only event ahead of him was breakfast at the diner with his dad and a group of his dad's cronies. He walked to the entrance and went inside.

Business was brisk, with people waiting to be seated. His stomach rumbled as he inhaled the aroma of rich coffee.

"Right this way, Jason," said a petite blonde. "The boys are expecting you."

Jason studied the older woman who crackled with energy. "Dee? Dee Barnes? You're still bossing this place?"

"Dee O'Brien now." She nodded at the big guy on the end of the circular booth she was leading him to.

"The Chief? You and the chief are married?" Rick O'Brien had been chief of police all during Jason's childhood. Every kid knew him. And had been lectured to more than once by him.

"Sweetie, it's been a crazy year for weddings around here," Dee said. "But I'll let them fill you in."

He stared into the faces of men he recognized, but struggled to remember their names. There was Ralph Bigelow from the electric company, Lou Goodman—Rachel's father and high-school librarian. Doc Rosen…

"What are you doing here in the middle of the week, Doc? Shouldn't you be in Boston with your patients?"

"Not anymore," Doc replied, while chuckles came from the others around the table.

Jason looked at Joe Cavelli from the garage, and Mike Lyons, an environmental engineer. "Still working for the aquarium?" asked Jason.

"After a fashion," the genial man replied.

And next to his dad sat Bart Quinn, whose blue eyes studied Jason greeting the group. Jason extended his hand to Bart and was jolted at the power of the man's response.

"Sit down, sit down. Take a load off. And let's get a good look at you." Bart Quinn's big voice.

With one sentence, Jason felt like a kid again. And then everyone was talking at once. Asking questions about him. Updating him about the town. Somehow breakfast platters appeared along with two pots of coffee, with the chief's wife directing the table service.

"So, Dee," said Jason when there was lull. "I meant to ask, what's with the sign on the door? Who are the ROMEOs?"

"You're sitting with them," said Bart. "Take a

look." Quinn pointed at the Reserved sign in the middle of the table, which was almost lost among the napkins, cutlery and dishes.

"Retired Old Men Eating Out. ROMEOs." Jason looked at the eight men with him. "You guys?"

Sam clapped him on the back and looked at his friends. "We're a semiretired bunch. We work a little, volunteer a little and spend the rest of our time keeping Pilgrim Cove in order."

Nods all around. Then Bart focused on Jason once more. "Time doesn't stand still, boyo. But you know that now. And it's too darn precious to waste." Quinn's voice was strong with meaning. The table became quiet, the silence a bit uncomfortable. Bart didn't seem to notice. "So when are you moving back home?"

Covering his surprise, Jason pushed his coffee cup away, curious to see where Quinn was leading. "What makes you think I am?"

"Because, my lad," said Bart, "every single person you love lives here. And every single person who loves you lives here. And if that's not reason enough, then I've lived seventy-six years as a fool." The old man paused for breath. "And Bart Quinn is no fool."

Jason had been around creative people long enough to recognize that Bart was putting on a show. A damn good one. And Act II was coming up.

"And because I know you're a smart fellow— smart enough to find your way home, finally—I'm going to make you a deal you can't refuse while you make your arrangements to move back."

The play was getting better and better. Jason was starting to enjoy himself.

"It'll cost you a few bucks, but I'm the one taking all the risk," Bart said.

What was Quinn talking about now? Jason glanced around the table. Every ROMEO was eyeing every other one there.

"Spit it out, Bartholomew," Jason said.

The old man waited a beat. "Sea View House."

His world crashed. Waves pulled him under. Sea View House. Making love to Lila. Moonlight on her hair. On her gorgeous body. Walking the beach, hands intertwined. So in love with her, he hadn't considered another relationship since.

But how did the old man know about Sea View House? He inhaled deeply, then asked, "Why Sea View House?" His voice cracked; he coughed quickly to cover it up.

"That's an easy one to answer," replied Bart, his tone gentle now. "You qualify."

WHATEVER THE MYSTERIOUS qualifications might be, it didn't sound as though Bart knew anything specific about the part Sea View House had played in his and Lila's lives. Next to him, however, Jason heard his dad murmur Bart's name and saw him shake his head. "Do you know what you're doing?"

"Merely providing opportunity," Bart replied. "Jason will have to provide motive."

What were the men talking about now? Jason was about to ask when his cell phone vibrated. Before he answered it, however, he heard his dad say to Bart, "You've provided Maggie with plenty of motive— Motive to kill you."

Bart nodded. "I suppose it's a chance I'll have to take." He didn't seem too worried.

"Your daughter might not be the only female in your life to feel that way," Sam replied.

With his ear to the mobile, Jason didn't hear Bart's reply or the men's further conversation. Instead, he heard his agent's voice, and was surprised.

"Mitch! What are you doing up so early? Must be only, what? Six o'clock on the coast?"

"It's still dark," came the husky reply, "so I figure, why should I be the only one getting calls so early? I'll call J.J. and wake him up, too."

"Much too late for 'early' around here. I'm already at breakfast, surrounded by a bunch of ROMEOs."

"Romeos? You auditioning for Shakespeare now? Forget it. Hollywood's crawling with wannabe actors. They don't need you!"

Jason laughed. He could always depend on Mitch to be quick on the uptake. "The youngest ROMEO in this group is about—" Jason looked up at the men "—let's just say they qualify for senior discounts."

"So you're with your dad, huh? How's it going?"

"Good, Mitch. Some unhappy surprises, but generally good."

"Glad to hear it. And here's more good news. Radio stations have been promoting like crazy and the phone calls from listeners are out of sight. When the CD goes on sale, you'll be covered in platinum. Now, what do you think about that?"

"If your prediction is true, you can thank Luis Torres."

"Bull! He can thank you!"

Jason chuckled. Mitch Berman's belief in him had never wavered. "Let's say we're a good match," Jason replied.

"You are," said the agent. "But it wasn't an accident. You studied the guy's voice and wrote with him in mind. Just like Paul Anka did for Frank with 'My Way.' That's what's happening here with you and Torres."

Inside himself, Jason knew it, too. He'd written "At the Water's Edge" from his heart, but had wanted Luis Torres to sing it. "And your point is?"

"My point is that I've gotten calls… No, *we've* gotten calls. Two agents of big-time stars. They recognize talent and want to know what else you've written. And…get ready for this…Disney is looking for songs for several projects. I called and told them to send storylines."

Jason had hoped his career would grow, but

hadn't expected any of this so soon. "I just got here, Mitch. And I still have a lot of unfinished business to take care of."

The sudden silence at the table caused Jason to glance up. Eight pairs of eyes stared at him, his dad's creased with worry. Eight pairs of ears were tuned to every word. ROMEOs knew no shame.

"Can you hold them off for a while?" Jason said into the phone.

As he listened to his agent's excited protest, his thoughts whirled, but then he managed to relax. "Just a minute, Mitch. We might have a solution, or the means to one, sitting right at this table."

Sure, the solution might kill him. But what the hell? He couldn't walk out on his dad again, not so soon. Matt would be pissed, too, not to mention disappointing his nephews.

He looked at Bart Quinn. "I'd have to haul in a piano so I can work—which for me is day or night, so a motel won't do. If you have no objections to that, then draw up a lease—for *any* house you've got available." It was a last desperate effort to divert the Irishman.

But Quinn's eyes brightened. "Everything else is rented, boyo, so Sea View House it is. With an open-ended lease."

The Realtor was pushing it. "A month should be long enough for me to produce something." He glanced at Sam.

His father's smile reinforced Jason's decision. "I'll work here, Mitch. A month in Pilgrim Cove should keep us right on track."

LILA STRODE TO HER CAR, the keys to Sea View House dangling from her hand. She shook her head in disbelief. Her granddad really did have the luck of the Irish. Hadn't they just spoken about finding another special tenant for the place? And in just twenty-four hours, Bart had found one.

The sunny day was accompanied by a brisk ocean breeze. Too gusty for her granddad, or so he'd said. She bit her lip. Sometimes the arthritis in his knee kicked up, and because he didn't want to admit it, he looked for the means to avoid abusing the joint. And then there were times—she gripped the keys in frustration—that she could hardly believe he had arthritis at all! She'd put nothing past her grandfather when it came to getting his own way.

She slipped behind the wheel and pulled out from the curb, sighing in resignation. Her granddad loved his family so much, he'd go to any lengths to help them. When she and her mom had fought constantly after Katie's birth—Maggie trying to take over, and Lila trying to be independent—Bart had insisted Lila and the baby live with him. And Lila's dad had backed him up. Maggie needed to be a grandma, and Lila needed to learn how to be a mom. Both men had been right, and it had all worked out beautifully.

She and her own mom maintained a good relationship. Her dad had helped Maggie to accept the new arrangement. The saddest one at the time, she'd thought, was her thirteen-year-old brother, Steve. He was fascinated by the newborn and wanted Katie and Lila to stay at home.

Katie had certainly been surrounded with love from the moment she'd been born, with grandparents, aunts, uncles and cousins, as well as a mom who adored her.

And soon, she'd even have a daddy.

Lila turned onto Beach Street and studied the two-and-a-half-story saltbox on the corner. Sea View House had a majesty to it, with its gray weathered shingles, a deep porch reaching across the entire front of the house, and a white picket fence where a mass of red roses would soon be in bloom. It was one of the few houses divided into two apartments.

She checked the slip of paper Bart had given her. This man was renting the first floor, also known as the Captain's Quarters. Oh…he was paying the full price! No wonder her granddad wanted to close this deal. She had all the information she needed to speak intelligently about the house except the man's name. She shrugged. In the real-estate business, she met new folks every day and had enough experience to avoid awkward moments over introductions.

A dark sedan was parked in the driveway, but as Lila pulled up behind it, she saw the car was empty.

No big deal. If she'd been a first-time visitor, she'd explore the beach, too.

She grabbed her purse, put on her sunglasses and made sure the key was in her pocket. Then she started down the driveway toward the back of the house. The wind was stronger here, and she wished she'd brought a rubber band to hold back her hair. The new tenant wasn't on the back deck, nor in the yard. She continued toward the sand, instinctively inhaling the unique fragrance of salt and sea, listening to the sound of the waves.

The low tide meant the water's edge was a long way off. In the distance, however, she saw someone looking out over the ocean. One hand rested on his hip, while something dangled from the fingers of his other hand. Probably his shoes. He'd never hear her voice over the sound of the wind, so she didn't bother to call out. Instead, she'd wait a minute for him to return before attempting to walk on the loose sand in her pumps.

She was rewarded almost immediately when he turned around and saw her. He waved, and she held up the key. He started toward her.

Broad shoulders in a dark shirt or sweater—she couldn't tell which—lean body with dark hair blowing in all directions. Dark glasses hid his eyes—a smart move against the glare of both the sun and water. As he got closer, she saw a scruffy beard and a slow smile cross his face.

"Hi," she called, when he was in hearing range.

She waved the key. "Quinn Real Estate. I'm Lila Sullivan."

Had he hesitated before continuing toward her? "I know," he said, slowly removing his sunglasses.

Dark eyes. Just as she remembered. Just like Sam Parker's. And Matt's.

Hungry eyes. That devoured her, barely blinking, searching every square inch of her face… while she stood still, feeling powerless to move….

Powerless when he leaned closer, when his lips gently touched hers and—for a moment, a mere nanosecond—the past nine years melted away, and she was eighteen again.

She stumbled backward. "No," she whispered, throwing the keys at him. They hit the ground.

Pain-filled eyes. She was tired of pain. So tired of it.

"What do you expect to find here, Jason? At Sea View House? The past is gone. I'm not Penelope, content to wait twenty years for her hero to come home." Her breath came in gasps, her anger spiraling on itself as she lashed out at him. "You said it yourself in your damn song. It's 'Too late and much too dark.'"

He stood immobile as a statue. "You're right, Lila." His words were barely audible. "I guess I was hoping—just a tiny hope—to find my best friend."

Had she heard correctly? "Your best friend? Me? Don't be so foolish. Haven't you learned that friendship is for children? What we had is over, Jason. And that was your call. So go back where you came from. Please." Did she sound as desperate as she felt?

His brow furrowed. "I will—in a month, Lila. One short month. Would you deprive my family of a visit after all this time?"

Of course she couldn't do that to the Parkers. "Just stay away from me," she said. "Don't come to the office, my house or the Lobster Pot."

His eyes twinkled. "Not even for the best clam chowder in New England?"

She knew he was trying to lighten the tension, but with Katie in the back of her mind, she ignored his efforts. "Stay away, Jason. I don't want to see you."

He put both hands on his hips, his smile gone, his eyes narrowing. "Do you think I'm going to beat up your boyfriend or something? Is that why you're in such a sweat?"

That remark got her attention. "You mean, my fiancé?"

He nodded. "I saw you with him the other night at the steak house. Your diamond shines a block away."

The steak house. Too bad there was only one good one around. Too bad her clients had cut the evening short. Lila looked down at her hand, at the ring sparkling in the sun. Okay. She could handle this. "I have no concerns about a fight. That's teenage stuff, and we're way beyond that."

"Right. So what's the problem?"

A question she couldn't address with Jason, so she didn't.

CHAPTER FOUR

WHAT'S THE PROBLEM? One simple question that wasn't very simple at all. It was complex enough to linger in Lila's mind all day, even now as she drove Katie and Sara to their baseball practice.

How was she going to keep Jason from learning about Katie? Pilgrim Cove was too small, and her family was too big.

Why couldn't he have surprised them with a quick weekend visit—a time frame she could manage? But a whole month? Never. She was realistic enough to know that much.

So she'd tell him—in a straightforward, impersonal manner. He might even think he had a right to know. Lila wasn't so sure. After all, he'd chosen to stay away from everyone who loved him. Her mouth tightened. She, also, had memories to deal with from that night and from their whole senior year. But she didn't like digging deeply. Too painful. Guilt about Jason's brother haunted her, too. She and Jared had been opposing forces, each pulling Jason in different directions. She hated looking back. But she'd finally moved on with her life…and now this.

She glanced in the rearview mirror at the giggling little girls. Delightful children and such good friends. They were the only two girls on their team; Sara as eager as Katie to whack that ball into the outfield. And Katie, of course, had to keep up with her cousin Casey, who loved baseball. Or was it Casey who had to keep up with Katie? Lila's smile came naturally now as she thought of the Parkers. Matt had been a loyal friend to her over the years, and had been one of the primary male figures in Katie's life.

Fortunately, Katie was ready to embrace Adam also. Combining families was a good idea. She admired Adam. He was a good man, a devoted dad and the only man she'd been attracted to since….she jerked the car to a stop in the parking area next to the ball field.

"You both okay back there?" she asked, turning around.

Her concern was misplaced. The girls were chatting away while unbuckling their seat belts. Then, with gloves in hand, they said their goodbyes and raced from the car toward home plate where their coach was waiting.

A few parents were sitting on the bleachers, and Lila was surprised. No scheduled game today. This afternoon was only a practice, but it seemed everyone was ready for baseball season. After a hard day's work on a beautiful spring afternoon, why not?

She got out of the car and headed toward the bleachers herself until she saw her daughter turn around, lift her arm and run toward the two males she'd pointed at. "Casey's here already, Mom. And Uncle Matt."

Lila grinned and strolled closer, waiting for Katie's ritual launching at her uncle. Matt would swing her around, pretending to be surprised, always groaning that she was getting w-a-y too big. Her daughter loved the attention, and Matt didn't seem to mind, either.

"Hey, Uncle Matt! Here I come." Katie's voice.

Casey's voice came next. "Catch her, Uncle Jason!"

The man turned around, caught the flying Katie in his arms as smoothly as his brother did. Lila could clearly see his surprise and his grin. She rushed over as Katie began to speak.

"Hey! You're not my uncle Matt!"

"I guess I'm not."

"But you look like him, except he's fatter."

Jason lowered Katie to the ground and began to laugh. He laughed with delight, making a delicious sound that invited other voices. Soon, Katie joined in with equal glee; Casey's giggles were next.

Jason saw her, and his eyes lit up. "Lila! What a terrific kid." He smiled, a warm, genuine smile. "Your folks really know how to turn out beauties. And she looks just like you, except for the darker hair."

What had he said? His words started to sink in. He thought Katie was her little sister. Oh, my Lord! Were men usually this dumb? Or didn't he want to know? Or… She studied him carefully, thoughtfully, and sighed in relief. Not a crease, his expression open. He really didn't have a clue.

The kids ran to the field, and Lila changed the subject. "Have you moved in yet?" When he shook his head, her hopes soared. "Have you changed your mind?"

Now his eyes narrowed. "Sorry to disappoint you. I'm having a piano delivered tomorrow."

"A piano?" Such a big, permanent instrument.

"It *is* how I make my living," Jason replied dryly.

"But a piano's so…so…*not* portable! Why can't you just use an electronic keyboard or something like that?" *And not get so comfortable in Sea View House that you'll never want to leave.*

"I've got one of those, too. Why? Have you finally learned to play?"

She chuckled easily at that. "No, no. We leave all the music in Pilgrim Cove to the Parker family."

He stared out at the ball field where the kids were throwing and catching. "Yeah," he sighed. "The Parker family. But without Jared… He was the best of us."

"No!" Her protest was instinctive. "No, he wasn't," she repeated more quietly. "You were both—so special. And you still are. Jared just…wanted it more at the time."

Jason continued to watch the children in silence.

"Don't make Jared into a larger-than-life person," Lila said. "What happened was tragic, but he wasn't a hero. I was there, remember? He dragged you from behind the wheel and got in. He was drunk and angry."

Jason looked down at his hands, and Lila followed his movement. They were strong hands, big and broad and very masculine. "But I should have been able to stop him. I should have been stronger." A thread of frustration, of blame, lingered in his voice, making her wince.

"How can you say that?" asked Lila. "You pulled me from the back seat before he took off. I was so scared. Thank goodness *you* weren't drunk. I'd never seen either of you with more than a light buzz on."

He barked more than laughed. Shook his head. "A light buzz? Lila, Lila…you don't know anything. And, sweet girl, you don't have to."

Sweet girl? Pet name from the past. A boy's way of being grown up to his girlfriend of the same age.

They stood behind the fence at home plate, just the two of them with no one else in earshot. The kids were taking turns at bat now.

"I'm glad you made peace with your family, Jason. And I'm so sorry about your mom and Valerie. It must have been…just overwhelming yesterday."

"Yes, it was," he replied. "But I got through it."

His face was shadowed, stark. A tic throbbed in his jaw. She wished she could kiss the hurt away, at least put her arms around him, but that wouldn't work now. "Look, Casey's at bat."

She saw him blink, then grin at the familiar line. He focused on the boy, cheering with her as Casey connected and sent a grounder between second and third.

"Good job, Case," he called. His nephew turned and grinned, his new top teeth half-grown in. "What an imp."

"For sure. Just ask him."

He chuckled, then pointed to Katie, whose turn had come. She stood at home plate and allowed two pitches to go by.

"Good eye, Katie," murmured Jason. "They were high."

Then the girl connected, and the ball repeated the same trajectory Casey's had taken. Hard grounder between second and third.

"Your sister may look like you, but she must take after your dad and brother. Tom must get a huge kick out of her."

Her dad, Tom Sullivan, was athletic director at the high school; her brother, Steve, was a senior at Boston University and played football for them.

"Oh," Lila said, her stomach in sudden knots, "we all get a real kick out of our Katie."

LILA HEARD THE SOUND of a car pulling into the driveway and sighed with relief. Adam had arrived a few minutes early as she'd asked when she'd dropped Sara off after practice. She opened the back door before he could knock.

"All scrubbed and ready for dinner?" Lila directed her question to Sara and gave her a hug.

"Yes, I am. I'm hungry. Where's Katie?"

Lila nodded toward the back of the house. "Hopefully in her room getting dressed." The child ran off, and Lila looked at Adam. "Time is short and we have to talk about something important."

"Sans children?"

She nodded. Then bit her lip. "It's big."

He reached for her. "Whatever it is, we can deal with it together."

She so admired his calm, rational approach to life. "I hope so," she replied. "It's about…about Katie's dad." She had his attention.

"O-kay. What about him?"

She took a breath. "He's in town. After so many years, he came back. No letter. No phone call. No warning. He simply showed up."

"Does he want Katie?" Adam's whispered question gave Lila chills. She shook her head.

"No. He thinks she's my sister. Has no clue."

His quiet chuckle surprised Lila, but he anticipated her protest. "I know it's too serious to be funny. Your folks, however, must feel flattered."

"I didn't tell them. But I'm not finding his reappearance a laughing matter at all."

Adam stepped in front of her and took her hands. Kissed her softly. "There's nothing to worry about. You're her mom. You've got sole custody. He cannot take her away from you…from us."

His sincerity rang true in his confident tone, and Lila felt herself relax. "I wasn't really concerned about custody. It's just that he'll start hanging around her, getting involved in her life if I tell him."

"Lila! Of course you have to tell him. You can't keep his daughter a secret. Especially in this town."

"I know, I know," said Lila. "But I'm not looking forward to telling him."

Adam's eyes narrowed. "Are you afraid?"

"Not physically. No. But…" She dismissed her concerns with a shrug. How could she explain the intensity of the love she and Jason had shared back then? It wasn't something to share with a new man.

THE LOBSTER POT did a brisk business every night of the week, and that evening was no exception. When she arrived with Adam and the girls, Lila noted that the wide wraparound terrace sported a few full tables even though early May was still cool in New England. As they walked through the restaurant, a steady hum of conversation emanated from the three dining areas. With its wood-paneled walls and nautical theme, the place was known by some folks as the Good Ship Lobster Pot.

Her folks were already at the family table. Lila waited while the girls greeted Maggie and Tom, and then sat the children between herself and Adam. The girls were immediately lost in their own world of chatter.

Adam glanced at the kids, looked at Lila and rolled his eyes. Lila grinned in acknowledgment, taking in the whole picture they presented. They *did* make a good family. She just wished the little nervous tremor that shot through her stomach occasionally would disappear as quickly as it came. It would…as soon as she told Jason about Katie. And as soon as *he* disappeared.

"Sara's never been happier—at least not since Eileen…hmm…passed away," said Adam quietly. He inhaled hard, then looked at her over the kids' heads. His poignant smile touched her heart. "Coming to Pilgrim Cove was a good choice."

His hearty tone reassured her, and she reached over the girls and squeezed his shoulder. "I think so, too." Adam was fighting to move forward, just as she was, and if they could help each other, so much the better.

Maggie's laughter rang out just then, and Lila glanced at her mother who was teasing Lila's dad, her eyes sparkling like a youngster's.

"Your folks actually look young enough to be

Katie's parents," Adam said softly, his voice laced with admiration.

As if to prove his statement, Maggie jumped from her seat to talk to one of the servers. Her energetic mother was never happier than when handling five tasks at once. The Lobster Pot was her baby—hers, and Lila's aunt Thea's—and nothing escaped either woman's notice.

"One fact about this family," said Lila, "is that everybody works hard."

"I noticed," said Adam, standing up to greet Bart.

"That's because they all take after me!" Her granddad lost no time jumping into the conversation—and taking any credit he could grasp. "Look at this place," he said. "My girls did everything. Even to the posters on the wall."

Lila smiled at Bart's unabashed pride. He didn't believe in false modesty and was used to speaking his mind. But in this case, she had to admit he was right. Not only had her mom and aunt built the business from the ground up, but they imbued it with their personal touches outside the culinary area.

"Have I ever given you a guided tour of the decor?" she asked Adam. The wall decorations were special—a humorous tribute to the citizens of Pilgrim Cove.

He shook his head. "Of course I've seen the motto. It's everywhere!"

Lila grinned and quoted, "The Lobster Pot—

Where No Lobster is a Shrimp!" The words were written on the menus, on the door and on a large wall hanging in each of the three dining areas.

"But now check out the posters," said Lila. "Look carefully and you'll recognize people you've met." She watched as he studied one, saw the moment when recognition dawned.

"That's Katie's uncle from the hardware store," said Adam.

Lila nodded. "Every time a new poster gets added to the wall, I love it the best," said Lila. "Look at the one about Jack Levine and Rachel Goodman. He's a marine biologist from Maine, and she's the assistant principal of the high school."

She pointed at a large print with a caricature of an overly muscled Jack standing on the deck of a boat, and Rachel with extremely long, shapely legs, fishing from the beach. The tagline said: "Jack floundered around the seven seas, Till Rachel said, 'He's my Maine squeeze.'"

"I wonder what they'll come up with for us." Adam smiled at Lila.

She shrugged. "Couldn't venture a guess."

Her mother's voice came from behind her as Maggie walked back to her seat on the other side of Bart. "Don't you worry, Adam. My sister and I will think up something very special."

Bart glanced at his daughter, then grumbled something to Lila. "Say again?" Lila asked.

"Have you spoken with Jason yet?" He spoke quietly, nodding toward Katie.

Her granddad's meaning was clear, but it was Maggie who spoke from the other side of her father. "There's no hurry about telling him," she said. "And he won't be in town long. Maybe we could just—" she rippled her fingers through the air, a question in her voice "—overlook it?"

"Are you nuts?" Tom Sullivan half-stood up, sounding appalled, and Lila saw Bart lean against his chair, a satisfied smirk on his face. He'd let someone else run with the message as long as he'd planted the thought.

The two girls looked up at the sound of Tom's voice, and Lila caressed each child's shoulder, paying special attention to Adam's daughter. "You know, Sara, that with this family, there's always a lot of noise and conversation. Everything's cool."

Katie nodded. "She's right." The children went back to coloring their place mats.

Lila glanced at Adam. He created a circle with his thumb and forefinger in the universal gesture of "good job." But he quickly glanced back at Maggie.

"You're only kidding, right, Mrs. Sullivan? A man is entitled to know about his own child." He glanced at Sara, his love for the little girl clearly visible, then resumed the conversation. "And the child has a right to know him."

Maggie's eyes flashed before she banked her

anger. "You're naive, Adam," she said gently, "if you think the truth won't change the balance here. And I like things just the way they are. You and Lila and the girls. I guess I was merely indulging in some wishful thinking."

Adam visible relaxed. "Balance? No worries there. With children, visiting rights are no problem. Millions of kids live primarily with one parent while the other abides to a schedule."

A schedule? The Parkers? Lila's mind raced. The Parkers loved hard. Every one of them. The men had loved Katie since she was born. She was part of their lives. Lila couldn't picture any of them living or loving according to a schedule.

"After all," continued Adam. "Three thousand miles is a lot of miles."

"That's certainly true." Lila turned to her mother. "As usual, you're putting the worst spin on everything. I'm an adult. I'll handle it and maintain my 'balance.'"

"Then why haven't you told him yet?"

Lila lifted her chin. "Because the time wasn't right."

"Ha!" replied Maggie. "The time will never be right. Admit it, Lila. You'd be better off if he'd never come home."

Lila turned to Bart. "How did you manage to produce such a selfish daughter?"

"Hold it," interrupted Maggie. "I didn't say *Sam*

would be better off, or *Matt* would be better off. I merely said, *you* would be better off. I'm not selfish. Only truthful."

The immediate silence was interrupted by Adam. "Why should it matter that this man is back? Lila's leading a different life now." He reached for her hand and caressed it.

Lila smiled at him, happy for the support, but her attention was fixed on her daughter as Katie whispered to her friend.

A minute passed…or a year, before Lila turned to Bart. "I'll find Jason tomorrow." *And her comfortable life would change.*

"Lila," said Adam. "My offer's still open. If you're afraid of his reaction, I'll be more than happy to come along."

She wasn't afraid. Just not eager for an emotional upheaval.

"I'll be fine," she said, and even Maggie agreed that Adam's suggestion, while understandable, wasn't appropriate. But her mother's eyes glowed with satisfaction, and Lila knew that Adam's status had risen on Maggie's imaginary scale.

So she'd track Jason down the next day…third item on her morning agenda. After she returned phone calls and after her ten-o'clock client. She wasn't moving him to first place.

JASON PARKER BEGAN THE DAY by checking out of his motel, shopping at the supermarket and moving into

Sea View House. The Captain's Quarters provided more than enough room for his needs. The place was nicer than he remembered with its wide-planked gray floors and oval area rugs, which provided some color. Chintz-covered upholstered furniture and a large brick fireplace decorated the living room.

He'd unpacked and stored his groceries and now stood in the entrance hall trying to decide where to put the upright piano he'd ordered the day before and which was due to arrive from Boston at any moment. He'd had to pay a surcharge for the quick service, but it was worth it.

The back living-room wall was perfect. When he returned to California at the end of the month, the music store would sell the piano on consignment for him. Satisfied with his decision about the piano, he began searching for stereo components but found only a VCR underneath the television. No external speakers anywhere. He thought of the case of CDs he'd brought with him and sighed. Seemed like quality music systems were not part of a rental house. But who could blame Bart? Quality cost money, and tenants came and went. Although sometimes they came and stayed, like his new sister-in-law.

Laura was a delight, and Matt was a lucky guy to have found a second wonderful woman to love. Laura insisted that Sea View House had helped her to heal emotionally.

And now here *he* was in Sea View House. Perhaps being here right on the beach would be perfect for him, too. He hadn't had time to dig his toes into the sand, hadn't listened to the ocean's soothing murmur up close in far too long. He'd make running along the shore as much a morning ritual as breakfasting with his dad and the ROMEOs at the Diner.

Of course Sea View House also was steeped in memories for him. But if he dwelled on them…if he dwelled on Lila…he'd not only torture himself as he'd done the night he'd seen her at the steak house, he'd ruin the relationships he was starting to rebuild with his family. His dad, his brother, the kids, Laura—those were the people he needed to think about.

Jason glanced at his watch. It was after two, and the piano had been due at one. He opened the front door to check the street. He saw nothing, but heard the rumbling of a motor. A truck appeared at the corner, and Jason went outside to wave the driver over. Twenty minutes later, the instrument had been carefully maneuvered into place by the driver and his helper.

"It was tuned this morning," said one of the men as Jason handed him a tip at the door. "But with all the moving and road construction…"

"No problem. I can make adjustments myself."

Suddenly he heard high-pitched voices from the area near the truck. Two kids on bikes appeared and pedaled to his front steps at full-speed. Casey and Katie.

"We came to see your new piano," said Katie.

"Yeah, Uncle Jason."

The delivery guys left, but two jean-clad eight-year-olds remained, walking through his open front door as if they belonged there.

"Whoa!" Jason dipped down, wrapped one arm under each child's tush and lifted them off the ground, grinning at their squeals.

"Do your moms know you're here? Or do you usually take off on your bikes all over town?"

"My mom's in B-Boston," said Casey. "She's doing a taping. A big story. But it's for girls." He wrinkled his nose, and Jason laughed out loud.

He looked at Katie. "And where's your mom?"

"Working. But Grandpa Sam knows we're here," said Katie.

Grandpa Sam? Probably a courtesy title since she hung around with Casey so much. The children wriggled to the floor, and went into the bathroom to wash their hands without being asked. His dad's influence? Teaching them respect for an expensive instrument? But why Katie?

He watched the kids run through the living room, at home as could be. They'd obviously been to Sea View House in the past. Jason decided to remain quiet and watch what happened next.

"Let's practice for the Memorial Day program

first," said Casey. "And then we can do funner stuff."

Katie turned to Jason and wrinkled her nose the same way Casey had wrinkled his earlier. "We have to do a Memorial Day program *every* year at school." She turned back to the keyboard before he could answer, which was just as well, since all he wanted to do was laugh.

"You want the bass or the treble?" asked Casey.

"Either one."

"Okay, you take the low part first, then we'll switch."

The girl nodded and stood on the left side of the instrument, while Casey stood on the right.

And then Jason's amusement turned to amazement as Casey led with the melody line, and Katie carried the beat. Four hands never left the keyboard, not even when they switched from "Yankee Doodle Dandy" to "You're a Grand Old Flag." As they changed songs, they also changed positions, each child keeping one hand on the keyboard, and the music never stopped. Now Katie was above middle C and Casey below. They'd turned the change into a challenge.

Jason watched them closely. They had no music sheets; they played by heart. But playing wasn't a silly child's game to them. Rather, it was a skill they took pride in. He could see and feel how attuned they were to each other. Just the way he and Jared had been.

He and Jared. Suddenly, his heart began to thud as he stared at Katie. The image of Lila. But neither Tom nor Maggie nor anyone in that family played a musical instrument as far as he knew. True, they could all sing a pretty tune, but was that enough to produce…this talented child?

"So, whaddyathink, Uncle Jason?" asked Casey.

Katie spoke next. "I don't like the part where we change songs. Something doesn't sound right."

"Yeah," said Casey. "That's the problem."

Jason refocused to the business at hand. "That's because you changed keys. The songs were written in two different keys, and that's how you learned them. But now you're trying to put them together like a little medley, so just transpose one of them."

"Huh?"

"Like this." He walked to the piano, pulled the bench out and played for them. "Hear the difference? Start with your hands here and follow me." He showed them. They copied him. And played through the two pieces again.

Wide grins this time. "Yup," said Katie. "I like it better."

He decided to go one step further. "Good job. But you've got another choice." Two sets of eyes stared at him unblinkingly.

"Let your ears take your fingers for a walk between the songs. Make up something to connect them, the way a flight of steps connects the first floor to the second floor. So when you get to the new key, it'll sound good."

"Show us," demanded Katie.

"All right. Here's the end of 'Yankee Doodle Dandy.'" He played the last few bars, then composed a short transition to "Grand Old Flag."

Two young heads were watching his hands and nodding. They both insisted on creating their own transitions—at the same time. This experiment ended with a cacophony of sound and a lot of laughter. Jason wouldn't bet money against them coming up with something that worked.

"Now we can have some real fun," said Casey.

He whispered something to Katie who looked at Jason and said, "Grandpa taught us this one, too. It's ragtime."

Jason pulled the bench back to give them room. He'd already learned that they preferred to stand next to each other. He and Jared had done the same thing when they were very little.

They played Scott Joplin—"The Entertainer." Jason remembered driving his parents crazy playing it all the time. And now…these two. Katie and Casey. The next generation of Parkers had made themselves known.

Katie had to be his daughter. A Parker. Nothing else made sense. At that moment, his brain froze. He simply stared at Katie, needing to catch his breath.

Every move she made seemed miraculous. A child. He had a child!

His thoughts began to flow again. He felt a smile grow across his face. While he had been gone, his dad and older brother had made sure Katie knew she belonged with them as well as with Bart and the Sullivans. In fact, thought Jason, putting more pieces together, the whole town had realized the truth, had realized that Katie was Jason's child.

Lila had no reason to deny it. She'd assumed Jason would be returning. He'd made that promise on the night he'd left, and she'd believed him. He'd believed it himself. He'd asked her to wait for him, and she'd said "Yes."

How could he have known he'd break that promise? That he'd go on an alcoholic binge with no hope for a future? God, the things he'd done in order to forget the past. If he hadn't recovered…he would have missed this miracle before him.

The kids slid into a duet of "The Candy Man." This time they were singing as well as playing. And were right on key.

Jason couldn't take his eyes from Katie. Katie Sullivan-Parker. His daughter. His clever daughter who referred to him as Casey's uncle Jason.

LILA HEARD THE MUSIC as she stepped through the front door. So Jason's piano had arrived. Maybe he'd be in a happy frame of mind to absorb the news she was about to share.

She had to admit that her nerves were singing, but she thrust her chin up, walked to the living room. And stopped dead when she saw the children.

Too late. She was too late. A crazy day at the office. The third item on her morning agenda had evolved into the thirteenth, and she'd gone along with the work flow, thrusting Jason to the back of her mind. Now she was too late. And it was her own fault.

She watched the kids going to town at the keyboard like they always did. Jason's attention was on Katie. He hadn't even heard Lila come into the house. She took a deep breath and waited.

Jason stood behind the kids, almost blocking them from Lila's view. He started to speak when the kids finished their number. "So Grandpa Sam taught you both how to play?"

Two heads bobbed. "And Uncle Matt helps sometimes," said Katie.

"Brian plays lots of instruments," added Casey about his big brother. "The piano, the trumpet and the flute."

"Wow!" said Jason, looking at his nephew. "Does Grandpa Sam teach all the kids in town?"

"No way!" replied Katie, staring up at him. "He helps Uncle Matt in the store sometimes. But he don't help anyone on the piano except us. 'Cause we're special, 'cause we're his family. Brian, Casey and *me*. That's what he said." She sounded adamant rather than boastful—staking her claim.

"You sure are special, Lady Katie," said Jason, scooping her into his arms and giving her a kiss. "I can see that easily. And you're as beautiful as your mom."

She started to giggle. "Everybody says that!"

"You know what I think?" asked Jason, not giving the child time to answer. "I think you're a sweetie pie and very smart. Smart enough to know what time your mom gets home from work."

Lila's cue. "Her mom's right here." Lila stood as straight as an oak tree and hoped she wouldn't faint.

He turned to her slowly, still holding Katie. "I wondered how long you'd take to announce yourself. How long I'd have to keep the conversation going."

She felt heat rise to her throat. "I was politely allowing them to finish their piece."

"Right." Skepticism colored his tone and expression. "You should have remembered my hearing is very acute."

"Hi, Mommy!" Katie waved from high in Jason's arms. "Casey's uncle showed us a lot of stuff today."

"That's great." She never interfered with Katie's musical education. That was Sam's department.

Katie turned to Jason again. "But you know what's not great?"

"What, sweetheart?" asked Jason.

Lila winced. She knew what was coming.

"Casey and Brian have a piano and I don't! It's not fair 'cause Casey can get better'n me and what if I can't catch up?"

The incredible look Jason sent Lila almost made her stagger. "We were getting to it on her next birthday," she protested. The excuse sounded lame, but it was the truth. And she was more than ready to prolong this conversation in order to delay the one she was sure would come next.

Jason, however, had already turned toward his daughter, still in his arms. "I guarantee that you'll have your own piano very soon. In the meantime, you can use mine whenever you want. Will that work?"

She responded with a kiss on his cheek and a hug around his neck, before resting her head against his shoulder and sighing a deep sigh. Jason's expression was easy to read. A mixture of love, wonder and regret. In mere minutes, he'd become totally connected to this child.

Lila bowed her head. Jason's return had changed the status quo. No going backward. Despite her future with Adam, Lila knew it was time for truth. For Katie's sake.

When she looked at Jason again, his dark eyes held a question. A question laced with hope he couldn't hide.

"She is, isn't she?" he finally asked.

Lila's throat closed. Katie had been hers alone for eight years. She'd been the one to cuddle her, feed her, nurse her and play with her. She'd been the one to tuck her in at night with a hundred kisses. And now, she'd be the one to introduce her to her dad.

"Yes." One word whispered on a thin breath of air. She gave Jason the one word that would change the world for both of them. She said it again and watched his smile emerge. The smile that could melt her like rich chocolate on a hot summer's day. His grin widened, a dimple appeared. And God help her, she was eighteen again.

"Then there's no time like the present," said Jason.

His meaning quickly dissolved her daydreams. She forced herself to inhale, then exhale. She and Jason would have words—later. And she'd learn to deal with him as the father of her child—later. Right now, however, their daughter came first. They'd tell her the truth together.

Jason walked toward the couch, glanced at Lila and inclined his head at Casey before he sat down. Lila bribed the boy with chocolate-chip cookies and milk in the kitchen. When she returned, she saw that Jason and Katie hadn't moved. Her daughter, who lived life at Mach speed, was content where she was. Cuddled in the arms of her dad, her expression as peaceful as an angel's. Jason's countenance, however, revealed his concern about the next few minutes.

At that exact moment, Lila understood what Jason didn't. She stepped closer to the sofa, looked at the worried man and whispered, "Relax. She already knows."

CHAPTER FIVE

JASON KISSED his daughter's cheek, forehead, neck. "Katie?" he whispered.

"Hmm?" She didn't raise her head.

"Do you know what your Mommy and I are talking about?"

Instead of replying, Katie snuggled into the sweet spot on his shoulder, right under his jaw, where she fit perfectly. He could have stayed with her forever on that sofa in Sea View House. He didn't care if the rest of the world faded away. Everyone could disappear at that moment... Everyone, that is, except Lila.

The other end of the sofa shifted as Lila sat down. He looked at the mother of this remarkable child, the woman who'd held his heart from the time they'd been children themselves, sitting side by side in fifth grade. Her eyes held uncertainty, a furrow marred her brow.

"This water's deep," she murmured as she reached over and stroked Katie's leg.

She'd get no argument from him.

"Remember when you were a little girl," began Lila to her daughter, "and you'd ask me about your daddy?"

Jason felt Katie's head move up and down against him. Then she turned partway and stuck her thumb in her mouth. Lila startled—her jaw dropped, her eyes widened—and Jason understood that his child, whom he'd observed only as an outgoing and vigorous youngster, was now a frightened little girl.

Lila leaned over and kissed their daughter's cheek, her own smooth skin so close to his mouth he could barely breathe. He fought the instinct to slide his lips across the silky surface and gather her in his arms, right next to her daughter.

"Everything's fine, Katie," Lila crooned. "Everything's fine."

The child nodded.

"Remember long ago I told you that your daddy…"

"Went away on a trip," the child continued, allowing her thumb to slide from her mouth. She raised her head and looked at Jason. "But you got lost, and…" She sighed. "Very, very lost. And couldn't find your way home."

How could he make an eight-year-old understand? "Not exactly lost, sweetheart. I was searching for something. Something that was extremely hard to find."

She remained quiet as she considered his statement. "Did you find it yet?" she finally asked.

"Oh, yes. I certainly did. Definitely."

Katie's smile was followed by her cheers. Back in normal form, she bounced from his lap onto the couch next to him. "So you don't have to go away anymore, right?"

He glanced at Lila, saw her face pale as she waited for his response. His presence would shake up her life, and they both knew it. But a shake-up would suit him just fine. What was the old saying about all being fair in love and war? She may have matured to womanhood in his absence, but Lila was the same sweet, bright-eyed girl who'd made his blood roar through his veins. The girl whose smile could turn him into mush. The only girl he'd ever dreamed about and who'd ever shared dreams with him. The only girl who'd believed that anything was possible together.

How could he consider walking away when he'd just discovered his daughter? When he'd made so many new beginnings with his family? With Lila?

Lila. It always came back to Lila.

He spoke to Katie, his words aimed at both females in his life. "I intend to be here for a very long time, Lady Katie. Do you know why?"

She shook her head.

"Because I'm your daddy forever and ever, and I love you." He leaned over, rubbed noses with her and kissed her again. "You can count on that, sweetheart."

He raised his head and captured the blue-eyed gaze of the woman who perched in his heart. "And so can you," he said quietly.

LILA LEFT SEA VIEW HOUSE on legs made of rubber. What had he meant by those last words? She moved like a robot, absently noting that dusk was settling in. More time had passed than she'd anticipated when she'd first arrived. She stowed Katie's bike in the trunk, then leaned into the back seat to fasten her daughter's seat belt, glad that Jason was driving Casey home.

What had he meant? she asked herself again. And why should she care? In fact, she didn't. Not at all. If Jason still had feelings for her, he'd have to get over them. Just like she'd gotten over him. People did it every day…they simply put the hurts behind them and marched on. And if they were as lucky as she was, they'd find a happy ending.

"Mommy! Is Grandma feeding us at the restaurant again tonight?"

Lila wished the answer was no. But Friday evening was the designated family dinnertime at the Lobster Pot and had been for years. "You bet, sweetie. But first, we'll clean up at the house."

"Is Daddy coming, too?"

Oh, boy! She glanced into the rearview mirror and winced at the eager expression on her daughter's face. "Not tonight, Katie. But you'll see him tomorrow at your game."

Katie's mouth tightened, and Lila braced for an argument or at least a question-and-answer session. But none came. Katie sat back looking thoughtful.

Lila focused on her driving, grateful for the reprieve.

"Mommy?"

A short reprieve.

"Hmm?"

"You don't have to buy me a piano anymore."

Uh-oh. She didn't have to ask why.

"I'm going to Daddy's house after school every day from now on and use his. He said I could. And we can play together," Katie prattled on.

A rock settled in Lila's stomach. "We'll see, Katie. We'll see…."

In the mirror, Katie's happy face morphed by stages into a thundercloud as Lila's words penetrated. "That's the worst answer. I hate, 'we'll see.' And Daddy said I could go! He said I could…."

Lila pulled into her driveway next to Bart's Lincoln. She could feel a headache coming on. She parked, got out and took Katie's bike from the trunk as her daughter scrambled around the car to her.

"But I want to go to Daddy's house…"

"Enough!" said Lila. "I heard you. And we'll figure something out later. Right now, please put your bike away." Her headache sharpened to the same degree as her voice. She rubbed her temple.

Katie glared at her as they waited for the garage door to rise. After Katie positioned her bike against the wall, Lila motioned to her. "Come here a second before we go in."

Katie, suddenly looking unsure of herself, trudged toward her mother. "What?"

Her snippy tone was so unlike her normal self that Lila wished Jason had never set foot in Pilgrim Cove. Everyone else might be pleased that he was back, but his presence was already complicating Lila's life. Katie—usually happy and cooperative— was looking at her own mother with anger and suspicion. Lila bent closer to her daughter.

"You've had a big, big day, haven't you?" she asked in a soft voice. "It's not every day that a girl meets her dad for the first time."

She'd caught Katie's attention. Interest replaced fear in her daughter's eyes, and Lila continued speaking. "Daddy is not going to disappear again," she said, gently pulling the child to her. "You heard him yourself. He'll be here for a long time and you'll see him often."

She felt Katie's weight against her as the girl relaxed, felt two small arms come around her waist. That was more like it. "So we'll set up a schedule of when you go to Sea View House," she continued as she began stroking Katie's hair. "I have to know where you are every day. You just can't take off all by yourself whenever you want."

"I'm not all by myself. Casey's with me. And sometimes Sara."

Her daughter never gave in without an argument. "None of you guys are allowed to disappear without telling anyone. Got it?"

"O-kay," Katie sighed. "Just put Daddy on my schedule every day."

Lila chuckled. "Come on in," she said, leading the way through the inside door to the brightly lit kitchen. "I bet Papa Bart is wondering what's taking us so long."

Her grandfather answered from his seat at the table, where the newspaper lay open to the daily crossword. "I'm as curious as a cat," he said. "And as hungry as a bear."

And had eyes like a hawk. Lila saw his glance move from Katie to herself and back to his great-grandchild.

"How are my girls today?"

"Guess what?" asked Katie, dancing to the man she adored and who adored her, and plopping herself on his lap.

"What, Katie girl?"

"I got a daddy. That's what."

"You *have* a daddy," said Lila automatically.

"Well, of course you do!" replied Bartholomew Quinn.

"I *have* a daddy, just like Sara. Just like Casey." She began to giggle. "And you know what else, Papa

Bart? It's Casey's uncle Jason! That's who! And I'm glad!"

Her grandfather's sharp gaze pierced Lila. And she nodded, quickly filling him in whenever Katie took a breath.

"Wonderful! Wonderful." He rubbed his hands together, his eyes glowing. "Let's get this show on the road. The family's waiting."

THEY WERE ALL WAITING at the corner table nearest the kitchen. Although family members might have dinner at the restaurant on other evenings, on Friday nights, the corner table was the gathering place. Not that Maggie or Thea ever remained seated all the way through the meal. But the standing dinner date meant everyone got to see everyone else at least once a week.

What was it about her granddad that commanded attention? Lila watched Bart approach the group, go from person to person shaking hands, slapping shoulders, giving hugs. Asking questions as though he hadn't seen them in years. Taking inventory. That's what he was doing. He was checking up on the Quinn-Sullivan-Cavelli branches of his family's tree.

Her aunt Thea and uncle Charlie were there as well as Charlie's dad, Joe, who still helped run Cavelli's Auto Body Shop. Her cousin, Andy, was with them. He was a senior at Pilgrim Cove Regional High and would be graduating in two weeks and going to Boston University. And that made a total of three sons in college at the same time for the Cavelli family. Three young men who could take apart a car's engine or bus tables at a moment's notice.

"Hi, Dad," Lila greeted her father with a kiss on the cheek.

Her father stood, pulled her close and led her in a dance around the table.

"Wow, you're in a good mood," said Lila. "What's happening?"

"We're coming to the end of a great school year. I'll tell you about it later."

He didn't have to. His satisfaction was clear to anyone who cared to look. Tom's leadership as athletic director of the high school had made a difference not only to the teams, but to the entire school. Her dad's promotion was well deserved, and he had Rachel Goodman-Levine, the new assistant principal, to thank for pushing his name forward.

Tom twirled her out, then pulled his wife up. "Maggie, Maggie," he sang, as he waltzed with her in the aisle. Her mom's complexion turned pink, and she laughed like a girl. A pretty girl with her honey-blond hair and sparkling blue eyes, like her daughter's. Lila smiled, enjoying the natural camaraderie between her parents.

Nine seats surrounded the table. When her cousins and brother were home, there were more.

"Where are Adam and Sara tonight?" asked Maggie, now released from her husband's arms.

"At home," Lila replied. "He thought Sara was coming down with a cold and wanted her to have an early night. I'll call him later."

"He's such a good father," said Maggie.

Lila nodded briefly. Her mom was right. The love Adam felt for his daughter was obvious. He was a family man. A dependable family man. Unlike another man who'd insinuated himself back into her life.

Her nails dug into her palms and she winced, then quickly uncurled her fingers. She wouldn't think about Jason. Especially not about how happy he'd made Katie today. Of course, the novelty of reunion was still fresh, she reminded herself. Jason had no idea what parenthood entailed. Really entailed. And Katie had no idea what having a dad was all about. What it was like to have a man in the house who would not indulge her as much as Papa Bart did. To have two people—a dad and a mom—who would share the responsibility of taking care of her.

Well, Lila would experience that sharing as soon as she and Adam got married. As for Katie…she'd have two dads. From zero to two in the time it had taken Jason Parker to say "Remember me?"

Damn it! She wouldn't cry. No maudlin scenes for her. Thank goodness for her family. They'd keep her mind occupied, and no one more so than Katie.

Lila chose the seat next to her daughter's. Tom sat on Katie's other side. No one used a menu.

"Do you know what you want, Katie?"

"Yup. Chowder, please."

A tureen of clam chowder was always brought to the family table. It was one of the Lobster Pot's specialties.

"What else? Fish and chips? Clam cake? Hamburger?"

Katie leaned against her chair and shook her head. Then she looked Lila directly in the eye, her megawatt smile stealing Lila's breath. "Mommy, I'm so happy! Hap-py, hap-py. I don't want to eat." The little girl sighed deeply, and a dreamy expression crossed her face as she quietly gazed around the table.

Lila watched her daughter's uncharacteristic behavior. When Katie was happy or excited, she usually shouted from the rooftops. This reaction was different.

She wasn't the only one to notice and a quiet settled on the table as one by one each family member's attention focused on Katie.

Tom spoke first. "Did you hit a home run today, Katie-girl?"

The child shook her head back and forth. "Tomorrow's the game, Grandpa."

"And I'll be there cheering you on!"

The girl beamed at him. "And you know who else, Grandpa? My daddy! Daddy's coming to the game, too."

The quiet turned to a surprised silence as every person stared at Katie first, and then Lila.

"You mean Adam, don't you?" asked Maggie in a soft voice tinged with anxiety. "Sara's daddy who will soon be yours, too."

"No! No! Not Adam," protested Katie. "I don't need Sara's daddy anymore. I got my own now, and he's coming to the game. Sara has a dad, and I have a dad."

Lila filled them in on the visit to Sea View House. "Jason is definitely in the picture with Katie," she said as though reporting a news story.

"But for how long?" asked Maggie, her mouth tightening. "He'll run back to California at the end of the month. Which is just as well if you ask me."

"Mom!" said Lila. "That's enough."

Maggie's mouth thinned as she nodded.

Katie spoke up. "But my daddy's staying a long, long, long, long time, Grandma. He said so. And I'm going to see him every day." From happy to troubled in the space of a blink, the quaver in Katie's voice was audible.

Lila's own heart squeezed. She leaned over and kissed her daughter's forehead. "That's what he said, sweetheart. And he'll definitely be at your game tomorrow."

Katie's eyes cleared. She turned to her grandfather and started chatting about her team. Katie had great respect for Tom, the coach, and their conversation would continue for a while.

"Let it be, Mom," said Lila quietly.

"Not on your life!" replied Maggie. "There's too much at stake." She glanced at her watch and started to rise.

"Keep out of it, Margaret!" Bart's voice boomed across the table, and Maggie froze in position. But not for long.

"I will not keep out of it! I'll talk to Sam and Matt. They'll see reason even if the boy won't."

The boy. That's the way her mom thought of Jason. The boy who left her daughter when she'd needed him most. The irresponsible boy. The boy Maggie wouldn't call by name.

Lila signaled their server. "Please make my order to go. My daughter and I will be leaving." She stood up and reached for Katie. "Come on, puss. Let's make sure your uniform's clean, and maybe we'll have a big storytime before bed tonight."

Without a protest, Katie stood and raised her arms to be carried. Surprised by the silent request, Lila hoisted the child to her hip. "Man, are you growing!" She exaggerated her daughter's weight by bending her knees, causing Katie to giggle and hold tight. Much better.

She turned toward her family and this time, it was

she who glared at her mother before transferring her gaze to her granddad. "I see two stubborn people who don't know enough to mind their own business. I'm telling you both, stay out of my life."

Her mother's expression set into stone. But Bart leaned back, hands up in mock defeat. "That's exactly what I was telling her, wasn't I?" His protested innocence would have made Lila laugh ordinarily, but the circumstances were far from amusing.

"I don't trust either of you." Lila lowered Katie to the floor, took her hand and their dinner, and walked out of the restaurant.

She breathed deeply as soon as she stood in the crisp night air. Sweet New England springtime air. Stars twinkled in the dark sky. The noise of the restaurant became fainter as she and Katie walked to the car. Funny how she could be surrounded by family who loved her and still feel that she was alone in the world. Alone and invisible.

Her mom didn't see her as she was. Maggie still thought of her as a helpless teenager with a child to raise. As for her granddad, well, he offered unconditional love no matter what was happening. They both, however, definitely had their own agendas, definitely for her own good! That's what they'd both say. She sighed in exasperation as a veil lifted from her eyes and consciousness.

She would no longer allow herself to be buffeted by the forceful personalities in her family. No more taking the path of least resistance to avoid an argument. She wasn't a nineteen-year-old with a new baby anymore, so relieved when her granddad intervened between her and her mom. She was a grown woman now. It was time for her to decide her own future, to decide what was best for Lila and her daughter.

She secured Katie in her seat belt and slid into the driver's seat, her hands on the wheel. Her engagement ring sparkled in the moonlight coming through the window, and her heart warmed with affection for the man who'd placed it there. She'd call Adam as soon as she got Katie into bed.

SARA MADE HIS LIFE worthwhile. Adam finished the bedtime story, kissed his daughter on both cheeks and on her belly to make her laugh, and tucked the cover around her.

She smiled up at him. "Won't it be fun when Katie and Lila come to live with us? I can't wait to have a sister."

"I'm glad you're so happy, sweetheart. I'm happy, too."

She nodded and yawned. "Good."

Before he left the room, he positioned the door to remain partly open. All the bedtime rituals he and Sara had developed since Eileen had died.

Look forward, not back. His mantra for personal survival. He turned his thoughts to Lila just as the phone rang. He glanced at his watch and smiled. With an eager step, he went into his home office and checked caller ID.

"Hi, Lila." He sat back in his large leather chair, ready to reconnect with the woman who would be his wife in the not-too-distant future. "Is Katie tucked away for the night, too?"

"She fell asleep as soon as she hit the pillow. But not before reminding me about tomorrow morning's baseball game."

"I'm not sure Sara should go," he replied, his stomach tightening. "She still has a runny nose."

"Any temperature? Any chronic coughing? Sore throat?" Lila's cheerful questioning wasn't what he expected. "If the answer is 'no' to all three items," she continued, "let her play. A few sniffles don't warrant a day in bed, and Sara won't want to be left out."

He wished he could adopt that carefree, confident attitude Lila managed, but it was hard for him. "It took me a full thirty minutes to choose a children's cold medicine at the pharmacy yesterday."

"Probably because you really know what all those ingredients mean!" He heard Lila chuckle. "Medical school, even veterinary school, will do that to you, I suppose."

He felt a reluctant grin cross his face. "You always manage to make me laugh. I don't know how you do it. But, thanks."

"You're welcome. It's what we do for each other, isn't it, Adam?" Her cheerful tone had become quieter, more serious. "We help each other find balance and make life work."

"Yes," he said without hesitation. "We make a good team, Lila. And Sara and Katie are happy. *I'm* happy." Although his relationship with Lila was different than with Eileen, he wasn't lying. He envisioned a future with Lila, and he was content. More content than he'd been in three long years.

LILA HUNG UP THE PHONE in a thoughtful mood. Marriage *was* a team effort. She'd just never thought about it that way before. Of course, she'd had no experience with the married state, and Adam had. Perhaps teamwork was the key. A sensible approach. Rational. Organized.

Unexpectedly, a full-color picture of her parents came to mind. Sensible? Her mother? Lots of laughter and noise there. But each relationship was different. Her aunt Thea and uncle Charlie's was calmer. Maybe.

Did her past relationship with Jason count as an example, or did teenage hormones rule out any semblance of normalcy? When it came to Jason, she didn't know what to think. She suddenly realized, however, that Adam hadn't asked her about her meeting with Jason that afternoon. Well, his mind was on his daughter, and he was distracted.

The phone rang ten minutes later just as she finished getting undressed.

"I forgot to ask you how it went with Katie's father today. Was he angry when he found out about her? Should I have been there after all?"

Lila propped a pillow against her headboard and stretched out. Adam truly cared; he wasn't taking Lila for granted. And she needed to prepare him for Katie's adoration of her dad. Didn't want Adam's feelings hurt if Katie paid him a lot less attention in the next few weeks.

"He figured it out on his own, actually." She told him about Katie and Casey playing piano. "And I think he was more in awe about her than angry with me."

"Hey, I'd be, too, to discover I had a wonderful child like Katie or Sara. So how long will he be in town?"

"The lease is for a month. But he told Katie he'd be here 'a long, long time.' Maybe he figures a month seems like a long time to a child. I don't know."

"A month? Hmm…a month is long enough for Katie to get used to him. And then she'll have to adjust to him dropping in and out of her life."

Lila's stomach knotted. "Do children ever get used to that?" she whispered.

"I'm afraid that sometimes they have no choice. But…" His voice trailed off.

"But what?"

"Maybe we could give Katie something else to think about. Let's set a date, Lila. Soon. A summer wedding would work for all of us."

Caught by surprise, she didn't answer for a moment. "I—I think we can figure something out… Find a date that won't leave my granddad to cope alone for too long.…"

"Oh…right," said Adam. "I forgot that the summer is a frenzy for you and him." He sounded disappointed.

"I'll see what I can arrange," said Lila. "You may have a good point about Katie."

And what if Jason disappeared completely again? What if having a daughter was just a lark to him? What if…Katie was no more important to him than Lila had been? What if he broke Katie's heart? No!

She said good-night and hung up before she gave voice to her whirling thoughts. She heard the kitchen door open. Granddad was home. Good. Pulling on a sweatshirt and jeans, she ran to the kitchen, kissed Bart and said, "Stay with Katie. I'll be back later."

CHAPTER SIX

LILA GUNNED THE ENGINE and almost hit the mailbox as she backed out of the driveway. Hunched over the wheel, with the pedal to the floor, she wondered how a scarce three miles could take so long to travel.

She didn't knock at the door. She pounded. She pounded until it opened. Until Jason Parker—scruffy beard, wavy hair and wearing nothing but a T-shirt and sweatpants—stood there exuding his own damn brand of masculinity that she'd been a sucker for from the beginning—or, at least by junior high.

"My God! What's wrong? Did something happen…?" He tried to grab her arms, but she pulled away, then realized she was still pounding. Not on the door, but on him. And it felt good. Very good.

She got in another thwack, then jumped back. "Do you intend to disappear on her, too? You do, don't you? You're going to get on a train or a plane and you'll disappear and leave Katie with a broken heart. You'll leave her just like you left me." Both hands curled into fists.

"If you had called…even once…during the last nine years," she continued, "you wouldn't have come back to find what you did. To such nasty surprises.

"But no! Not Jason Parker!" She swung at him, but he was fast. She connected with the palm of his hand. "Jared was dead, so you had to disappear, too? Wasn't there enough pain in this town? You had to provide more, didn't you?" She wished she weighed three hundred pounds so she could bash him to the ground. Her voice would have to do.

"Well, I won't let you do that to Katie. Do you hear me? Not to my daughter! You're not going to disappear and…and break her…h-h-heart. Like…like…" Suddenly, she couldn't go on. She needed air. Twirling unsteadily, she stepped toward the door.

And was stopped by a pair of gentle hands on her shoulders. "Like I broke yours." A gravelly whisper. A statement of fact. A sigh filled with sorrow.

Lila froze, then inched around. To her amazement, tears trickled down Jason's cheek. "I am so sorry, Lila. I never meant to be gone this long."

Now she held up her hand. "I don't want to know the reasons, and I don't want your apologies, but if you want to make amends, just leave town. Leave now. Before Katie truly loves you. Before she thinks she can count on you. Before you cause more pain."

But now she saw that it was *her* words that caused the misery in his eyes. *Her* words that caused the telltale tic in his jaw. She saw it all, but didn't regret saying what she had. Then Jason took such a deep breath, she heard it whoosh to his lungs.

"I dreamed about you a thousand and one times," he said, "and every dream was different, but none were like this."

A thousand-and-one dreams? And not one letter to her! Only a handful of Christmas cards to the Parkers. She started to say so, but Jason didn't seem to notice.

"I'm in for the long haul, Lila. I'm not going anywhere." He tapped his forehead, then wiggled his fingers. "I have portable skills."

She shrugged. "You'll get bored here, and you'll be gone. Portable skills or not. And then I'll be the one to console Katie. I'll be the one who'll have to pick up the pieces."

He reached over and stroked her brow. "I wish I could wipe your fears away. I wish your eyes were shining with happiness instead of clouded with worry. I wish I could make you believe me."

His fingers traveled along her jawline, his eyes held hers fast. "But I can't give you what you want now, sweet girl. I can't leave again. Not after being away for so many years."

She felt his touch near her mouth. Over her bottom lip. Could his eyes actually deepen in color? She thought so, but then she couldn't think—couldn't see—because his mouth gently covered hers. And,

God help her, she couldn't fight him. She inhaled his familiar aroma, enjoyed his arms around her and thrilled to the sound of her whispered name.

Her heart thumped to a beat she hadn't felt in forever. And when he crushed her to him, she soared high and fast like a bird in flight. A heady sensation. Delicious. Unique. And so much a part of her own fantasies, she got lost in a time warp. For a moment.

Then she pulled back. "We're not eighteen anymore." Her throaty whisper carried its own message.

"We don't have to be. A hundred years of this wouldn't be enough." His words, too, came on labored breaths.

What was he talking about? Lila shook her head. "No, Jason. We have no future. Only a past. Our daughter is the only part of that past I want to hang on to. Nothing else."

He stood in front of her, his hand trembling as it rose to stroke her hair. "You're fooling yourself, sweet girl. What we just shared was not your run-of-the-mill ordinary kiss. You know it. I know it. Soon all of Pilgrim Cove will know it."

She laughed without humor. "That's where you're wrong. You're out of my system now. And if you thought that kiss would distract me from the real issue, you've underestimated me. I warn you, Jason, if you leave Katie in shreds when you return to Los Angeles, I'll get a court order barring you from seeing her. I'll hire a lawyer...."

Jason shook his head. "Lila, Lila, Lila," he sighed. "Haven't you been listening at all? You won't need a lawyer, honey. I'm not leaving."

She turned from him then and took a step closer to the door. No sense getting into a "yes, you are, no, I'm not" kind of argument.

"And do you know why I've decided to stay?" he asked.

She looked back, head tilted, to see his expression. His concerned, gentle expression. "Why?" she finally asked.

"Because everyone I love lives right here in Pilgrim Cove." He paused for a heartbeat. "And, as I've been reminded since I've arrived, everyone who loves me lives here, too."

His explanation was too simple. The Parker family had always lived in Pilgrim Cove, and that hadn't kept him from staying away.

"It took me nine years of running to realize it," he said. "My mom… My mom blamed me for Jared's death."

Lila paused. "I know. It wasn't fair of her. I guess the pain of losing a child made her a little crazy."

"Did you know she couldn't bear to look at me afterward?" He pointed to his face. "When she did, she saw Jared. Being an identical twin…can sometimes be a disadvantage. My dad made excuses for her." He shrugged. "I didn't know that mothers could say stuff like that to their kids. Finally, she told me to get out. I never told my dad the details. He had his hands full with her grief and his own."

He stared at her then. "And I never told you, either. Not even on that last morning we said good-bye." He blinked quickly. "I simply left. And managed to survive."

Lila looked sharply at him. "Survive" was an accurate description. She hadn't known exactly what the grief-stricken Margaret Parker had said to her son, and now saw that the pain of those comments still lingered in Jason's soul. Interesting how well she could read him. "And now you're back," she said. "Successful career, too. But time doesn't stand still."

His grin was more like a grimace. "Think I hadn't noticed?"

"I'm sorry for your…your exile," she said quietly. "That you chose to stay away. But why didn't you tell me?"

"Why? Because maybe you'd agree with her. Maybe she was right. I should have saved him. I didn't try hard enough."

"No! Don't think that. I was there. Oh, God. Your mom was unfair." She impulsively reached for his arm and squeezed it. "I'm so sorry, Jason. But she was. You *couldn't* control your brother."

"I accept that now. In fact," he said, looking at a faraway spot over her shoulder, "my dad carried a message from my mom asking for my forgiveness.

At some point, she'd confessed to him. Probably when she became ill. My poor dad. So much to cope with. He loved her, then had to swallow his anger because she was dying. He stayed by her side until the end. I hope she's at peace now. It's all right."

Lila blinked and felt her own tears well. Tears for Jason. The first ones she'd shed for him rather than for herself. "I brought Katie around for visits when she was a baby. Your dad took joy in her. Your mom, too. But then she'd always cry. Now I understand why. Katie reminded her of you and that she'd sent you away."

She took a breath, but she wasn't finished. "If Pilgrim Cove is where you really want to be… If it's where you really need to be…then, welcome home. But, Jason, believe me when I say you and I are leading different lives now. We're different people. I'm involved with someone else. Your return doesn't change that."

"I'll make a note of it," he said. A warm smile took the sting from his words. A warm, sexy smile with the power to heat her blood. She turned away.

"I won't take responsibility for your disappointment," Lila said, her hand on the doorknob. "Think carefully before you commit to this place."

"There's nothing to think about," he replied. "I'm back for good."

She left him then, glancing back only after she was behind the wheel of her car. He stood in the doorway, silhouetted against the light, and waved when she started the ignition. As she reached the corner, she checked her rearview mirror. He hadn't moved.

JASON STOPPED at his brother's house to pick up Casey the next morning, glad to be able to do such a small favor. He knew Saturday was the busiest day of the week at Parker Plumbing and Hardware.

"The Golden girls will work the registers today," said Matt over a cup of coffee at the kitchen table. "Dad and I will help customers, Brian'll do stock in the morning. After lunch, he has a game."

"I'll bring lunch," offered Jason, "and take Brian to his game. Maybe I'll have both Casey and Katie with me."

"Well, all right!" said Matt. "We'll fill up the company kitchen."

"She's some kid, isn't she?" asked Jason, immediately feeling heat rise to his face. Was bragging allowed? When he saw Matt's grin, he knew he needn't have been concerned.

"She's a great kid, Jason. Never doubt it."

"Just l-like me!" Casey's voice. "I-I'm a great kid, too."

Jason chuckled, but twelve-year-old Brian shook his head. "Was I ever like that?"

Matt eyed his son, the corner of his mouth lifting. "You were worse."

"No way!"

Jason settled back into his chair, studying the members of his family around the table. "This feels very good."

Casey leaned over and patted his arm as though to comfort him, then looked at his dad. "Can't you build another room for Uncle Jason?"

Jason chuckled, hoisted the boy to his lap and hugged him tight. "You are an amazing kid! Not just a great one. How's that?"

Casey squirmed away, and Jason recognized the child's sudden embarrassment. "So let's see how amazing you are on the ball field," Jason added, hoping it was the right thing to say.

The kid grabbed his glove. "Come on, Brian. Throw me a couple while they finish eating."

Suddenly the kitchen was quiet. "Whew!" said Jason.

"They *are* lively. Keep us busy. And I love it."

Jason stood up as Laura walked into the room. He looked hard at the big, black cat resting on her shoulder. Laura's eyes lit up with laughter when she noticed, and she waved him back to his seat. "We're not formal in this house, Jason." She lifted the cat and set her on the floor. "Go on, Midnight. Go find Jason."

"Middy's a cat, Laura, not a dog," Jason said.

"Well, for heaven's sake, don't tell her that!"

Laughter all around, and once again, Jason enjoyed the loving vibrations in the house. "I assume Dad's at the Diner with his buddies."

"Almost every morning at eight," replied Matt. "The ROMEOs. What a bunch." But his comment was laced with admiration. "I hope I have their energy and curiosity when I'm that age. They really do a lot of good for this town."

"They did a lot of good for me," said Laura. "Not only did Bart rent me Sea View House, but they all made me feel so welcome. Lou Goodman remembered my parents from years ago. And then, of course…Matt came to fix the plumbing."

"One look and I fell…hard."

Jason believed it. Their feelings for each other showed every time Matt touched Laura's arm in passing, every time their eyes met. He drained his coffee cup and stood up. "I'd better get Casey there on time for his warm-up."

"Behind the middle school," said Matt.

Jason nodded and walked to the door. "Oh, I almost forgot to mention—" he paused "—that I saw Lila last night."

Could two people hold their breath at the same time?

"And?"

"And I told her I intended to buy a house in Pilgrim Cove. So you're off the hook about adding a room for me." He winked and closed the door behind him, glad to hear their exclamations through the wall.

At least he'd made some people happy with his decision.

"Wait a minute." Matt was at the door. "What did she say?"

Jason took at moment. "To put it succinctly, she's not crazy about the idea."

"Oh."

"So I sent her some red roses this morning."

"Oh-h-h." Matt's voice rose in interest, and he gave Jason a thumbs-up.

Jason grinned and jogged to the street to collect Casey. The odds were stacked against him, and from what he'd heard, Lila's boyfriend was a nice enough guy. But was "nice" good enough? He had doubts. Big doubts. In the end, he might fall flat on his face in his pursuit, but it was gratifying to know his brother was in his corner.

"GOOD MORNING, JANE," said Lila to the office manager at Quinn Real Estate and Property Management. "Had to drop Katie at my mother's, so I'm a little late. Any new appointments? Any cancellations?" She spoke over her shoulder as she walked quickly to her office across the hallway from Jane's desk. She liked to be right where the action was, and that meant near the front door. "Is my granddad here yet?"

"No, no and yes."

Lila turned and grinned at the woman who'd taken to her first office job at the age of forty as though born to it. And that had been less than two years ago. Now Lila and Bart wouldn't know how to survive without her.

"You had a delivery, and Mr. Quinn was here when it arrived. He is now in a very good mood."

Lila yawned. "I'd also be in one if I'd gotten more sleep."

"I'm going to keep my mouth buttoned up here," said Jane. "Oh, good," she added as the phone began to ring. "Saved by the bell."

Lila crossed the threshold of her office, then froze for a moment when she saw the stunning vase of roses on her desk. Gorgeous red roses. Adam was such a generous man. She rubbed the ring on her finger. He seemed serious about setting a wedding date. She couldn't think of a reason for the flowers, however, except as a surprise. Surprises were usually out of character for Adam, but maybe…

She walked closer, stroked the velvety petals and bent her head to inhale their fragrance. Heady, sweet. Feminine. "Hmm…" she almost purred as she inhaled again and brushed her cheek against the velvet.

Nine roses. Hmm… An odd number for flowers. The number nagged at her. Nine. The number had significance for only one person. And it wasn't Adam.

Her hand trembled as she reached for the card.

"You're as beautiful as ever—inside and out. And as my friend, Luis, would say, *'Mi casa es su casa.'*" It was signed "J."

My house is your house. Once upon a time, it would have been. But now, "'It's too late, and much too dark,'" she murmured. New chapters had begun.

"It's never too late if you love him."

Startled, Lila pivoted and looked at her granddad, his blue eyes filled with interest, question and hope. It was all there, along with the love he'd always shown her.

A wry laugh preceded her words. "Love," said Lila, "doesn't seem to be enough." She looked Bart straight in the eye. "I want a man I can trust. Jason Parker is not that man."

"You're wrong, lass. Give him a chance."

A chance? She'd given him years. "Is that your famous gut instinct talking? Or is it your own heart, Granddad? You're Sam Parker's best friend, and you want a happy ending for him and everybody else, too. Well, I can't help you with that script. Not this time. I don't believe in fairy tales." She held up her hand. "I'm happy wearing Adam Fielding's ring."

"No, you're not," he replied without missing a beat. "You're lying to yourself. And that's not like you, lass."

Did he think he was a mind reader among all his other talents? Well, she'd had enough of people telling her what to think, how to feel, what to do. "I'm trying not to be rude, Granddad, but it really isn't your business!"

The silence in the room pulsed against her ears.

The expression on Bart's face…shock, anger, disappointment. Mostly shock.

"You're wrong again!" he retorted. "My family is my business! Every last one of you down to my little Katie. The boys at college—they're mine! Your mom and dad—they're mine, too." His voice rose. "The Quinns and the Sullivans and the Cavellis, too. They're all in here…in here." He banged on his chest as he spoke. "My family is everything."

Now it was Lila who was in shock. "Granddad. Stop!"

He waved his hand at her and pulled himself up straighter than a soldier at attention. "Nothing's wrong with me, lass, that a little common sense wouldn't cure—some common sense on your part."

"I am being sensible!"

"Real love doesn't have to make sense. What it must have is *passion!*" He pointed to her and then to himself. "Just look at us."

He left her then, left her mind in a whirl, and actually went whistling down the hall. Lila recognized the happy Irish folk tune. She stared after him through her open door. Then looked at the roses on her desk. "What in the world just happened here?"

WITH CASEY CHATTERING NONSTOP, Jason arrived at the middle school thirty minutes before the game. His mind, however, was not really on baseball. It was on Lila. He hoped she'd be at the game with Katie, and he wondered how she'd liked the roses.

He drove to the lot behind the school.

"Look. Coach is here already!"

"Hang on, slugger, until I'm parked." Jason heard the clicking of Casey's seat belt as the kid unstrapped himself. And as soon as he shut the motor, he heard the back door open.

"You know what, Uncle Jason?"

Jason turned his head. "What, Case?"

"I'm so glad you're here! It's fun!" Slam went the door, and Jason watched his younger nephew scamper to the dugout.

"I'm glad, too, Casey," he murmured, getting out of the car.

He stood on the rise overlooking the field and inhaled the crisp spring air. Today the sun held the promise of warmth as it shone in a clear blue sky. The baseball diamond gleamed a bright green, grass trimmed close to the baselines. And young voices chirped like birds. Jason could sense the excitement.

He'd missed this. This small-town memory now come to life. Wasn't it only a minute ago that he and Jared had raced around the bases, their mom and dad cheering in the bleachers?

He took a step toward the field and heard another door slam. A deep voice. And a high-pitched one. Turning slightly, he saw Lila's boyfriend with his daughter in tow. Jason nodded in greeting, and the child's eyes lit up.

"Oh, good. Is Katie here already?"

"I brought Casey today, but I'm sure Katie'll be here any minute." Sweet little girl. Chocolate-brown eyes tilted at the ends and a dark head of curls. They'd seen each other at the practice during the week. "Does Katie's friend have a name?"

"I'm Sara," she replied with dignity as she turned to the man next to her. "And this is my dad."

"Adam Fielding." Sara's father stepped forward, his hand extended.

They were of a height, but Fielding was more slenderly built. He had straight brown hair, the kind that always falls on the forehead. Jason watched him brush it back. His brown eyes, tinged with yellow, were now taking inventory of Jason.

"Jason Parker." Jason clasped the man's hand. "Katie's father. Matt's brother."

Adam Fielding nodded. "Can't mistake that resemblance."

"I guess not," replied Jason with a quick grin. "But you should have seen my other brother." His smile deserted him as a pang shot from his heart. Why, for God's sake, had he mentioned Jared to a virtual stranger?

But Adam just stood quietly. "It doesn't get easier when you've really loved someone, does it?" he replied. "No matter what people say." Grief-filled eyes stared at Jason. Eyes reflecting so much pain that Jason lost his breath.

And then Fielding blinked. An easy smile appeared and he nodded at the kids. "Let's go watch baseball."

"Good idea," said Jason. But he turned back toward the parking lot. "I wonder where Katie…"

"Dad-dy!" And there she was flying toward him, her glove dropping on the ground, her blond hair blowing behind her as she ran. "Dad-dy. You came." Her arms were raised, and he scooped her up and twirled her around, the same way he'd done the first time on the field when she'd thought he was Matt. No mistaken identity today.

"Hi, Adam," she said from her perch in Jason's arms. "My first daddy came back." She wiggled to the ground.

"I see that," replied Sara's dad. "You're a lucky girl."

"Yup. Where's my glove? I'm gonna be late and that's no good."

"Your glove's right here where you dropped it." A new voice. Female.

Jason studied the older version of Lila walking toward them. Maggie Sullivan. He remembered her well. A very attractive woman who'd managed to remain so. Lila could thank her mom for passing on some good genes. Maggie handed the fielder's glove to Katie. "Have fun, honey."

"Thanks. Bye." And the child was off to the dugout.

"Morning, Mrs. Sullivan," said Adam. "Staying for the game?"

"Hi, Adam. Sara feeling better today, I hope?" She bestowed a warm smile on the man, turning toward him so that her back faced Jason.

"She says she does, so I let her play. It's hard to know what to do sometimes."

She nodded. "Yes, indeed. And being a single parent makes it even harder. But…you won't be single for long. Soon you and Lila will handle things together. And I couldn't be happier."

Jason realized that he was meant to hear every word Maggie spoke. He rested back on his heels, his curiosity tingling, wondering what her next line would be. Wondering if the woman would acknowledge his presence at all.

"If you could bring Katie back to Lila's office after the game," Maggie continued to Adam, "I can watch her play for a while now and still have enough time to prepare the Lobster Pot for later."

Time to intervene. "Katie will come with me." A quiet statement. Jason waited until Lila's mother finally turned around. "Hello, Maggie," he greeted in the same quiet tone. "You're looking well."

She ignored his remark. Instead, she looked from him to Adam and back. "Have you two met?"

"We have," replied Jason. "And the earth continues to spin on its axis."

Adam waved. "And that's my cue to mosey on down to the bleachers. See you around."

"Tactful guy," said Jason.

"That's only one of his many fine qualities." Lila's mother delivered her comment like a lecture, her lips pursed.

Jason burst into laughter. "So sorry, Maggie," he said to the affronted woman. "But with every sentence, you sound like you're reading from a script. A bad one at that. You want to tell me to go to hell, so why don't you just do it and sound more like yourself?"

The woman's eyes flashed, the mouth narrowed. He'd been around Lila's house plenty of times in the old days and remembered Maggie's mercurial temper. Tom Sullivan had called her his firecracker…at least, he used to. And Jason couldn't think of a reason he'd stop. Maggie Sullivan hadn't changed a bit.

"Not hell, Jason. California would be fine." She spun to stand in front of him, tilted back to look him in the eye. "Just get out of Pilgrim Cove. Visit your family for a day or two, and go back where you came from." She sounded desperate.

"What are you afraid of, Maggie?"

"You ask that! Haven't you caused enough problems? Too many nights crying herself to sleep? Rais-

ing a child. And now, when her life is good…the best
it's ever been…with a good man…You show up. My
daughter deserves the best, and Adam Fielding is
perfect for her. If you're any kind of man, Jason
Parker, then leave her and Katie alone. Get out of
town."

Jason saw her whole body shake. She'd poured a
hundred percent of her feelings into her speech, and
the effort had cost her. But she was wrong. Adam
Fielding was not perfect for Lila. The man wasn't
perfect for any woman yet. Jason had seen the pain
in his eyes. He was still grieving for his wife.

"Would you like to sit down?" He nodded at the
bleachers and at the parking lot, giving her a choice.
He'd deal with her words later.

"Not likely. No cozy chats with you."

Seemed that "later" would have to be now. "I'm
back to stay, Maggie."

HE'D PUT UP A GOOD FRONT for Maggie, but her
words lingered as he watched the game. Was he
being selfish? Maybe he should rethink his decision. Maybe holiday visits or monthly visits were all
he deserved. If Maggie was right and Lila was
happy…

Then he remembered the kiss. The kiss he and
Lila had shared at Sea View House. Could Lila respond like that but still love someone else? He didn't
think so.

Of course she'd been a single parent for so long now, responsible and hardworking. Maybe she needed more than physical attraction and a long held love. What the hell did he know about relationships anyway?

CHAPTER SEVEN

"WE HAD LUNCH with Uncle Matt and Grandpa Sam at the store. And then Brian went with his friends, and Casey and I went with Daddy to Sea View House."

Katie's voice was muffled by the force of the shower. Just as well as far as Lila was concerned. The child had been chattering nonstop since Jason had dropped her off at the house. Daddy this, and Daddy that. Her only topic of conversation. "A regular Johnny one-note," Lila mumbled.

The water stopped. "Huh?" said Katie.

"Never mind. Let's get you dried off and your hair combed."

"Quick, Mom. I gotta get ready for the poker game."

Lila rolled her eyes. "I hope you don't bother Papa Bart and his friends. You stay out of their way, don't you?"

"M-o-o-m! I hafta stay at the table with them 'cause I'm Papa Bart's helper. But not for telling him about everybody's cards—I only did that once—but for passing out the food. And beer." She stopped wiggling, and looked at Lila. "Beer tastes terrible…but they like it. How come?"

"I have no clue, puss." She leaned closer to her daughter and whispered, "I don't like it, either."

Katie giggled and wrapped her arms around Lila's waist. "Oh, I love you, Mommy."

Lila nuzzled her daughter's neck, inhaled her sweet fragrance. "And I love you forever and ever and ever."

"And I love you forever and Daddy forever, too."

Katie smiled up at Lila. And Lila knew then that Jason was going to be a part of the rest of their lives. She'd have to work something out with him, just as Adam had suggested. Not the worst thing in the world. Adam had said that, too. Lots of families had scheduled visits, and her family would soon be one of them.

She glanced at her watch. "Come on, Katie. Let's do your hair and then you can scram. I've got to get ready. Adam will be here soon."

"Cool. Then my two dads will be here. My first and my second."

Lila dropped the brush. "What did you say? Two dads?"

Katie nodded. "Yeah. Daddy's playing cards, too. With Grandpa Sam and Papa Bart and…you know…the ROMEOs."

Lila did know. She recalled that the men had

moved their regular game to this evening. Their Friday night tradition had been in place for as many years as Lila could remember. Bart always joined the family for dinner at the restaurant, then went to his card game. And tonight, Saturday, Jason was joining them. Nothing she could do about it. In fact, she'd have to get used to Jason popping up around town and around her—their—daughter.

She stood under the hot shower imagining her discussion with Jason over scheduled visits. She hoped he would be cooperative. Finally, she dried herself off and chose a silk turquoise sweater paired with black slacks and black wedge sandals. Her hair fell past her shoulders, and hoop-style turquoise-and-silver earrings completed the ensemble. At least she looked well put together on the outside. She dabbed on some pink lipstick and ventured into the front of the house, just as Jason walked through the door.

Her heart ricocheted in every direction as she watched Jason and Sam greet her grandfather. Once again she saw that the lanky boy had grown into a broad-shouldered, solidly muscled man, now exuding self-confidence in conversation with Bart. He filled out his sea-green sport shirt in a way that made her want to slowly slide the buttons through their openings—one at a time—and let her fingers walk across bare skin.

She forced herself to move. Break the spell. She'd

have to stop behaving like a teenager every time she saw him. The present would have to erase the past, erase her memories of the younger Jason. Those memories didn't hold true anymore.

She stepped forward and Jason turned around… then froze when he saw her. She paused. Couldn't breathe. Wondered if crowded rooms really could disappear. She saw only him.

"My God," he whispered. "You're more beautiful than in my dreams."

His thousand and one dreams.

The doorbell rang, jerking her from the dream state. "Adam's here, Mommy."

Lila pasted a smile on her face and walked to the first man she'd felt comfortable with since Jason had left Pilgrim Cove. She tilted her head back for a kiss and looped her arm through his. "I'm ready."

"You sure? It always took Eileen three tries before we actually left the house." His teasing grin took any hint of criticism from his words, but Lila was surprised. He rarely mentioned Sara's mother. Maybe this was a good sign that he was more and more comfortable in their relationship.

"Lila's a very organized person," said Jason coming forward to shake the other man's hand. "If she says she's ready, she's ready. How're you doing, Adam? Is Sara knocked out from the game?"

She was more than ready to leave.

"Dozing off when I left her with the sitter."

Lila felt herself scowl. What did Jason think he was doing? Befriending the competition? She didn't know how his mind worked anymore. Perhaps he was simply insuring that Katie and Sara remained good friends regardless of their parents. Now, *that* idea she could appreciate.

"Bye, all," she said, blowing a kiss to Katie. "Be good, pussycat."

"That's easy. Daddy's here, and we're gonna figure out where to put the new piano when he moves out of Sea View House."

She'd forgotten about the piano. "Just talk about it. Don't any of you dare move furniture." She threw a concerned glance at the ROMEOs.

"Of course we won't, Lila." Jason approached. "You'll have the final say-so. Promise."

She gave him a meaningful glance. "Promise? You shouldn't use that word."

His eyes darkened instantly and the tic in his jaw returned, but the rest of his face showed no expression.

She'd scored a cheap hit, and they both knew it.

As soon as the door closed behind the couple, the room erupted with activity as everyone moved into the dining room. Everyone but Jason. Lila's parting shot reverberated in his ears, and he knew immediately that he had no chance of having any relationship with her. The truth was she didn't trust him as far as she could throw a piano. And without trust, they had nothing. Not even friendship.

He finally took a seat at the table between the M&M's and the potato chips. Katie was busy carrying small bowls of goodies and placing them strategically around the perimeter. He began to laugh.

"What's so funny now?" asked Sam.

Jason shook his head, still chuckling. "The absurdity. I've sat at more poker tables than you guys will ever know, but never have I been served in such style! Thanks, Lady Katie."

She beamed at him. "You're welcome, Laddie Daddy."

"Ha! I like that, lassie." Bart pushed the deck of cards to Jason. "You want to take these first? My arthritis is acting up today."

"Sure. Dealer's choice?"

Bart nodded.

Jason unwrapped the new deck. "This is seven-card stud, and just to keep everybody interested, the high spade-in-the-hole splits the pot. If you've got the best hand and the high spade, you get it all. Any questions?"

"Nope," said Bart. "We've played this before."

Jason allowed the fifty-two cards to flow back and forth in his hands with hardly a sound. Expertly he cut, shuffled and cut the deck again before dealing. Every card landed exactly in front of each player.

He picked up his own deal and realized that no one else had moved. "Something wrong?" he asked looking around the group.

"Uhh—tell us about how you learned to do that," said Sam. "I'm thinking we're all mighty curious now."

Four men nodded along with his dad. Bart Quinn, Joe Cavelli, Rick "Chief" O'Brien and Lou Goodman. Jason had known them all his life. How much did he want to tell them?

"After my money was gone—"

"That was ten days after he left home," Sam inserted.

"—I got a job washing dishes on the Mississippi riverboats. Gambling boats. It was hot, awful work." Jason paused, thinking back. "But I didn't notice. I was like a robot—numb—just did what I was told. As long as they paid me in cash, I stayed." He looked around the table at each man. "You'd think kitchen work would tire me out, but I couldn't sleep. Maybe I dozed five minutes every so often, but I'll tell you, I've seen the sun rise day after day over that big river. Never missed a morning. And I'd think, jeezez, I've got to get through another damned day."

He heard the anguish in his own voice, and it shocked him. A deep silence filled the room. Painful silence. No one at the table moved. Or seemed to breathe.

Jason held up his cards. "Then I found these." He

shuffled his seven with precision. "And I practiced." He wriggled his fingers. "I figured I probably had the hands for it."

Now the men nodded, and Jason picked up the tempo of his story. The spotlight was starting to feel hot.

"I wound up dealing in the casinos in Louisiana for a time. But I didn't like staying too long in one place."

"Why not?" asked Sam.

"So we couldn't track him." The chief replied to his friend while giving Jason one of those slow once-over looks he was famous for. "You did a damn good job of not being found."

"It's not that hard to disappear," said Jason. "Easy to get fake IDs. But I was worried about private detectives."

"Your dad said no to hiring them," replied Rick.

A pang of hurt raced through him, but he erased all expression before glancing at Sam.

"I trusted that you would come home when you were ready," said his father. "Except sometimes we passed your picture around to Rick's police-force friends in other cities."

"Matt went running to New York on more than one occasion, I can tell you that," Rick added.

His brother hadn't said a word about it.

"And Lila," said Bart, "insisted on being told about everything we did." The Realtor's voice was softer than usual. "Those red roses were a beautiful gift, Jason. Beautiful."

Bart glanced at his cronies, before turning to Jason. "Now, that's the right way to start courting a girl!"

Jason's ears felt as red as the roses. "Shall we play cards, gentlemen?"

In five minutes, Jason knew that the only one with a true poker face was Rick O'Brien. Reasonable enough for a cop. He also realized that he hadn't before sat at a table where people were having such a good time. He was having a good time himself, but it wasn't only the cards. It was the company.

For the first time since coming home, he finally felt that he was picking up where he'd left off.

"Who wants a beer?" asked Bart, getting up from the table after collecting half the kitty.

Jason stood. "Where's our little helper?"

"Look in there." Bart nodded toward the living room.

Jason stepped into the room, eyes zooming to the sofa where his daughter lay sleeping, her open book facedown on her chest. He tiptoed to her, gently removing the book and covering her with a blanket he found at the end of the couch.

He inhaled her clean shampoo and little-girl scent, and marveled at the perfect, miraculous gift he'd received. A healthy, lovely and lovable child. He watched her little chest move up and down as she breathed, and found himself breathing along with her.

Maybe he shouldn't tempt fate. Or be greedy. Maybe Katie was enough of a gift. Maybe she was more than he deserved. After all, Adam Fielding seemed like a nice enough guy. Maybe Jason should let well enough alone. But…

He'd think about it later. Now he returned to the table through the kitchen, bringing a can of soda from the fridge.

"Nothing stronger?" asked Bart.

"I'm fine," said Jason.

He felt his dad's eyes on him, shining with approval. And scenes from the last few days shuffled in his memory until he was back at the cemetery telling Jared about his life. Sam had been there listening to everything he'd said. His dad knew about the binges, how he'd tried to erase all the pain with alcohol. Being blitzed sure felt better than being tortured by memories. Happy memories. Painful memories. Jared. His mom. Two years wasted in a stupor. And throughout all the years away, memories of Lila. The only memories with the power to bring calm to his soul.

"Shall I carry her into her bedroom?" he asked, once again looking down at his daughter when the game folded at midnight.

"Well, sure, boyo. You're the dad, aren't you?"

"That I am, Bartholomew, but you'd better show me the way."

He carefully scooped Katie into his arms, but her eyes fluttered open. "Shh, honey. It's all right."

She smiled. "My first daddy. Good." Her eyes closed again.

"I love you, Katie," he whispered.

"Me, too-o-o." Her voice trailed away, and she slept. He carried her as though she were made of porcelain.

He tucked her in, then joined Bart in the hall. "Sweet, isn't she?" said the older man.

"How can you ask? There's no one sweeter."

"Not even her mother?"

Jason said nothing until they reached the kitchen where his own dad waited. "Nothing has changed about the way I feel about Lila. But what happens next is between her and me."

"Jason." His dad's voice was raspy. "Don't push her. Lila has shared Katie with us a hundred per-cent…and Lila's not had it easy, either. So let her be. She's met a nice guy. She'll have a good life. And Katie will still be part of us."

"Sam, be quiet!" spoke Bart. "Your boy knows what he's doing. He's courting her, like he should. Starting with the flowers. He's the one for Lila. Al-ways was since they were babies, and you know it. I've lost count how many times Lila fought with her mother throughout the years every time Maggie tried to push her toward another man."

"Until she met Adam Fielding!" said Sam with

vigor. "And that's my point. Adam Fielding is special to her. Let her find happiness with him. Let well enough alone, Bartholomew."

The two old men stared at each other, each looking surprised, maybe a little shocked.

Jason felt sick. His presence was causing conflict between two lifelong friends. Maybe he shouldn't have come back to Pilgrim Cove.

"You gave Matt such good advice when he was afraid to commit to Laura," said Bart, first looking at Sam, then Jason. "She'd had the breast cancer, and your dad pushed Matt out of his shell shock into some good action. And now look at the lovebirds!" He turned once more to his friend. "You were so sure of yourself, Samuel. And you were dealing with life and death. Why are you holding back now?"

Sam Parker poked his finger at the Realtor. "I'm not so in my dotage that I can't tell the difference between two people madly in love with each other like Matt and Laura, and two people who aren't. And that's the difference here. If you don't believe me, ask your granddaughter! And I'm done. Good night."

He walked straight to the front door, then turned. "Are you coming, Jason? I'm tired."

"Right away." He glanced at Bart. "Don't you dare ask Lila anything, or you'll push her into a corner. I appreciate your support, but you're sidelined now. Understand?"

Bart pointed at Sam. "What about him?"

"Dad? Are you kidding? I'm putting duct tape over his mouth."

He walked to the door, keys in his hand. "Come on, Dad. I'll take you home."

He couldn't blame Sam for speaking his mind. "So you were a pretty big Cupid for Matt and Laura, huh? I didn't know that."

Sam opened the passenger door and got in. "Oh, pooh. A blind person could have seen how crazy they were about each other. I want you to be happy, too, Jason. But to be happy like your brother, the woman's got to love you all the way. That's all I was trying to say in there to that stubborn old geezer!"

Jason got into the driver's seat and turned the ignition key.

"Lila's not the sweet little girl you remember, Jason. She had to become a woman and a mother very quickly. A lot of responsibilities for a teen."

"She's done a magnificent job," said Jason quickly.

"She certainly has. And while she was raising Katie, she learned that she could survive without you. She's built a new life. Let her be."

Jason dropped his dad off and made his way along Beach Street back to Sea View House, glad he had his own place, away from the opinions and emotions aired so easily by everyone in his life. He'd caused a whirlwind by coming home. Home to small-town living where everyone knew each other's business, and no anonymity existed at all.

"Just buck up and swallow it," he murmured, as he stood at the back porch railing staring at the ocean, enjoying his solitude.

The moonlight glistened on the water and the ocean's rhythmic movement sounded like a lullaby. A lullaby of the waves…of the wind. Of the sea. "A Lullaby for Katie." "A Song for My Daughter." One thought flowed into the next. One connection to another. A melody emerged. He entered the house and made a beeline for the piano.

He finished at 5:00 a.m. and left his music sheets on the bench before staggering to bed. If his work sounded as good to him when he awoke as he thought it did now, he'd call his agent.

HE WAS ALMOST AFRAID to play it again the next day. Had he really hit the mark, or had he been afflicted with maudlin madness in the middle of the night? His watch said eleven o'clock. He needed coffee. His stomach rumbled as he set the small pot to brew. Okay, he needed food, too, but he decided to take a shower first. Procrastinating. That's what he was doing. He knew it, but he also knew he'd get to the piano when he ran out of excuses.

Shower. Shampoo. Dry off. He pulled on a pair of soft worn jeans, grabbed a T-shirt from his drawer and padded to the kitchen. A mug. He needed a mug.

Sea View House provided all the essentials including mugs. When he downed his first swallow, the world came into sharper focus. He slapped some cheese on bread and took it and his coffee onto the porch.

The sun shone and the ocean still whispered. The vastness, the rhythm, the waves cresting over and over. He started to hum what he'd written the night before. Started to sing it softly with the ocean as backdrop. And he knew it worked. He'd tell the producer they needed to be at the water's edge to record this one.

He punched a number on his mobile. "I've got something, Mitch," he said to his agent a minute later. "You might think I'm crazy, but I want to send it to Celine Dion's agent."

"Do you know what time it is here?"

Jason glanced at his watch. Ouch. "I keep forgetting."

The other man growled something.

Jason remained unperturbed. "Why don't you just rest back against your pillows and listen to some pretty music. It'll relax you."

"Just a sec. Vivien's going to listen, too. You'll get a woman's reaction. And besides, why should I be the only one in L.A. up at this hour on a Sunday?"

"No reason at all, but I'm glad I'm three thousand miles away from her."

Vivien was really a peach, and she had good instincts. But Jason had no idea if she was a morning person or not. "Okay. I'm putting my cell phone right on top of the piano. It'll have to do for now."

He played and sang his four verses of "A Song for My Child," which told about the love of parents for their children. He tried to make the piano act as a full orchestra. He wanted this song to work.

Three and a half minutes of becoming one with the music left him wrung out. Drops of perspiration dotted his face when the last refrain faded, and he actually felt weak. Slowly he reached for the mobile.

"It's beautiful." The soft words came from behind him. He spun on the bench and saw the two females who made his life complete. Tears trickled down Lila's cheeks. Katie was clutching her mother.

He stood and walked toward them while speaking into the phone. "Well, Mitch?"

"Vivien's crying."

"So's Lila." He gently thumbed away her tears.

"Lila?" His agent's voice rose with interest. "*The* Lila?"

"That's right. *The* one and only Lila."

"Very interesting."

Jason didn't comment, but Mitch didn't seem to notice.

"I'm going to call Dion's agent and tell him to buy Luis's CD! Then I'll tell him you wrote this new song with Celine in mind."

"Good. I'll cut a demo for her. There must be a

sound studio in Boston I can rent for an hour. Just the eighty-eight keys and me."

"And me, too. I want to see a studio." Katie was leaning against him, looking up, curious and eager. He leaned over and kissed her. "Good morning, Lady Katie." Then turned his attention back to his agent.

"I suppose you can ship a CD," said Mitch. "But you'd be better off here."

Jason spoke into the phone, but his eyes never left Lila.

"Mitch, listen carefully. From now on, my trips to the West Coast are business trips only. I'm relocating here. My hometown."

He saw Lila swallow hard. Her eyes narrowed. "You're really doing this?"

"You bet I am."

"What?" Mitch shouted into his ear. "You're not even gone a week. There's nothing there. If it's Lila—bring her to L.A. She'll love it."

"She'd hate L.A." He pointed at Lila.

"Tell him everything," she said through tightly drawn lips. "Whoever he is."

"Yes, ma'am."

He spoke to Mitch again. "Settle down and listen." He took a breath and winked at Katie. "I have a daughter. The most wonderful little girl you can imagine. And I'm staying right here. Congratulate me, Mitch, and congratulate yourself. You're an honorary uncle!"

He hung up with a promise to call later, and turned to Lila, who'd seated herself on the couch.

"Didn't you believe me when I said I'm moving back?"

"You hadn't defined 'long, long time.'"

He hoisted Katie into his arms. "But I bet you knew, didn't you, sweetheart?"

A big nod, up and down. "Yup. Daddy's home again. Forever and ever."

He lowered Katie to the floor, then strolled to the sofa. He looked directly at Lila, whose lovely ivory skin had paled to milk-white. He waited a heartbeat before casually saying, "Since I only have Sea View House for a month, I'd really appreciate you lining up some properties for me to see."

CHAPTER EIGHT

LIKE HELL SHE WOULD! He could live in a shack for all she cared. Lila glanced around the comfortable room, hoping for inspiration to strike.

"Why don't we extend the rental on Sea View House for the summer? Then you won't have to rush into buying anything." *And maybe the novelty of living in Pilgrim Cove would fizzle out by Labor Day. And he'd leave town again.*

Rising from the couch, Lila began pointing out features of the house. "Look at these wonderful oak floors. Twelve-inch planks. People envy this kind of construction. Not to mention the brick fireplace running all the way to the ceiling. And your piano fits perfectly on that wall." Babble, babble, babble. She heard the words pour out of her mouth and couldn't stop before striding to the center hall, Jason a step behind her. She flung her arm toward the kitchen and back door.

"And as if those features weren't enough—where else could you live next door to the Atlantic Ocean—right at the water's edge?"

His eyes glowed at her words, and she slapped her palm over her mouth. Good Lord! How could she have quoted from his own song?

"Then find me a house at the water's edge, Lila," he said softly. "Where the song of the sea provides the perfect musical background for making love."

Like they'd done nine years ago in this very house.

Their shared memory was evident in his raised eyebrow, in his smiling mouth and in his eager stance. His body language said "Remember?" Desire lurked behind his eyes, but humor lurked there, too. And at that moment—for just one moment—she saw the happy boy, the loving boy Jason Parker had been. Here was her Jason—the Jason she remembered. And the Jason she'd tried so hard to forget.

The Jason she could no longer trust.

She turned from him, looked longingly at the front door, wanting to make her escape. "I don't think about those days anymore. And I advise you to follow suit."

He stepped around her, blocking her escape. "And *I'd* advise *you* to begin thinking about that time in our lives," he replied, his voice quiet but firm.

She shook her head. "No. No reason to go there."

"Yes, there is," he whispered, his fingers gently raising her chin so that their eyes met. "Because what we had together, Lila Sullivan, is the way it's supposed to be."

Soft music drifted in the air from Katie who sat
at the piano. The lilting notes wrapped around them
like a delicately woven veil and provided as much
privacy as if they'd truly been alone.

Jason's words came from his wishful thinking,
from his wanting to turn the clock back, Lila
thought. "You've got to live in today's world, Jason.
That time in our lives is over. You can't get it back."

He said nothing for a moment, just reached for
her hand—her left hand—and tapped the ring she
wore. "He's a decent guy, Lila," he said, "but he's
the wrong man for you."

Too stunned to speak, she could only gasp at his
words... At his nerve! Her anger began to build.
"And you, I suppose, are the right man? You're in
town for five days and you think you know everything? But you don't know me anymore, Jason! I'm
not the same girl you remember. I've grown up. And
it's time you did, too."

She didn't expect him to chuckle, though the
sound he made wasn't very happy. "Grow up?" he
asked. "Lila, Lila...you're preaching to the wrong
person. If growing up means getting to know yourself, I can assure you that there isn't a part of my soul
I haven't examined intimately. It's the only way to
survive after you've hit rock bottom and discover
that you really do want to live."

What was he talking about?

"But the most important thing I learned climbing

out of the mire is that the person I was hiding from had been with me all the time. Right in here." He touched the left side of his chest. "I know who I am, Lila. And what's important to me."

She couldn't turn away this time. Instead she did the opposite. Studied him from haircut to shoes. He spoke with a calm assurance she envied—no fidgeting, coughing, slouching or avoiding her gaze. A man comfortable in his own skin.

"Why did you return to Pilgrim Cove, Jason? Why now, after all this time?"

His natural smile returned. "That's an easy question. I had no choice but to come home. I have to face whatever waited here in order to move forward."

No doubt he'd been on a rough road. She didn't want to imagine the possibilities. His last words, however, gave her pause.

"But you're not moving forward," said Lila, her voice tight. "You just want to pick up where we left off, and that's not possible."

Jason leaned one shoulder against the wall, one foot crossed over the other, looking more relaxed than ever. She didn't understand him. "Where I come from, sweet Lila," he almost drawled, "anything is possible."

His words echoed those from a younger Jason planning a future. His familiar smile, warm and loving, sent her pulse racing. Although he'd grown physically, he remained just as she remembered him. Jason Parker. Her Jason. The boy who'd adored her. Who'd serenaded her outside her window until the whole neighborhood had come out for a concert! Memories flooded her—a thousand bits and pieces—treacherous memories.

Tears filled her eyes, and she ran out the door, not glancing back. But she heard his voice. Heard him call, "This running away is getting to be a habit with you."

And then she heard him chuckle again.

But darn it if he wasn't right! When she pulled away from the house, she realized that she hadn't even asked him if he could take Katie for the afternoon. She shrugged. He wanted to be a dad. Time he learned the job ran 24/7.

THANK GOODNESS Sunday was the busiest day of the week for a Realtor. Lila's clients had received superb service, had gotten her undivided attention. And by dinnertime, she'd convinced herself that her response to Jason that morning had been more imagined than real.

She ran through the door of Quinn Real Estate and Property Management. "Is my granddad in his office?" she asked Jane.

"With a client who just arrived." The woman grinned at her. "But I'm sure you can join them."

Lila and Bart made a practice of introducing

themselves and being friendly to all clients, regardless of which one of them was the primary agent. Jane's remark was nothing unusual, and Lila walked to the end of the corridor and made a left toward Bart's office. She heard Katie's voice before she reached the door.

"We had such a great day, Papa Bart. Where's Mommy? I want to tell her, too."

"I'm right here," said Lila.

Katie's eyes brightened and she skipped over to give Lila a kiss. "Guess what we did today!"

Lila glanced from her daughter to Jason, who leaned against Bart's desk looking happy. Her eyes narrowed as she studied them. "This one's easy, Katie. You both went out in the sun without any protection."

"I wore my baseball cap," her daughter protested.

"But the big old sun still found you." Lila swooped down for a kiss. "Next time, you must wear sunscreen."

"I need a list," said Jason.

She glanced at him. Guilt was written all over his face. His gorgeous sun-kissed face with his square jaw and thick dark hair falling into his eyes. She swallowed and nodded. "That's a reasonable request."

"I'm a reasonable guy, Lila. Believe me."

The problem was that she didn't want to believe him, but she could see his distress was genuine. He'd fallen in love with his daughter…who hadn't finished her recitation yet.

"First we went shopping," said Katie. "You know what I got? Daddy and me chose bedroom stuff…"

"Daddy and I," Lila corrected automatically.

"…for my bedroom in his house so I can sleep over in my own room. Just like at our house. We got sheets and a bedspread and a pillow and towels. And I got a new nightgown and slippers. For Daddy's house."

Whoa, whoa. Sure it made sense, but she wasn't ready to hear "for Daddy's house" quite so often. "So did you pick out a bedroom at Sea View House?"

"Yup. The one with the big desk so I can do my homework in there if Daddy's working."

"Working?" A job? For a moment, she was confused.

"The piano could disturb her," he said. When Lila looked at him, he continued. "I don't watch the clock. If everything's coming together, I keep on going. If I'm struggling, I step back."

"I'm sorry I didn't ask before I left Katie with you today. You might have been working."

"Katie's welcome at any time. Day or night. No need to be sorry." He tousled the girl's hair. "As a matter of fact, Katie's going to check out any new house I'm considering before I buy. She's going to have at least…half a vote."

Lila watched as Katie waltzed around the room, a big smile on her face, then plopped herself on her great-grandfather's lap. She stretched up to tell him a secret with her hands cupped around her mouth.

"Papa Bart, I'm so happy, happy, happy." Somehow, eight-year-olds had a hard time controlling volume. But not their love. Katie tucked herself close, turned into Bart's chest and hugged him.

"We should have a camera," said Jason. "That's quite a picture."

His quiet voice startled Lila. But then she smiled. "They are quite a team. His unconditional love and her total trust."

"Unconditional," he repeated. "I wish you'd—"

She interrupted. "It works for parents and children only."

"I'll have to think about that."

"Well, you do that while I close shop." She started to leave Bart's office.

But Bart stopped her. "Not yet, Lila. You need to book an appointment with Jason. The boy's come to his senses and wants to move back home."

"That's right, Mommy. You hafta help Daddy find a house."

She hadn't expected Katie's remark, but Lila was undeterred.

She turned slowly to her grandfather. "You're the one for Jason, Granddad. You two have a great rapport, and he wants a house right on the beach. Everybody in town tells you everything first. You'll have wind of properties way ahead of me."

She pasted a smile on for Jason. "Beachfront properties are spoken for within a day of being on the market. But don't worry. My grandfather will take care of you."

"Your granddad's okay in my book," said Jason, "but I'd prefer you."

Lila took a deep breath. "Now, tell me again why you can't rent Sea View House for the season?" She looked at Bart. "Do we have another tenant for it yet?"

Bart's eyes narrowed. "We never have a shortage for that house."

"But do we have anyone right now?" She knew Bart could dance around a question in double time and make a person believe the fault was theirs if they hadn't understood his answer. Lila had learned to be short and direct. "Do we have anyone right now?"

Bart glanced at the ceiling, a furrow creasing his forehead. Then he turned his swivel chair toward the window and watched the sky darken.

Despite his ability to bend a story, Bart never lied. "Okay," she said. "We don't have anyone right now, so there's no reason not to extend Jason's lease." She brushed her hands by each other to indicate she'd solved the problem. No house hunting. No regular visits with Jason. Perfect.

"Sorry to disappoint you," said her client. "It's very wasteful for me to pay double rents for three months."

"Double?"

"I lease in California. Could never bring myself

to buy property there." He paused. "I'll give notice the minute you find me a house. The sooner the better."

LILA'S PHONE RANG later that evening as she prepared for bed. She ran to answer it. Maybe it was Adam, home from the visit to his parents' house in New Hampshire. Adam, the calm, sane part of her life.

"Hello," she said with enthusiasm, her voice almost musical.

"Now, that's a greeting I can appreciate."

Jason. The turbulent, crazy part of her life. "Don't get used to it. I was expecting someone else. What do you want?"

She heard his deep sigh through the wires. "Sorry to disappoint you, but you're my house hunter, and I need some dates so I know when I can arrange studio time. My agent just called. He's been busy today."

"On a Sunday?"

"*You* work on a Sunday," he said, but then continued. "When Mitch likes something, he acts fast…. Celine Dion's agent wants to hear the demo that's not yet made. So, hi-ho, hi-ho, it's off to work I go."

"It's just as well," said Lila. "I can't fit you in until the end of the week anyway." Which was great. She'd have a few days for her life to get back to normal before she saw him again. "I'll review the listings we have in the meantime. See if anything on the beach is available." And if there were no properties, maybe he'd postpone the move. Return to California at the end of the month. She could live with that!

"Make sure you search hard," he said. "But if there's a problem, I'd consider the bay side of the peninsula."

Darn! "I'll keep that in mind," she said. "Good night."

She almost slammed the receiver down. The phone rang immediately. "Hello," she barked.

"Hi, Lila. What's wrong?" The calm voice of Adam Fielding.

"Oh, Adam. Sorry for snapping. The real question around here these days is 'what's right?'" she said.

"Uh-oh. Katie's dad?"

"You got it."

"What's he done?"

"Well, he…" What could she say? That Jason bought his daughter gifts? That he'd played soccer on the beach with her? That he wrote a song that would probably be recorded by a major star? Even to her, it sounded ridiculous. "He wants to buy a house, and I'm his Realtor," she finally said.

"A house? He can't mean it. His whole life—his career is in California."

"That's just what I said, but it seems as though I'm scheduled to show him properties." She shrugged. "I got coerced by my granddad and him."

"Relax, Lila. He won't go through with it." Then

Adam started to laugh. "You're simply adorable. You sound just like the kids. Except Sara wouldn't have used the word *coerced*. And Katie would have said, 'They made me do it.'"

His analysis was exactly right, but somehow, Lila didn't appreciate his humorous insight. Although Adam had several years on her, Lila wasn't sure she enjoyed being grouped with the children. For the first time, she wondered if Adam saw her as merely an older version of Katie. Someone he enjoyed and admired, but also someone who needed to be taken care of.

"Adam," she said, "how about you and I having dinner tomorrow night. Alone."

"On a school night it's hard to get a sitter," he replied. "But I love the idea."

"Then let's take the girls. I'll settle for second choice."

"Sold. But not the Lobster Pot, if you don't mind."

She hadn't wanted to be around her family, either, but his words were so unexpected, she took a moment to reply. "Are you tired of the food?"

"The food's great," he said immediately. "And I like your family, but you have to admit they can be…a little overwhelming. I'm an only child, Lila. I'm not used to all the commotion. Or emotion."

So it wasn't personal…exactly. "Why haven't you mentioned this before, Adam? If you've been uncomfortable, you should have told me. I'm so used to charging in full steam ahead...."

"And that's one of the traits I admire about you. You and Katie. What a great influence you've both been on Sara. She's been so much happier since we've moved here. She's really come out of her shell. In fact, my parents were talking about it today. They send their regards, by the way, but they understand you had to work...."

Lila barely registered the rest of their conversation. Something in Adam's words disturbed her, but she couldn't quite identify the problem.

By the time she hung up the phone, she wanted to crawl into bed and sleep for a year. She got undressed, brushed her teeth and finally slipped between the sheets. But when she laid her head down, she began to cry uncontrollably. She cried until she thought she'd never stop.

Finally she ventured a look at the clock. The hands glowed 1:00 a.m. Sitting up, she wrapped her arms around her bent legs, holding them close to her chest. "I'm scared," she whispered. "I'm so scared. And I don't know why."

MONDAY DRAGGED. Not that Lila didn't have a bucketful of work to do, but her heart wasn't in it. Follow-up phone calls, preparing some offers, and actually reviewing properties that might be appropriate for Jason. Reluctant as she was to deal with this latest client, she had no choice.

When the phone rang a little past three, Lila reached for it while looking out the window for the school bus. On the other end of the line, she heard the cheerful voice of Laura Parker informing her that Katie had gone home with Casey and Brian.

"Without asking first?" She'd have to speak with her daughter right away. "I'm so sorry, Laura. She shouldn't have done that."

But Laura brushed aside her concerns. "You can scold her later. But, honestly, Lila, I love having the kids here. The more the merrier. They're so adorable—even Brian, although he'd hate to hear me describe him that way."

"Brian's a great kid," said Lila, picturing Matt's twelve-year-old son. An almost-spitting image of his dad.

"You should see him with Katie right now," said Laura. "He's helping her with schoolwork. I'm going to get my camera."

Lila grinned. Laura Parker, loving her role as mother, was known for keeping her camera handy at all times. But then Laura's words penetrated. "Schoolwork? Katie never mentioned anything to me about a project. Or about a problem."

"Hmm. Then I'm just going to mosey on over right now... Ahh, I see...it must involve learning al-

phabetical order. They are deep into a big dictionary."

Lila filed the information away. "If you're sure
it's okay, I won't interfere now and disturb them. It's
nice of Brian to help her, but I hope he's not leaving himself short of time for his own work."

They chatted for another minute before Lila
thanked the other woman again.

"Please, Lila, no thanks are needed. I've never
been so happy in my life. Between Matt, the kids and
even the ROMEOs…" Her voice trailed off.

"And don't forget your own career," said Lila.

"Of course not," replied Laura. She paused and
softly said, "Life is good, Lila. Very, very good. And
I'm so glad you're part of it."

"I'm glad, too." Laura's happiness was so well
deserved; she and Matt were so perfect for each
other. The phrase stopped her. *Perfect for each other.*

The words echoed in her mind after she'd hung
up the phone. Her mother thought Lila and Adam
were perfect for each other. And until last night,
Lila had thought so, too. She idly wondered how
Maggie would feel to know her future son-in-law
needed time away from the Sullivans. Lila, while
surprised and a little hurt, couldn't hold it against
him. Not everyone was cut out to be a part of large,
noisy groups. Not everyone reveled in the tumult the
way Laura Parker did. The way Maggie Sullivan

did. No, Adam's feeling about the noisy family wasn't really at the heart of her discontent.

She rested her head in her hands and stared unseeingly at her paperwork. What had changed? What was wrong with her? A week ago, she hadn't a cloud in her sky, but ever since Jason had come home…

She slapped the desk. Jason. He was the root of this malaise. He was the only new variable in her life. Her usual confidence returned as the thought jelled. Identifying the target for her anxiety meant she could do something about it.

LILA DROVE NORTH on Beach Street, quizzing herself on who lived in which house—she really should know them all—until she arrived at the Parker home. Laura and Matt's new house was a two-story, natural-shingled affair at the end of the four-mile stretch of beach heading toward the Point. Bart would say that the Point was the fingernail of the peninsula pointing toward Boston. To Lila, the "fingernail" looked more like the heel of an upside-down boot when she viewed it on a map, but she didn't argue with her grandfather.

For his wife's happiness, Matt had literally moved the earth to build this house. And now Laura could start every day with a run on Pilgrim Beach. Early morning runs had helped the woman put her life back together after her bout with breast cancer, and she'd kept up the activity.

Lila pulled up in front of the house and made her way down the driveway to the side door. She knocked, called Laura's name and let herself into the mudroom. Three steps later, she was in the large country kitchen, with Laura approaching and greeting her from the hallway entrance.

"The kids are in the music room," she said waving behind her. "Great idea putting it on the opposite side of the house. I swear, we have enough instruments for our own band."

Lila chuckled. "Did Katie behave herself?"

"She was too busy not to." Laura walked to the table and pointed to Katie's books. "The dictionary project... Take a look."

The tone of the other woman's voice raised Lila's curiosity, and she opened Katie's three-ring binder. On the top line of the first page was the title "Lila's Song." Beneath that were listed several words with definitions laboriously printed in Katie's large writing. *Ledge, pledge, dunes, haunts, aching...lover.*

"Lover?" whispered Lila, glancing at Laura, then down at the entry. *Lover: a person in love, esp. A man in love with a woman.*

"Brian stopped her there," said Laura. "Before *Webster's* got to more intricate definitions. Paramour was fourth, I think." Laura's chuckle rubbed Lila's nerves.

She started to pace. "Damn it! Why did he write that stupid song?" She tilted her head toward the music room where the kids were. "You know Katie. She gets an idea and doesn't let go. And I'll have to deal with it."

Before Laura could reply, footsteps preceded Katie's entrance into the kitchen. "Mommy! Come hear what Casey and I figured out. Come on, come on." Twirling like a ballerina, she disappeared again.

"Forewarned is forearmed," murmured Lila following her daughter. She looked back at Laura who'd remained at the table. "Oh, no. You're coming, too."

Laura joined her immediately. "I wouldn't miss it."

Katie's eyes shone when the two women stood in the doorway. "Oh, wait till you hear how we do Daddy's song. We're doing an introduction and everything."

Brian looked at the women and sighed. "We just took it from the radio. No big deal." He looked at Laura. "Mom, we've got to get the CD as soon as it's released. Luis Torres is the man. It's gonna fly off the shelves."

"Not to mention your uncle writing three of the songs," replied Laura. "Of course we will."

"Three?" asked Lila, turning toward the other woman.

"Yes," Laura replied, drawing out the word. "Lila, honey," she said, taking Lila's hand and squeezing it. "Isn't it amazing? Jason's doing so well. He's writing for the best in the business now. He's got a serious career going. Not that I know much about the music world."

Jason and a serious career. Lila had to think about that. Jared was the one who'd wanted the big music career. Not Jason. And she'd been glad. Despite the tension…. No, she wouldn't go there. She thought instead of the bits and pieces of conversations, the song by Luis Torres and the rental of the piano, and how all of that still hadn't added up in Lila's mind to a long-term career. A serious career writing for truly big names.

"Mom, are you ready?"

Lila nodded and watched Katie and Casey take their usual places next to each other in front of the piano. Brian stood behind them, flute in hand. But there were no notes to read. Only the sheet of paper with the printed verses leaned on the piano above the keyboard.

The introduction was simply the last line of the chorus, but Lila found herself listening. She made her way to a chair, sat down and concentrated. She heard Katie and Casey play together, four small hands making a large sound. She heard their soprano voices blending sweetly. But it wasn't until Brian played alone on his flute, capturing the essence of the song as clearly and soulfully as a nightingale, that she felt the power of the music. She felt it for the first time since she'd heard "At the Water's Edge" on the radio one week ago.

When the children finished, she couldn't move. Laura sat quietly, too, for a moment, and then started calling, "Bravo, bravo." Lila began applauding and adding her voice.

A twinge of guilt assailed her when she realized how she'd taken Katie's talent for granted. Hadn't really wanted to acknowledge it as a major part of her life. Left it to Sam and Matt without ever getting involved. She blushed to realize she'd rarely thanked them. She'd taken their love for Katie and their involvement in her daughter's life for granted, as well.

It wasn't Katie, however, who caught her attention then. It was Brian. He walked over to his mother, and glanced shyly at Lila. He pulled Laura's hand. "Come here a minute, Mom."

Laura stood and followed him a few steps. "What's up?"

"That song," whispered Brian.

Lila hid a smile. Brian's excitement had made the twelve-year-old's whisper audible to the room.

"What about the song?" asked Laura.

"I know what it means now. I think he loves her. I think Uncle Jason loves Aunt Lila."

The breath whooshed out of Lila's lungs. Could Brian's interpretation be true? Then she remembered that Jason's version of love was that of an eighteen-year-old trying to pick up where they'd left off.

A door slammed in the near distance. "Anybody home?"

Lila's stomach plummeted to the floor. Jason's voice. She glanced at her daughter, who was staring at her with eyes open wide. Curious eyes. Questioning eyes. Eyes filling with wonder, then hope.

"In here," Laura called as she stepped to the door. Lila saw her pivot back to Brian and whisper, "Drop the topic."

Another door sounded, a car door this time followed by a second and third male voice calling out. And suddenly the room was filled with people. Talking, laughing. Low male tones and higher female ones. Squealing children. Family reconnecting at the end of the day.

Lila wasn't part of this family. Not technically. For the first time in years, that truth pricked her senses. She stood and inched her way toward the door, while watching Jason stride directly to Katie. He picked her up with sure hands and swung her around, while she clung to him in delight.

Matt hugged his boys, kissed Laura. And Sam grinned from ear to ear. "This is what I love the most," said Sam to the room in general. "The whole fam-damily enjoying each other. The noisier, the better. As long as we're together."

This should have been her life. And Katie's life. A happy life. A secure life. Where the whole world could go to hell and it wouldn't matter. Nothing would matter because within that family circle, the love she and Jason had for each other would transcend anything. Even the guilt they'd accepted for Jared's death on that awful night. The guilt she didn't dwell on.

Disappointment slapped her anew. All her hopes and dreams—gone. The deep love she'd given Jason, destroyed by him. Anger choked her. She couldn't kid herself anymore. Not when his presence was turning her inside-out every day he remained in Pilgrim Cove.

Jason Parker had been the love of her life. They'd been a couple. And no one had questioned it. Not their families. Not their friends. They'd laughed together. Dreamed together. Made plans together. And made love together. Had a child together.

As she stared at him now, she allowed herself to remember it all. A kaleidoscope of pictures and feelings, vibrant and wonderful, teased her mind—and began tearing her into little pieces. Until the only person she saw in the room was Jason.

"I gave you my heart," she cried at him. "And my soul. And you didn't give a damn!"

CHAPTER NINE

LILA RAN THROUGH the family room, through the kitchen to the mudroom. Her hand was on the door when she was caught by two strong arms around her waist. She twisted against them, tried to reach for the knob.

"You're wrong, Lila," said Jason. "But let's take this outside, away from the family." He relaxed his grip for a moment to open the door, and she pulled away and flew down the driveway toward the beach. He caught up to her—to her annoyance—but didn't stop her. Didn't touch her. Simply ran beside her. If she veered to the left, so did he. If she changed direction, he stuck close.

She ran down the thirty-foot ridge to the dunes, kicking her shoes off along the way. Amazingly, the farther she ran, the more vigorous she felt. Strong and eager for a confrontation.

They reached the dunes and the natural beach, where seagrass grew in tufts at nature's whim. The sand was hard-packed here from the tidal wash and felt cool under Lila's feet. The Atlantic loomed ahead of them, the bluff blocked them from behind. There was nowhere else to run.

But she was ready to challenge him. She spun toward Jason, her breath coming fast, her blood racing.

"If it weren't for Katie," she said, "maybe I could have forgotten. Maybe I could have started over. Made new memories with someone else." She gulped a big breath. "But I couldn't do that because every time I looked at our daughter, I saw you. I thought of you."

"What?" he asked, his face incredulous—a comical picture of disbelief. "Have you looked in the mirror?"

She snapped her hand at him, impatient. "Don't you see the way she moves, how she walks, her self-confidence, her sense of humor? A dozen times a day, I'd think—my God, that's just the way Jason juts out his chin. Or, that swagger is just like Jason's." She paused a moment. "She wasn't even two years old when your dad sat her at the piano. The instrument's been an extension of her ever since."

She raised her eyes to his and saw the grief. "I couldn't forget you, Jason. And I tried so hard." She started to laugh, but the sound was heavy. "Just to satisfy my mother, I went out on a few dates every year after your message came."

He winced. "I mailed that during my worst time. Did I just say, 'Forget about me?' I can't remember."

She nodded. "That and, 'Get on with your life.'" His terse note was etched in her memory.

"So you did—get on with your life. And eventually you hooked up with Fielding." A statement.

"That's right."

He reached for her hand. "Come on. Let's walk for a minute."

She glanced at her watch. "That's about all the time I have." But she allowed him to take her hand, intertwine fingers like they used to with his thumb stroking the top of hers. So familiar. So good. And such a mistake.

"Adam Fielding…" began Jason as they strolled a few steps.

"What about him?" Suspicion laced her voice.

"Nice enough guy, Lila. But he's not the one for you."

"Wha—" He gave her no chance to reply. Suddenly, she was in Jason's arms, her mouth covered firmly by his. Firmly, but gently, he tasted her, explored her, finding his way again. His touch—so familiar. And when she inhaled his familiar scent of spice and man, her senses exploded. She burned. She ached. And she responded, returning every kiss.

After years of sleepwalking, she was alive again. Jason's touch was a lit match against dry wood. The flame burst to life, and she spiraled skyward amid a potpourri of bright color twirling in patterns she'd never seen before. She couldn't think. Couldn't plan.

She simply fell into his kiss, deeper and deeper. Into his embrace, her arms latching around his neck until she didn't know where she ended and Jason began.

Just like in the old days, they were as one.

But the old days were gone. Lila jerked back, and Jason released her. She heard his raspy breath. When she looked at him, his dark eyes glowed with want. And with satisfaction.

"Do you see what I mean?" he asked. "Why you can't marry Fielding."

"I have to leave."

He shook his head. "No. No more running away. For either of us."

He had a point, but she wanted to ignore it.

"Face facts, Lila." He spoke directly, but his voice was kind. "You can't marry Fielding when your kisses are for me. What kind of marriage would you have?"

"That's none of your concern."

He tipped her chin up toward him, stroked her jaw. "Of course it's my concern." His eyes softened, their deep sable color warm and rich, reawakening other memories, and her heart thumped in double time.

"I love you, Lila," he said. "I always have. I never stopped loving you, no matter what you might think. Through all the years. Through all my bad times." His words fell away, and he studied her. "My guilt about Jared almost killed me, Lila. I couldn't stop blaming myself, and I tried to ease the pain in the wrong way."

She felt her mouth open in surprise. "What do you mean?"

He placed a gentle finger over her lips. "Another time, sweetheart. I just want you to know that you were with me—always—in here." He pointed to his head. "And in here." His heart. "I love you, Lila. Always have. Always will."

Her tears flowed then. "I believe you," she whispered, but shook her head quickly when she saw his smile. "But love is not enough. You hurt me terribly, and I can't take another chance. I may not survive the second time around."

IF SHE WAS QUIETER than usual that evening when they took the girls for pizza, Adam didn't seem to notice. Lila was relieved but not surprised, not when Katie and Sara were chattering away beside them in a booth at Three P's Pizza on Main Street. Not when the place was busy with a dinnertime family crowd.

The door opened and a chorus of "Hi, Benny," and "We won," resounded in the air. An older girls' softball team automatically lined up in front of the proprietor to the side of the counter as if they'd done it many times before.

"I'm going to play on that big girls' team when I'm older," said Sara, her eyes shining.

Adam beamed at his daughter.

"Not me!" said Katie with such certainty that Lila was surprised.

"I thought you loved your baseball team," Lila said.

"Yup." The child nodded, lifting a slice of pepperoni pizza. "Baseball. Not softball. I want to play baseball with Casey and the boys on our team."

"Girls don't play baseball," said Sara matter-of-factly.

"Yes, they do!" responded Katie. "And I'm going to play. Girls can do anything boys do. Daddy said we live in an age of eq-eq—We're equal! So there."

Animated. So alive. Lila bent down and kissed her daughter. "You can do whatever you want, sweetheart. As long as you work hard at it."

"And you know what else?" asked Katie. "When I get big, I'm going to write songs just like Daddy. I'll write one for you, too, Mommy. But not sad, mushy stuff. Won't that be fun?"

Motormouth Katie. Lila glanced at Adam and shrugged in apology.

Adam held her gaze, his expression thoughtful, but he smiled. "Her dad sure seems to have made an impression." He looked from one child to the other, then back at Lila. "I guess our little adoption plan won't work anymore, now that Katie's father has shown up in the flesh."

Jason's image flashed through her mind. The love he had for Katie. His pride in her. No way in the world would he allow Adam to adopt his daughter. Adam had volunteered in order to strengthen family ties after he and Lila were married. For Katie's sake, he'd said, because she'd never known a father and he wanted her to feel secure. He also wanted Sara to have a real sister.

"I'm afraid life is never tidy," said Lila to her fiancé. "It's messy. We think we can wrap pieces of it in neat packages, but I'm learning that it doesn't work. Things always change."

"And then we deal with it and go forward," he said in a strong tone as he clasped her hand firmly. "Have you thought about a date yet?"

She glanced at his earnest expression. A whisper of concern in his eyes.

Before she could respond, Sara interrupted. "We got another dog today. No one wanted him. He was too skinny and he had worms. But Daddy took care of him, and now he's eating, and he's going to get better." Her eyes shone as she looked around the table. "You know what? When I grow up, I'm going to be a vet with my dad. And I'll find homes for all the dogs and kittens."

"A stray?" asked Lila softly.

He nodded. "I'll try to find a good place for him."

Lila knew he'd do anything for his daughter. Sara was a gentle girl and still fragile, and Adam did deal with life and death in his animal hospital. He tried to keep the tougher situations from her, but Sara spent a lot of time with the pets Adam took care of, and it wasn't always possible. No wonder he liked Sara and Katie to hang out together after school.

"I'll ask around in school tomorrow," said Sara.

"Hey," said Katie. "Maybe my dad can keep him. He doesn't have a dog yet."

"I don't think your dad will want to fly him all the way to California!" replied Adam with a laugh.

Oh, Lord! Adam really had dismissed Jason's plans as unrealistic. Lila cleared her throat to speak. Too late.

"But he's not going to California!" said Katie, turning to her mother. "Is he, Mom?"

And there on her daughter's lovely face and in her voice, was just a thread of uncertainty. Just enough to mar her newfound happiness.

She patted Katie's hand and looked at Adam. "The man says he's moving to Pilgrim Cove."

Adam's eyes widened, his mouth thinned. "I can't believe this. He's really relocating here?"

She nodded.

"And Mommy's finding him a house. And I'm helping, too."

At Adam's consternation, Lila squeezed his hand, as well as Katie's. "There's nothing to be concerned about. For Jason, it's all about Katie." *The scene on the beach would never happen again.*

But his frown didn't disappear. "That's probably true." His voice, however, carried a note of doubt. "No wonder you seem preoccupied this evening."

"I had a busy day," she said quickly, "and was running late to meet you."

Adam sat back in the booth, his expression more thoughtful than concerned now. "Actually, it makes more sense for him to have two places. He'll have to split his time between the coasts. All his connections are in L.A. His agent...the singers..." His voice trailed off.

"That's what I said to him when...when he announced he was giving up his apartment out there. He can't afford...or doesn't want...to pay double rents or mortgages."

"I see." He gazed at her, a frown forming. "And I also see that you're disturbed about his decision. Frankly, I am, too."

Disturbed was putting it mildly. "Why shouldn't we be?" asked Lila, surprised at his self-critical tone.

"Because many divorced couples sensibly put their children first and choose to live near each other. Your situation is very similar. As for me—I'd like to think I'm open-minded enough to take the high road for Katie's sake." He stroked her hand. "I don't want him coming between us. *We're* the ones forming a new family."

"Yes..." She pressed her lips together. She couldn't hurt Adam by saying she and Jason would have married and would still have been married if all had gone as planned. They wouldn't have needed two houses or two families. "I tried to get my granddad to take Jason house hunting," she substituted, interjecting a lighter tone. "The Quinn actually refused!"

Now Adam's eyes narrowed; he sat up and leaned toward her across the table.

Lila kept chatting, trying to smooth over the situation, realizing for the first time where Katie got her motormouth talent. "Even if Bart had agreed," she said, "I have no doubt he suddenly would have been unavailable when the time came to actually visit properties. You just don't know Bartholomew Quinn!"

"Hmm...I wouldn't say that. I know him well enough to like the man. And to know that you're the apple of his eye."

She couldn't deny it. "He loves all his grandchildren, but I'm his only female grandchild. Just the luck of the draw."

"I'm his apple, too, Mom," Katie said with a big yawn.

"Ahh, the signal to end the evening." Adam glanced quickly at Sara whose eyes were closing. "She needs to be in bed."

They paid the bill and got each child tucked into seat belts in their respective cars. Then Adam walked to Lila and cupped her chin with a gentle hand. "You're right about something," he said. "Something I've learned the hard way, but prefer to forget."

"What's that?" she asked.

"Life *is* messy. Nothing stays neat and tidy no matter how much we wish it would." He kissed her quickly. "And your grandfather does nothing without a reason," he murmured before returning to his vehicle.

She wasn't going to read anything into his remarks. Or be insulted by his fast good-night.

Suddenly Jason's words haunted her... *When your kisses are for me.* Her eyes searched the parking lot. Adam's SUV had left its spot and was heading toward her on the way to the exit ramp. She flagged him down.

He pulled over next to her and lowered his window.

"What's wrong?"

She leaned over, stroked his cheek and put her mouth on his.

A PLEASANT KISS. Comfortable. Good enough for her. Her spontaneity had obviously surprised and delighted Adam, and she was glad about that.

Lila tossed in her bed that night, thinking about Adam. Thinking about Jason. Thinking about kisses. She didn't need fireworks anymore. She needed calm. She needed someone she could depend on. She felt old—too old for fireworks, anyway. She'd leave combustion to her parents.

Her parents? What was she thinking? She pictured Maggie and Tom together. Laughing. Dancing. Fighting. Making up. Fireworks. For almost thirty years. Her dad as strong and steady as granite. Her mom strong, too, but as mercurial as the New England weather. She kept him on his toes; he held her steady. Opposites attracting. And acting younger than Lila felt most of the time.

Lila sat up and punched her pillow again. She couldn't remember when she'd spent as much energy thinking about relationships as she had recently. Had she put herself in cold storage for the last four years? Shut down the sensual side of herself? The romantic side?

She lowered herself against the pillow, eyes wide open. One scary thought followed another. Was she sexually inhibited with everyone other than Jason? She'd hate herself if she were. She was a modern woman. She and Adam would be fine.

But the hardest question of all made her shake and sweat. Had she lost the capacity to love completely? Was she so frightened of being hurt that she'd chosen to walk a very narrow safe path? A tear rolled down her cheek, but she left it there, too frozen by the possibility to move at all.

Then she thought of Katie, and her whole being filled with love. The child was her life. She adored her with everything she had to give. So that meant she, Lila Sullivan, still had a beating heart!

Lila sat up in bed and smiled, wiping her tears with quick, impatient hands. Until...*loving Katie didn't count!* The thought exploded with blinding force. Didn't every mother love her child unconditionally? Romantic love was not the same with its give-and-take. With its crackling and heat.

Tears trickled again. She lay back down, rolled on her stomach and cried softly into her pillow.

ON THURSDAY AFTERNOON, Lila couldn't decide who seemed more excited at the prospect of house hunting, Jason or Katie. It certainly wasn't her. She'd been dragging all week, and had made a last-ditch effort to coerce her granddad into taking over. A total waste of breath. He'd scheduled himself to be on the other side of the county, miles from Pilgrim Cove at the very time of Jason's appointment.

"We'll not turn down the business over there," Bart had said. "Not if we want to remain the best and biggest real-estate agency in the area. We're county-wide, lassie. Don't you forget it. And don't forget to show Jason the Linden house on Bay Road." At her stricken look, he'd given her a quick hug before taking off an hour ago with their videographer to shoot footage of the new listings.

More and more complicated. Sure, Bart was pushing for the Lindens' house. Only a block away from theirs on Pilgrim Bay. It was last on her list to show Jason, and she hoped he'd like something else before they got to that one.

Katie prowled Lila's office while Jason stood next to the window and looked out on Main Street. "It hasn't changed too much," he said with a nod at the street.

"How can it?" Lila replied. "We're on a peninsula. No room for big malls with a ton of stores and parking lots. People do business on Main Street in Pilgrim Cove. We're small potatoes, Jason."

"I know." He glanced from her to Katie, looking content but thoughtful. "It's perfect for her."

But not for you. "Having second thoughts?" she asked softly. Her heart picked up tempo, but she couldn't decide if it was caused by hope or regret.

He aimed a sexy grin in her direction. "Not a one. Sorry to disappoint you."

He didn't sound sorry at all. Didn't look sorry, either. In fact, his eyes twinkled and he winked at her. And darn if she didn't feel herself blush.

"Then let's go." Her curt tone matched her brusque movements as she grabbed her purse and the binder containing all her notes on the five houses she would show him. She let them precede her from the office and closed the door behind her. "My car's out front."

Jason leaned toward Katie. "Is she always this bossy?" he whispered loudly enough for Lila to hear.

Katie's blue eyes seemed to pop out of her head. "Dad-dy! She's nice." A remark which would have been redeeming, except that Katie started to giggle. "She's real nice, most of the time."

It didn't help to see Jane Fisher, sitting at her desk, sporting a wide grin on her face, either. "Shall I wait for you, Lila, or will you be very late?"

"Oh, you'll probably still be here. I don't think this will take too long."

Jason sauntered to the desk and shook the woman's hand. "We'll probably be late, Jane, so why don't you just lock up?"

She looked from one to the other. "Hmm-m-m. I guess we'll just have to wait and see. Time will tell. It always does." Her questioning glance lingered on Lila. Although her words were innocent, Lila had a strong suspicion Jane wasn't speaking about what time the house-hunting trip would be over.

Once inside her Explorer, she lost no time getting down to business. "You told me you'd prefer the ocean side—something on Beach Street—so that's where we're headed first. There's one property available now, and it will be grabbed up quickly because of the location."

Of course, it was a small summer-only type house that would need insulation and other work to winterize it. But it was a well-kept, pretty place with potential.

Jason did not see the potential. He stood in the middle of the hall, able to peer into every room from his spot, and said, "Cute is for daughters, not for houses. My apartment in L.A. is bigger than this. Where would I put my baby grand."

Lila made a note, then held his glance. "You'd have a much bigger selection in Boston. And the ferry to Pilgrim Cove runs every thirty minutes."

"Boston?" Katie squealed.

He glared at Lila. "Show me more."

"No more on the beach. Sorry."

"There are four miles of houses along Beach Street and no others are available?"

"That's right. People hold on to these homes, Jason. You know that. But I've got two others that are bigger nearby. Real family homes. And one's just a few blocks from the water."

"Does it get the ocean breeze?"

She wasn't sure. And after seeing the next two houses, she wasn't sure Jason would be happy with anything available. Or maybe it was Katie who held the power of decision.

By the fourth house, she caught on to Jason's routine. He didn't say much in the beginning. Just watched Katie as they all explored the house. When he walked into the kitchen, he watched Lila. The living room was sizable, however, and he spent a few extra minutes in it before doing a walk-through on his own.

"Nope," he said, coming back to the kitchen. "Let's keep going."

She shrugged. "Maybe if you tell me what you want…"

"Dangerous suggestion," he drawled, and the atmosphere changed instantly. *Want* glittered in his eyes when he looked at her, and she felt heat rise to her cheeks.

"Jason! This is business."

"Beautiful business." His voice caressed her, its

warmth like a fine cognac, rich and smooth, going down with ease. She turned from him, suddenly off-kilter. "Please, don't flirt…"

"Mommy, how about the house near ours?" Katie was on her way to the front door. "Papa Bart said that was the perfect one and to make sure you didn't forget. After four houses, we go to Bay Road. And we seen four already. I counted."

No wonder Bart had taken himself miles away. He knew she'd murder him the first chance she got. "Saw, Katie. Not seen."

The child rolled her eyes. "We *saw* four already," she said impatiently.

"Kathleen Sullivan-Parker." Jason's crisp tone would have gotten Lila's attention immediately, but hearing Katie's full name for the first time had her drawing breath. It evidently had the same effect on Katie. The child didn't move, just stared at her father.

"Number one, you were rude to your mother," began Jason, his voice softer. Lila began to interrupt, but he motioned her to be still. "And number two, if you want to write songs, you have to know the language well. English is your language, so you must learn it."

Lila watched an amazing contest of wills between father and daughter. Katie's eyes shone with unshed tears, but she didn't blink. Neither did Jason. The air hummed with silent communication. Then Jason inclined his head toward Lila while still holding his daughter's gaze. Katie looked at her mom. "Sorry."

"Come here, kiddo," said Jason beckoning the child. Katie took a running leap straight into his arms. If Lila had been reluctant to accept it earlier, she had to accept it now. Her family's dynamics had changed forever. Katie had a real father.

How had he known what to do? She'd need time to absorb, truly absorb, what all this interaction meant. But not now. Now, they'd be going to Bay Road. To a house only a block away from where she and Katie lived.

LILA WATCHED JASON'S EYES light up as soon as she parked in front of the Lindens' home. Two steps up was a welcoming front porch almost the width of the large Cape Cod-style house. They all scrambled out of the car and made their way into the entrance hall.

In the front area, the living room and dining room were across a center hall from each other. An eat-in kitchen came next and abutted the large family room overlooking the bay in the back. A master bedroom plus a second bedroom were on the other side of the hall. It wasn't identical to the one-story house she shared with Bart, but had been built at the same time by the same construction firm. It felt solid and sound.

"There are two dormered bedrooms and a bathroom on the second floor," said Lila. "So it's really a four-bedroom house. Maybe it's too big for you?"

He chuckled. "Let's explore." He led the way to the kitchen.

From where she and Jason stood, Lila heard Katie's footsteps on the staircase, up and down a half-dozen times.

"She never wears herself out, does she?" asked Jason, eyebrow raised as he continued to prowl the house.

"She's enjoying the novelty of stairs. But, nope. She's got energy for a hundred people."

"Good."

The man looked as proud of Katie as if he'd single-handedly invented her. Overjoyed to have found her. As happy as Katie was to have him in her life.

But Lila asked, "And you're really going through with this, Jason? This house hunting isn't a lark? You're sure?" She pictured Katie's expression if her dad changed his mind and took off again.

Jason turned toward her. "Hey," he said softly. "If I didn't know your question came from your concern for our daughter, I'd be very insulted." His eyes bespoke his sincerity. "I won't let her down, Lila. I promise."

"Not that word! Don't use that word." His "promise" tore her nerve endings like the screech of steel wheels against a train track.

Her meaning registered, and he looked as if she'd struck him. Stunned. All color blanched from his face. And then surprise turned to sadness.

"Does holding on to your anger make you happy, Lila?" he asked.

His tone was soft and gentle, but she felt herself bristle. "I have a daughter to protect!"

"Liar. You know Katie's safe with me. You've seen how she is when we're together. And kids have good instincts. They can sniff out a phony adult like a bloodhound on the trail of a fox. So there's only one conclusion I can draw about you right now."

The nerve. Lila pressed her lips together. She wouldn't give him the satisfaction of asking.

She didn't have to.

"You're protecting yourself," he said quietly. "From me. And my love, my sweetest love, it's breaking my heart."

"Don't call me that." She'd rather argue than think.

"Why not? It's the truth. And not even your nice vet uses those words."

She wanted to spring at him like a cat, but settled for conversation. "You have no right to speculate about Adam…. You have no clue about—"

"Don't I?" he interrupted. "Let's find out." He captured her gaze, his eyes burning dark. "Have you set a date yet?"

She twisted the ring on her fourth finger. "As a matter of fact, we just spoke about it. Probably in the middle of the summer," she replied. "Or maybe early in the fall."

"Probably? Maybe?" he repeated softly, his expression lighter. "Think about that, Lila." He tapped the tip of her nose. "So what do you think of this kitchen?"

Lila slipped into professional mode instantly. A good method to block out other thoughts. She actually liked the kitchen—good counter space, and the sink, stove and fridge easily accessible—and told him so. "This kitchen is in good shape. You might want to change the floral wallpaper, but the cabinets are solid, and the countertops were updated a couple of years ago."

"The other houses we saw don't compare to this."

"The ones we saw on the beach are used only in summer. This one is for year round with full insulation, storm doors and windows, a big fireplace. It's a house that can be a real home, Jason. Not just a temporary stop for the season."

"That's exactly what I want," he said. "A real home."

"Let's see the rest of it room by room."

He nodded, and then called out for Katie. "I want her to have a stake in it."

"Half a vote?" she replied.

"I'm here." Katie was indeed with them now. "The upstairs is so cool, Daddy. There's big, big windowsills to sit on in the bedrooms, and the ceiling's sorta pointy. It goes down."

"It slopes."

"Yeah, it slopes. In both rooms. But I know which one I want. The one where you can look out over the bay."

"So you like this house, Katie?" asked Jason, putting his arm around her.

She nodded hard.

"Jason!" Lila couldn't help her concern. "Eight-year-olds don't select houses. This is a lot of money. We're not finished looking at it yet."

Katie darted ahead of them toward the bedrooms. "But Mommy, Papa Bart said it was perfect! And look…it's got two more bedrooms. And more bathrooms. And besides…I could come here on my bike every day and sleep over whenever I want to, and…"

At least until Lila and Adam got married. "We'll figure something out, Katie. No matter which house Daddy buys."

They were in the hallway outside the bedrooms when Katie stopped chattering. But she hadn't stopped thinking. Oh, no. Lila watched her daughter glance toward one bedroom, then the other. Finally, she turned toward them, a smile as wide as a jack-o-lantern's.

"It *is* perfect. We're a family like the three bears." She pointed at the master bedroom. "That one's for Daddy 'cause he's the biggest." She then indicated the second bedroom. "And that one's for Mommy." She finally pointed at the ceiling. "And I sleep upstairs 'cause I'm the baby bear."

No one spoke for a moment. Lila just shook her head. Jason's eyes shone with laughter. But when Lila looked at Katie, she realized her daughter was still deep in thought. The child frowned, looked toward the bedrooms again and quietly stared at the floor.

"What's wrong, sweetie?" asked Lila, concerned about the troubled expression on her daughter's face.

Katie merely shook her head before beckoning Lila closer. "It's not right," she whispered. "That's not how it goes."

"Ahh. The story?"

"No. A family." Katie took Lila's hand and looked shyly at Jason. "In Uncle Matt and Aunt Laura's house, the papa bear and the mama bear are together."

Katie looked up at her father. "You got too many bedrooms, Daddy." Then she shook her head. "Nope. You *have* too many bedrooms."

CHAPTER TEN

"OF COURSE HE MADE AN OFFER on the house, pending an inspection." Lila sat across the table from Adam two nights later at the Wayside Inn's restaurant, the eatery he preferred to patronize when they went out on their own. Katie was with Bart that evening. "Katie is ecstatic," she continued. "Doesn't talk about anything else."

Adam took a swallow of beer, then put down his glass. "And let me guess. Your grandfather is beaming like a leprechaun with a pot of gold."

"That about sums it up." She gulped her own drink and coughed.

Adam got up quickly and patted her on the back. "Why are you so out of sorts? You and Katie won't be living on Bay Road soon, anyway. You're her only legal parent, and you can dictate her visits."

She heard the annoyance in his tone, but couldn't stop her flow. "It's not about legal when Katie lights up every time he walks into the house. She loves him, Adam. I'm not going to make her miserable about limiting visits. Pilgrim Cove is not the big city where travel arrangements can be difficult."

Adam took his seat again before replying. "And what about Sara?" he asked. "She and Katie have been together only once this week after school, and that was the day of their game." His eyes blazed. "I won't have Sara being hurt or ignored because of Jason Parker."

A shard of guilt pierced her. "I'm sorry, Adam. I'll talk to her. I know Jason won't mind if she goes to Sea View House with Katie sometimes."

"That's not the point. I don't want Sara at Sea View House!" His fingers drummed the table. "Why don't we kill this conversation? Life will be a lot easier after we're married."

At the moment, everything seemed too complicated. "How so?" asked Lila.

"We'll be a family, Lila. Nothing is stronger than that. And the novelty of having her father around will wear off. Katie won't be so excited to see him after a while."

He was wrong. She didn't want to hurt Adam, but sometimes the truth had to be faced. She squeezed his hand before she spoke. "Is Sara tired of seeing you every day, Adam? Are you a novelty to her?"

The air stilled between them. She saw in his expression that he understood, this man who adored his child. Who'd had to be both her father and mother for the last few years. Not an easy thing as Lila well knew.

But now, when Lila looked into his face, she realized her heartbeat remained steady—no aerobics—and that it always had. For the first time, she wondered how fast Adam's heart raced when he looked at her. If it did at all.

She took a breath. "Tell me about Eileen," she said softly. "Tell me about Sara's mom."

He startled, looking totally bewildered. Then, at her urging, began to speak. Haltingly at first, but soon with freedom. And now Lila saw and heard what deep love had been like for Adam. What true love looked like in his eyes.

She couldn't play games with this man, couldn't pretend. When he was finished, she said, "Our relationship is not what you had with Eileen. Is it enough for you, Adam?"

"Yes." He didn't hesitate to reply and engulfed her hands with his. "You're the first woman since Eileen that..." He shrugged. "You know what I mean."

She smiled. "Yes. Yes, I do."

"You're a lovely woman, Lila, and a good mom. You deserve happiness. So let me ask you the same question. Is what we have enough for you?"

A kaleidoscope of Jason images flashed through her mind. A complete history of their young lives. Her Jason. His Lila. Together. Could any relationship eclipse what she and Jason had once shared? Or had she embellished their love in her memory? Then she pictured the mature Jason, the one who'd returned to Pilgrim Cove…and excitement rippled through her. She tingled from head to toe. The attraction between them couldn't be denied. But as long as she was aware of it, she could bury it.

She pasted a smile on her face and looked at Adam. "Have you heard me complain?"

"No," he said. "I haven't." He studied her for a moment, then tilted his head toward an inside exit. "How about adjourning to the lounge after dinner? Dance for a while. Preferably slow ones!"

"All right," said Lila, eager to change the focus of the conversation. "I'd love to."

A half hour later, Lila and Adam joined the growing crowd out on a Saturday evening who came to socialize and dance to the music of the DJ the Wayside Inn hired every week. They walked in as the hard beat of the Rolling Stones' "Satisfaction," surrounded them, and Lila started moving to the music before they found a table. How long had it been since she'd taken time to have some fun? And dancing had always been on the top of her list.

Adam tried his best, but when the band went into a second fast number, Lila took pity. "Go on, grab a stool and get a drink. I don't need a partner for this." He shrugged and disappeared to the bar while Lila simply allowed her tensions to dissolve into the music. She recognized a lot of people—waved and nodded—but never lost the beat. She'd needed this. Some physical release.

She moved to the music, turning full circle, arms above her head, legs working in rhythm, until she was back where she started. Except, when she looked up, she wasn't dancing alone.

JASON WAS NO JOHN TRAVOLTA, but even if he'd had two left feet, he would be standing exactly where he was now—in the middle of the dance floor with Lila Sullivan. He watched her turn, throw her head back and open her eyes. Then open them wider.

He said nothing. Just worked the music. Small moves. Personal moves. In time and matching hers. His eyes focused on her. Only on her. Did she understand his message?

She replied with silence, but kept on dancing. Her eyes rested on him. Shone only for him.

Alone in a crowd. Now he understood that expression! How tunnel vision wipes out the rest of the world—people, noise, furniture, conversations—as though they didn't exist at all.

The tempo changed. Slower. Much slower. He opened his arms. She stepped into them.

And he held her. Finally. He inhaled her sweet fragrance and his senses burst alive. Soft skin, silky hair. Lila. "A thousand and one nights of dreams," he whispered. "Just like this."

"Shh."

This dream lasted for eighteen bars of music before he felt a pair of eyes watching him. He glanced over his shoulder and saw Fielding standing next to a small table at the edge of the dance floor chatting with Laura, but studying him and Lila. Jason nodded, but the vet made no move toward the floor. No move to cut in. A real gentleman and very trusting. Or very shrewd.

Jason led Lila toward the man when the song ended. "Here she is, Doc. Safe and sound."

"I never had a doubt."

"So you two have met?" asked Laura.

"Sure," said Jason, pulling over another chair. "Kids' baseball games bring folks together."

"So do half-frozen kittens," Laura said, telling the story of finding a skinny kitten shivering against the front steps of Sea View House last year in the middle of an ice storm. Of how she wound up spending the night at Adam's house.

"Skinny kitten?" mocked Jason. "Do you mean that don't-mess-with-me black panther who rules your house?"

A waitress approached amid the chuckles, depositing bowls of pretzels and chips, ready to take their beverage order. In his turn, Jason named his usual. "With lime, please. Not lemon."

"Gotcha," she said with a wink. "Club soda and lime."

He nodded but noticed his brother's raised eyebrow. And Lila's.

And that was another chapter of his life that would have to be revealed to his family sooner rather than later if he was to settle down in Pilgrim Cove with them. If he was to be a responsible father.

He glanced around the group and allowed his eyes to rest on Rachel Goodman-Levine, the new assistant principal of Pilgrim Cove Regional High. A native of the town, a few years older than Jason, she'd returned after thirteen years to take the position at the school. He'd run into her on a Mississippi gambling boat a long time ago after they'd both left town "for good." He liked her. Trusted her. She'd kept her mouth shut about seeing him.

"I can see married life agrees with you, Rachel," said Jason with a grin toward Jack. "But how's the job? My dad told me about some tests the kids have to take?"

"I'm a wreck about that," she replied. "They're scheduled for next week, and then of course," she said, slowing her words, a frown settling on her forehead as she looked from Jason to Matt and back again, before taking a deep breath. "We have to deal with the prom."

A hot iron on flesh. Jason winced, then stared at her. "Deal, in what way?"

"Well, hell," she said. "I can't tiptoe around it. Drinking and driving, guys. I've got a crashed up car scheduled to sit on the front lawn in warning. I've got someone from MADD coming down to talk and show a video. I've got chaperones for the actual event, including Lila's parents." She looked at Lila then. "Thank God your dad is so well respected by the kids. He's been a great athletic director since he took over last fall." She looked around the group again. "I've got things in place..."

"But you won't rest easy till it's over," said Matt.

Rachel nodded.

"What can I do?" Jason heard himself ask the question. Speaking in front of groups was not a problem for him. He'd been singing or playing in front of people all his life.

Rachel's eyes twinkled. "I knew you'd volunteer! Let's think up something special." She looked up at her new husband. "Didn't I tell you the best people come from Pilgrim Cove?"

"Or live there now?" Jack replied, and kissed her when she nodded.

Jason chuckled with the rest of the group, then looked at Lila. "Your mom chaperones the prom?"

"Yeah," said Lila softly. "She and my dad have been going every year since...since the accident."

Jason whistled in admiration and surprise.

"She's not an ogre, you know," said Lila, slapping her hand against the table and glaring at him. Then she sighed, her eyes softening. "Maybe she's just a bit too overprotective."

"Maybe?" howled Jason, wanting to kiss her square on the mouth. "There's no maybe about it.

Every time I see her, she wants to shoot me. I haven't even gotten a meal at the Lobster Pot yet, and I love that place!"

Genuine laughter erupted from everyone else except one.

"Maybe," said Adam Fielding, looking from Lila to Jason, "being an overprotective parent is not necessarily a good thing, whether the child is small or grown."

No laughter now. Jason's breath caught at the possibilities behind the vet's remark, and he stared at Fielding. But Adam's eyes were on Lila. Only on Lila.

Jason reached for his glass and stood up. "Think I'll get some air."

ALTHOUGH HE WAS ATTENTIVE, Adam was quieter than normal for the rest of the evening. They danced, they chatted. Lila checked the door periodically for Jason's reappearance.

But when he did show up again, he spent his time making the rounds of the room, catching up with old friends, being introduced to their friends. He returned to their group briefly to speak with his brother and finally to say good-night.

"I have to book a flight to the coast," he said. "Just got a call."

Would he wind up leaving Pilgrim Cove after all? How many times a month would he be taking the red-eye flight? To Lila's surprise, disappoint-

ment filled her. Distress. Then anger. Anger at herself for letting him affect her this way.

"One-way ticket?" she asked, injecting a hopeful
note into her question.

He laughed, not rising to her bait at all. "No such
luck, sweetheart. I'll see you in the morning. Have
to explain to Katie." He waved and was gone.

Ten minutes later, when Adam suggested they
leave, too, she had no objection. He remained quiet
on the ride to her house, and Lila was only a little
surprised when he pulled onto a side street and shut
the engine.

"What's wrong, Adam? If it's Jason…he's just
making himself seen and heard. He's not a serious
person…."

He shifted in his seat and took her hand. "Shh.
Just listen to me. And then listen to yourself. That's
the best advice I can give you."

She shut up.

"We both have ghosts in our background. And we
both thought we could handle them. I know you're
always comparing me to Jason…."

"I'm not… Oh, my dear…" He put a gentle finger over her lips.

"We have to be honest now…this is too important for games. And I'll readily admit that I'm guilty
too…of pretending, I guess. Eileen's in the back of
my mind, even when I look at you. And you don't
resemble each other at all!"

She tried to smile.

"More than Eileen, however, is Sara. She comes first. You and I thought we could make it work because my wife can never come back, and less than a month ago, we didn't think Jason would, either. We thought we were on our own and that our love would grow as we built a new life for ourselves and the children."

Now he took a shaky breath—Lila heard it—but he still didn't allow her to speak. "Competing with a memory—" he began, then coughed and cleared his throat. "Competing with memories," he said again, "is tough enough, but competing with flesh and blood will destroy us after marriage. And Sara most of all. She loves you already."

"I'd never do—"

"Please…just a moment more or I won't be able to go on." He took a deep breath. "I've had a great marriage. The best. And you haven't, so you don't know." He shook his head, and finally his composure totally deserted him. His voice trembled.

"When I see Jason Parker look at you, I know how he feels."

He stared into a distance that she couldn't share. "I know how he feels," he repeated, "because I see myself looking at Eileen. That was me…before."

Lila felt tears run down her face. Tears of compassion. Tears of sorrow for him. Admiration for his honesty.

"You are quite a man," she said, grabbing a tissue from her purse.

"But am I the right man for you?" he asked, rubbing his own face. "I won't compete with him, Lila. I have too much at stake for false pride. But I'm leaving the decision to you. I'm trusting you to think hard, be honest with yourself and with me and for the children's sakes. I'm trusting you to be sure." He paused and reached for her hand. "Love does grow, Lila. That I do know. So set a date, and I'm there!"

He turned in his seat, leaned toward her and kissed her gently, then more deeply. "This part will improve, too."

JASON WOKE UP EARLY the next morning with a sense of anticipation. He'd see his "girls" in a little while, spend some extra time with Katie while Lila went to the office, and then fly to California where he'd take care of some urgent business. Both personal and professional.

He showered, then padded out to the back porch of Sea View House, delighting in the sunshine, in the breeze. Delighting in the sense of familiarity. The Atlantic loomed before him, vast and majestic, its waves rolling in and out as they had since the world began.

Maybe Dorothy was right, and there really was "no place like home." Of course, his own home would be a lot better with Lila in it. Instead she was with a guy for whom she'd always be second best. Good God, if positions had been reversed last night, he would have taken Fielding outside and made sure he'd never dance with Lila again! Shoot! What was he thinking? He was too old for fistfights now. Those belonged to yesterday, to him and Jared. They'd had some doozies.

He went inside, put on running shoes and joined some early morning joggers along the shore. There were only a few now. The summer folks hadn't shown up yet, but they'd be arriving soon. Memorial Day weekend was only two weeks away or so, and that was the start of the big onslaught of seasonal visitors.

A familiar figure jogged toward him and waved.

"Hi, Laura." He turned around and headed back toward Sea View House with her. "How many miles do you do?"

"Oh, anywhere between three and eight. Depends on how much time I have every morning."

"I can't match that…yet!"

She laughed. "Did Lila reach you earlier?"

"Lila? I was in the shower. What's up?"

"She thought you might be having breakfast with us, so she called. The sellers made a counteroffer. They want another ten thousand."

"Then I guess I'd better get back to the keyboard and write!"

She eyed him and didn't speak for a moment.

"How badly do you want to be hurt, Jason, by sticking around?"

He understood what she meant. "She won't marry him." He spoke with conviction, but his teeth clenched, and he had to consciously relax his jaw. "They don't look at each other the way you and Matt do."

She reached over and patted his arm. "But that doesn't mean she'll marry you, either, Jason." As though to soften her words, she added, "You know Matt and I are rooting for you!"

"Thanks, sis."

Laura dimpled at the term. Waved goodbye to him as they approached Sea View House. "Breakfast awaits me back home. Today is Mother's Day—my first one as a mom—and the boys are cooking." She turned to go back.

"What did you say? Mother's Day?" Jason looked around wildly.

Laura was laughing. "No stores on the beach, I'm afraid. Go write her a song, and tuck it inside a card. You're good at songs."

He shook his head. "She hates the other one. It's all over the radio, and she's never said a word to me—at least a complimentary one."

"It's a gorgeous song, Jase. She'll come around." She took off.

"Happy Mother's Day, Laura!" he called. Sheesh, Mother's Day!

An hour later, he pulled up in front of Lila's house on Bay Road, and Katie immediately ran out to greet him. Must have been watching for him. A warmth filled him. His daughter really liked him. Now all he had to do was win over her mother.

Katie reached him, and he caught her up and tossed her a short way in the air. "I think you're getting too big for tossing, but not for being carried right here against me."

She laid her head on his shoulder and wrapped her arms around him. He didn't need a Father's Day. He had it every day.

"I'm in hot water, Lady Katie. I didn't know it was Mother's Day."

"Uh-oh. Papa Bart and I already got her favorite perfume. We get it every year." She wrinkled her nose. "She don't…doesn't like to cook. So, no pots and pans. She says Grandma never let her do anything in the kitchen except clean it."

Jason could believe that. "How about a hobby like painting?" he asked.

But Katie was shaking her head. "She doesn't have time. She only works and takes me places like dancing school. And reads. She reads."

"All right, then! We can go to a bookstore," he said as he slid Katie to the ground. "What does she like?"

But Katie shrugged her shoulders. "Just books with no pictures. But…maybe they're about magic.

About disappearing. Yeah. How people disappear.
That was one of 'em. Poof! They're gone."

Jason swallowed hard. "You know what? A bou-,
quet of flowers sounds good." No red roses this time.
Something lighter. Happier. Springtime.

"I like flowers, Daddy."

"Good, you can help pick them out."

He approached the front door with his daughter
just as Lila opened it. She wore a casual yellow suit
today, slacks and jacket, hair tied loosely at her nape.
Jason started to smile, until he looked closely at her
face. Not good. Her makeup couldn't hide the puffiness. Or the furrows on her brow. She seemed
aware of them, too, with a pair of dark glasses dangling from her hand.

He decided not to comment.

"Did you get my message?" she asked, leading
him inside toward the kitchen.

"I didn't check my machine. But I met Laura on
the beach. We jogged a couple of miles." He leaned
casually against the table, watching her pour coffee
into a cup for him. "Meet their terms, Lila. Offer the
ten thou. I want the house."

The carafe wobbled, coffee splashed on the table,
splashed on her. She quickly put the pot down, and
turned away. "Excuse me, I have to change my blouse."

Jason grabbed a sponge from the sink and wiped
up the mess. His daughter's eyes followed his every
movement.

"Maybe I should give her my present now," said Katie in a small voice. "Papa Bart won't mind when I tell him."

Sad and scared. Everything Katie felt was written on her face. His daughter was still too young to hide her feelings, and he hoped she'd never hide them from him or Lila. He reached for a chair and scooped her onto his lap. "Mommy's just a little mixed up now. She's trying to figure out a problem."

"Oh. Problems like in math? I'm good in math. Maybe I could help her."

He held his child close, snuggled her. "You're very good, Kathleen. In lots of ways. Just the best. But this math is full of equations you don't know about." Of course, it could also be very simple. How hard was one man plus one woman? And how complicated if the wrong man was substituted in the equation? He didn't want to think about Fielding now, and refocused on Katie.

"How would you like a special present today? It's something that every kid in the world wants even though you can use it only at special times."

She turned in his lap, and put both her hands on his cheeks. "What? What?"

He'd thought long and hard during the night about how to make his trip to L.A. easier on Katie. Short of taking her with him, he came up with one idea.

"Cell phone."

As if he'd offered her the world, her eyes almost popped from her face. "A cell phone? Like the teenagers have?" She jumped from his lap and started running toward the back of the house calling for her mother, who was just returning.

"A cell phone?" asked Lila, looking crisp and professional in a tailored white blouse. But her lips quivered, and she had to press them together.

Jason's heart went out to her—he recognized nerves wracked by indecision. Anxiety. Stress.

He glanced at her hands. The ring was still on her finger. Damn it! Anyone could see Fielding wasn't ready for a new wife. Lila would be shortchanged... unless, she didn't want the skyrockets anymore.

He thought of their kiss on the beach. The glow in her eyes every time she saw him. And felt marginally better. She wanted skyrockets. Just didn't trust them.

"When are we buying a cell phone?" asked Katie. She turned toward her mother. "Daddy said so."

"Come here, Lady Katie," said Jason pulling out a chair for her. "You, too, Lila. She may need your help to understand."

Then he told Katie about his trip to California, and felt his heart shrivel when he saw her expression. "That's why you'll have your own phone. So you can call me anytime, day or night."

She turned to her mother. "Is he going to get lost again?"

Lila shrugged, her expression bleak. But on

whose behalf? Katie's? Her own? "You'll have to ask him."

Katie turned toward him, her heart in her eyes. "Do you have a map this time?" Literal child.

He nodded. "My map takes me straight back to Pilgrim Cove and Sea View House. Then to Bay Road. And we'll practice using your new phone before I leave. If you give me a piece of paper, I'll write my number down for you."

That seemed to satisfy Katie. He pointed to the wall phone and asked Lila, "Can you call the Lindens now or their agent and get the offer down and accepted?"

"Sure," she replied, shrugging. "Money's the easy part for you, isn't it?"

Her eyes challenged him before she put her hand on the phone. Was she asking about his personal finances? Or was she afraid that if money was no object, he'd be able to pick up and move whenever he felt like it? He decided to be completely open with her.

"I'm not wealthy, Lila. But royalties are coming in regularly now, and my career is growing. Faster than I thought. However, it's only about two years old."

"That'll change when you get the royalties from that—that—water's edge song that's playing much too often if you ask me. Now, be quiet while I call."

She was right, but didn't know how right. Jason

listened with half an ear as Lila confirmed his offer for the house. His agent had told him last night that the first few days' sales of the CD looked very promising. Luis Torres knew how to woo the ladies. And with Jason's three songs on the album, earnings would roll in steadily for years to come.

Lila hung up the phone. "The house is yours pending an inspection that we'll arrange. Foundation, electrical, roof—all that. We can close June 15th. And then it's yours for however long you want it." She waited a moment. "Congratulations." Not a smile.

"Thank you." He tried to match her lack of enthusiasm, but he couldn't. "It's my first house, Lila. Be happy for me." He reached for her and whirled her around the floor while Katie cheered.

"Oh, give me a home, where the buffalo roam…" he sang.

She began to laugh. Her stiffness melted after one turn and her laughter turned to giggles. "That's more like it," he said.

"Oh, Jase," she said, leaning against him. "You always could make me laugh, and we always could laugh together." The furrows had disappeared. Her eyes shone.

He kissed her. Long and hard.

Katie cheered again. "I'm telling Grandma."

CHAPTER ELEVEN

LILA HAD THREATENED their daughter with the loss of the cell phone, and Katie had immediately pantomimed zipping her lips.

In that moment, Jason had understood the power of bribery.

But now he and Katie were on their way to Quinn Real Estate and Property Management with gifts for Lila and with a new phone in Katie's pocket. His child was beaming in all directions, even though she knew the restrictions.

"But *next* year, I can use it for friends," she said.

"I didn't say that." He felt himself start to drown.

"And next year's almost here because summer's almost here."

He didn't quite follow her logic, but figured Lila would know how to handle this type of situation. He also understood the relief of having backup. How had she handled everything alone? Every decision. Even with input from her family and his, the final say had always been Lila's.

He glanced at the bouquet he held—a colorful

mix—and decided he'd give her another one on Father's Day. He put his free arm around Katie, delighted at how comfortable she acted with him. She seemed to believe that he'd be returning to Pilgrim Cove without a problem. He'd explained about business trips, and that he'd have to go to Los Angeles sometimes. "Or my songs won't get on the radio."

Katie understood that.

They bounded up the steps to Bart and Lila's business and let themselves in. Jane Fisher greeted them from behind her computer.

Katie raced over to her. "Hi, Aunt Jane. I got a cell phone just like Amy and April. Look!" She pulled the mobile from her pocket.

"Pink! Oh, my. How beautiful!" She winked at Jason.

"Two daughters, huh?" said Jason.

"Twins. Graduating from high school this year."

Click. Click. Click. Jason's mind went into action making connections. "Tell me about them."

"They're good kids. My husband named one April because of their birth month, and one Amy because they were his 'Little Women.' He had sisters, you see, and knew all about that story."

The phone rang then, interrupting her recitation. Jason made a mental note to find out more while Katie led him toward Lila's office across the hall.

"Thought I heard you come in," said a deep voice from the back of the building.

"Bart! Good to see you." Jason detoured to shake Bart's hand. Katie showed off her phone.

"Congratulations on the house. I can't think of anyone I'd want more for a neighbor than you."

The man sounded sincere. No double meanings. No sarcasm.

"Thanks, Bart. I appreciate it. And look forward to being on Bay Road."

"Me, too." Katie had her say.

Bart nodded at the flowers and the wrapped gift left on Jane's desk. "You've been busy, it seems."

"That one's from Katie," said Jason, pointing at the package. "It's special."

The old man twinkled. "Our Katie's special, too. Let's go spread the cheer." He joined them as they walked into Lila's office.

She looked up from the notes on her desk and focused on Bart. In total business mode. "We've got electrical problems toward Land's End. Can you call Ralph Bigelow and give him a heads-up? Do you think he'll want the work, or should we call someone else?"

"I'll call him," replied Bart. "He likes to be busy."

"A ROMEO thing?" asked Jason. Ralph was retired from the local utility company, and contracted his services now whenever he had the time. As he'd said more than once around the breakfast table at the Diner, "Retirement takes up a lot of time. Can't remember being so busy."

Lila leaned back in her chair. "Yeah. A ROMEO thing. You should see them at breakfast, Jase. Figuring out how to solve all the problems of the town. Your dad, too."

He loved hearing her shorten his name like that, like his family often did. Meant she was starting to relax around him. "I've had breakfast with the boys already, sweetheart. I know."

And maybe he was too relaxed. He felt Bart's eyes shoot toward him. Saw his smile start to grow.

"Guess what, Papa Bart?" Katie chimed in. "Daddy kissed Mommy in the kitchen before. Ain't that great?"

And Jason learned that little girls couldn't keep secrets, even with the loss of a cell phone hanging over their heads.

"Kathleen!" said Lila.

"But you only said not to tell Grandma, so Papa Bart doesn't count."

He had to remember children thought in black-and-white terms. Everything had to be spelled out clearly.

"That's the best news I've heard in weeks," said Bart, walking toward his great-granddaughter and giving her a hug. "You're a fine lassie to share that."

"And it's time for me to catch a ferry to Boston," said Jason. He turned toward Bart. "Females are complicated."

"But you can't live without 'em."

"Wouldn't consider it." He gave Katie a kiss. "Got my phone number?"

She nodded. "But wait till Mommy opens my present."

Lila began ripping the paper fast. He got the message: leave! But then her hands stilled. Her mouth formed an O. "This is beautiful," she whispered. "She can almost walk out of the frame."

"Glad you like it," said Jason, stepping behind her and looking once more at the picture of Katie he'd taken with his digital camera that morning. They'd gone to a one-hour development place, and after he purchased a silver frame, he'd set the photo inside and voilà—instant Mother's Day gift. Perhaps better than the flowers.

"I love it. It's wonderful. Thank you. Thank you very much." Her blue eyes shone, exuding a warmth he hadn't seen directed at him lately.

All right! Finally, a home run. He kissed Katie again, shook Bart's hand and told Lila to stay well. Didn't want to risk spoiling the mood with another kiss. "See you on Thursday afternoon when I get back from L.A."

As he left the office, he felt a pair of eyes burning into his retreating back. Just like the night before, except this time there was no veterinarian around. This time, the eyes belonged to Lila.

WHAT TO DO. What to do. Lila paced her room that
evening after dining with her family at the Lobster
Pot, and after putting Katie to bed. Adam and Sara
had been to New Hampshire again with his parents,
and Lila realized she'd been granted a reprieve for
the day.

She looked at the ring she wore. A beautiful diamond symbolizing a pure love from the heart. But
was that what she and Adam shared?

Adam was a lovely man. And wise. Or at least,
more experienced. But he was also a parent, and Lila
knew like no one else did how much Sara meant to
him. For Adam, his child would always come first.
Heck, from their conversation last night, Eileen
would also come first—at least for a while. What
he'd said, however, made sense. They could have
moved forward together with a fair start. And until
Jason had reappeared, they'd had a fair start.

She absently twisted the ring with her other hand
as she paused in front of the window and looked out
on the night. The quiet night. Suddenly, she needed
to go outside. To see the moon and the familiar con-
stellations of the northern sky. To hear the water
gently lap against the rocks and the narrow shore of
the bay. To smell the salt and the seaweed, the aromas she'd inhaled all her life. She walked quietly
through the house, through the kitchen and onto the
back screened porch. Grabbing an afghan and lift-

ing the latch of the door, she made her way down to where the rock formations offered her a seat.

The problem with being a single parent and owning a business was the lack of time for personal thought. Tonight, she had to steal some of that precious commodity. An hour would be sufficient. Or maybe two. Maybe until sunrise. She didn't know for sure. All she knew was that she could not postpone her decision any longer.

She placed the folded blanket on the ground and lay back, resting her head upon it, searching the sky for her landmarks. Or skymarks. And there were the Big and Little Dippers. And the North Star. Cassiopeia. How many times had she studied the heavens over the years, wondering if Jason did, too? Had he spent evenings thinking about her, remembering how they used to walk along the beach at night sharing their dreams? Planning their future?

Don't think about Jason. Her decision was not about Jason. Her decision concerned her relationship with Adam. She blinked hard, but tears ran from the outer corners of her eyes. She would hurt a lot of people if her judgment was faulty. Adam, certainly. And Sara. Sweet, delicate Sara. Katie, too, but less so now that Jason was in her life. If he stayed, that is.

Adam was worthy of true love. He was young. Only thirty-four, and although he'd lost his Eileen, perhaps there was another woman out there who could give him her whole heart. *Lila was not that woman.*

A weight lifted. She breathed deeply, her body began to relax. Her eyes closed, her tears dried and she drifted. She'd be setting Adam free. And she would be free again, too, her heart bruised but basically intact. She'd make sure it remained that way. Adam deserved more than she could give him, and Jason deserved less.

She'd go it alone as she'd always done. Her lids fluttered open, and she glimpsed the heavens again. This time, however, the stars seemed distant and cold. Tears trickled once more.

JASON HAD LEARNED TO SLEEP whenever he had the chance, and he arrived on the West Coast rested, which was a good thing, he decided later that day as he walked into Mitch Berman's office and saw Luis Torres and the singer's agent already there. Good vibes floated in the air.

"Are we having a party?" Jason clapped Luis on the back before he greeted the agent.

"With the music, we always have a party," replied Torres, his dark eyes twinkling as though he had a secret.

Jason became still. "Okay…what's going on?"

Mitch turned to the others. "The man writes the title song for an album that just broke all sales records for the first week out, and he doesn't know what's going on. You'd think his mind would be on the business...."

"Wait a minute," said Jason, turning from one man to the other. "Maybe I have jet lag. What did you say?"

Mitch walked to a corner of his office and wheeled a cart toward the group. Champagne, flutes, cake and strawberries. "I say, it's time to celebrate—and make plans."

Goose bumps rose on the back of Jason's neck as he watched Mitch pour the bubbly drink. What plans?

After handing his guests their glasses, Mitch glanced at Jason. "I've got yours here." He pulled out a 7-Up, poured it and added a strawberry.

"Here's to future collaborations," said Mitch.

Jason raised his glass as the image of Lila sprang to mind. He could think of many ways to collaborate with her! And then he wondered if he were chasing an impossible dream.

"I'm taking the album on tour," said Luis, looking at Jason as he took his seat again. "For a year."

Jason put down his glass and shook his head. "I'm not going."

Luis grinned. "Don't want you to go." He looked at his agent. "Tell him what we want."

The man steepled his fingers and looked up at Jason from under bushy eyebrows. "Give us an album, J.J. Love songs. The sweet. The sexy. The romantic and the unrequited. Put in a Latin beat. Try a rhythm-and-blues style. Evoke the French chanson if you want. Mix it up. Just make sure it's all about love between a man and a woman."

His head swam. This was an unheard-of opportunity for a writer in the first blush of a career. A real jump start with the accompanying rewards, growth in reputation and bank account. Maybe he could pay off his mortgage quickly. Help Matt with his. He looked at Mitch. "What about Disney?"

"I've got the script notes right here. But they need an answer by next week. We'll talk later." He nodded toward their guests. Some discussions would be private.

"And Celine Dion? Have you heard from her agent? Or is it too soon?"

Mitch's wide smile gave away the news. "She likes it. Wants to record it on her next CD."

It was too much at once, being surrounded by good offers and good results. And all because of Lila's song. As though from a distance he heard Luis joke, "The writer just lost his words."

"Merely trying to absorb," said Jason.

"There is just one little thing," began Mitch. "And you won't like it."

"Ah," said Jason, taking a seat and leaning back. "Now this is more what I'm used to. Problems."

His cell phone rang.

"Let it go," said Mitch.

Jason glanced at the caller ID. "Not on your life."

He picked it up. "Hello, sweetheart. I'm right here just like I said."

He saw the interested gleams Luis and Mitch had in their eyes when they looked at him, then at each other.

"It's my daughter," clarified Jason, taking Katie's picture out of his wallet. "What's up, Lady Katie?"

He listened for a moment. "You did? You and Casey? Okay. Play it for me. Put the phone on top of the piano. I'll hear it."

He shrugged in apology at the others. "First things first," he said. Then he began to listen, and like the first time he'd heard the kids play, goose bumps prickled his arms.

"Wasn't that better?" asked Katie afterward. "We built a real bridge between the songs for the Memorial Day show, didn't we?"

He laughed, and his heart filled with pride. "More beautiful than the Golden Gate, baby."

"Grandpa Sam said it was the best we ever did."

Jason turned to Mitch. "Is that a speaker phone?"

Mitch nodded.

"Put Grandpa on, Katie, and you and Casey stick around. I want to hear it again on a bigger phone."

A minute later Mitch's landline rang. "Take it from the top, kids," said Jason, looking around the room. "You're in for a four-hand treat, my friends. My daughter and nephew."

He looked at their interested faces while the

music came over the speaker, and although the sound quality was deficient, Jason basked in their expressions of amazement, in their compliments later after he'd praised both children again and said goodbye to them.

"What goes on in that town of yours?" asked Luis's agent. "Maybe we should send a scout?"

Jason laughed out loud. "Not necessary. Your scout would wind up on the Parker family's doorstep." He turned toward Luis and then Mitch. "After listening to you guys brag about your kids all these years, I just had to show mine off, too." He paused. "Katie is just unbelievable. And being a dad…well, it's early days yet, but…wow, there's nothing like it. And now that I've bought a house, she'll be staying with me sometimes…."

Mitch cleared his throat. "So you actually bought a house?"

"I sure did. Told you I was relocating to Pilgrim Cove."

Mitch sighed and shook his head. "That was too quick. A bad idea…at least for now," he amended. "There's a lot on your plate."

The room became quiet. Jason searched the faces in front of him. He knew what they were thinking. Although Luis would be on tour, he'd grab days back home in Los Angeles when he could. Having J. J. Parks on hand would be the only way to touch base musically.

And if Disney studios liked his work, they'd want him available when the time came. There was a lot of material to coordinate when making a movie. A lot of people to work with, and they were all in California. He understood that. He also knew that if he was labeled as uncooperative, he'd be jeopardizing relationships with both performing artists and studios. "We love his work, but…" Performers were expected to be high maintenance, but musicians had better be available and have their work in on time.

Visions of eliminating debt for everyone in his family vanished quickly. Jason was not in the position to call the shots here, which was ironic considering that he produced what Luis sang. But there were thousands of talented composers on both coasts writing their hearts out.

You and I can do anything. We're the best. Jared's voice echoed in his mind. Jared, always more confident than Jason, more adventurous. But not more talented. And neither was Jason's competition.

Jason stood up and faced the room. "When you decide that you want the best in the business, feel free to call me in Pilgrim Cove."

He walked out the door and, too impatient to wait for an elevator, jogged down the five flights of stairs in the office building to the basement garage. As he headed for his apartment to pack it up, the reality of what he'd done sank in. He'd just made the biggest bet of his life. He'd put everything on the line and taken a huge professional gamble. Huge. But, he wasn't sorry about it. If the singer and the studio couldn't deal with him living on the East Coast, then he'd write for someone else. New York was a mecca. Or he'd find another way to earn a living.

It seemed he had a habit of putting himself in risky situations. He thought of Lila. What if she didn't come to her senses? What if she decided to marry Fielding after all? Then what? Would he be able to stand aside and watch them as a family even for Katie's sake? The thought made him grimace, and he shoved the idea away, as he'd done before. He'd handle it. Somehow, he'd figure it out.

There was always the possibility, however, he could end up with no contracts and no Lila.

JASON HAD PACKED BOXES, given some stuff away, cleaned the apartment and slept like a baby on the night flight home. He'd arranged for his car to be driven east, and was content with his accomplishments. He was back in Sea View House by mid-morning on Thursday and planned to pick up Katie and Casey at school at three o'clock.

Since the would-be celebratory meeting, he'd gotten one phone call from Mitch Berman telling him to "hang tight." Jason had shrugged. His heart's desire was in Pilgrim Cove, and if he had to… Well, his hands had pounded many a nail for the family's business while he was growing up. He'd find a way to earn a living in construction if needed.

Or he could play in piano bars again. J. J. Parks earned good money in personal lounge appearances at hotels, in clubs or even on Mississippi riverboats. Of course, traveling the river was out of the question now.

And then…niggling in the back of his mind… there was the path Jared had always wanted them to go. Writing and performing their own music. Billy Joel plus Elton John, except more unique. Jason and Jared. A double dose of whatever talent they had inside of them.

But Jason hadn't agreed with his brother's plan. At eighteen, he and Lila had made their own plans. First, college together, then get married and raise a family. He would have enjoyed his music on the side. He would've kept writing, but he'd have let Jared do the performing.

His twin, however, had been furious. Couldn't understand it. Called Jason a coward, afraid to leave Pilgrim Cove. Jared had been angry with Lila, as well. Thought she was keeping his brother down. Jason had said some bad things, too. Their senior year had been hard, fraught with conflict because change was coming. Childhood was over.

He understood all that now. At the time, their testosterone did the talking. And on the night of their prom, their hormones shouted. Everyone's future was in place. No more wiggle room. He and Lila had enrolled in school. Jared was going to New York City—alone. Edgy. Disappointed.

When the memories of that night threatened to overwhelm him, Jason did what he was accustomed to doing. He called for help. He picked up the phone in Sea View House, but instead of dialing a counselor, he called Rachel Goodman-Levine at the high school. She answered after only one ring.

"I was afraid you wouldn't have time for us," she said after greeting him warmly.

"On the contrary. Can't think of anything I'd rather be doing at the moment than helping Pilgrim Cove students stay safe next week. Tell me about Jane Fisher's twin daughters."

If she thought it an odd request, she didn't let on. Jason absorbed the information and promised to call her back the next day when he had his ideas on paper.

Before he had a chance to call Lila and let her know he was back, his cell phone rang. He recognized Mitch's voice.

"You pay me for advice as well as for opportunity, so listen up. When are you going to break out on your own and become a true self-contained artist?"

Mitch Berman on a mission.

"Is this what you meant by 'hanging tight'?"

asked Jason. "Or is this the 'lecture for your own good' I hear coming?"

"What are you afraid of?" the agent continued. "If you want more control over your time and your work, then write and record your own stuff. We'll get you on any record label you want. After 'The Water's Edge,' publishers will be beating down your door. You can almost write your own deal."

First Jared. Now Mitch. With their big-time dreams. Mitch blasted into his ear again. "What's to stop you? You'll write hits and make more money than you can spend. You'll have respect, fame. You'll be a celebrity."

Jason grimaced. "Jared wanted that part of it," he said in a sharp tone. "I didn't. I just wanted to compose the music."

"Well, your brother's not here," Mitch retorted. "And you are! With enough talent for the two of you. So what are you going to do about it?"

"Do about it? How can I steal my brother's dream?" His voice exploded with pain. "What you're talking about is what he wanted so much… that he died for it. And now you want me to waltz on in and take it from him?" Jared died and Jason lived. Mitch didn't know what it meant to be the survivor.

"I thought all that guilt crap was behind you."

He would have laughed if he could. Mitch was being Mitch. Instead Jason started to pace. "It only comes back when I talk to you! When I start to think about changing my career path—bringing it to new levels."

"I'm glad to hear that, Jason. Now, you… have…got…to…listen to me. And trust me." The agent slowed his words and delivered them with punch. "If you don't use all your God-given talent, talent that anyone else would kill for, you'll either explode or shrivel up. Or worse—you'll become a bitter man. I've been around a long time, kid. I've seen self-destruction in many forms when so big a gift is discarded whether from fear of success or fear of failure. You've tasted that fear already.

"I know you've been to hell and back," the agent continued calmly, "but you're a better writer because of the trip. On the other hand, the detour cost you time, and you're getting a late start. You've got to act now if J. J. Parks is to go forward and join the ranks of the single names in contemporary music. It's totally up to you. So think about it and call me." He clicked off. Just a gentle click. Hardly like Mitch Berman's usual style.

Jason tapped the recall button. The number barely rang before he heard his agent's voice.

"You've got something important to say?" Anxiety. Impatience. Concern. Hope. The emotional mixture hit Jason's sensitive ear.

"I've got five thick binders. Filled."

Silence. Deep and quiet. Then Mitch started to

laugh. Warm and joyous. "Only five, Jason? Well, it's a start!"

A new start. He'd allow himself that much. He walked to the kitchen and stepped onto the back porch, inhaling the ocean breeze, reveling in the warm sun, enjoying the clean sweep of the sand and sea. The water's edge. Just as he'd remembered it.

Peace entered his soul. It had taken a long time—fits and starts—to turn his back on the haunting guilt and become his own man. He was Jason Parker. And when he recorded under the name J. J. Parks, it would be to honor his brother's memory, not to assuage his own guilt by trying to keep Jared alive. He allowed his tears to fall. They felt damn good.

And now, more decisions. Which songs to pull first for the demos he'd make. Just him and the piano. Later, when it was time to structure the first album, he could figure out the tracks for the backup instruments.

Chills ran through him. His first album! He smiled and raised his arms in victory. Yes!

CHAPTER TWELVE

FIRST, HE'D OUTLINED his ideas for the high-school program, then he retrieved his notebooks, played through one of them, and realized he'd need some help selecting material. He went into the kitchen to call his brother at the store and simply asked if he and Sam would be available that evening for a guest.

Matt exploded. "You're not a guest, for crying out loud! You're my brother! Get yourself to the house for dinner." Then he slammed the phone down, leaving Jason with a buzzing dial tone. When had Matt gotten so bossy? Or was it his way of saying that Jason had not spent enough time with the family?

He called the store again. "I'm sorry, Matt, but I promise you that by the time I'm done, you and Pop are going to think I'm a piece of furniture in your house."

"Uh…I think we can take it, bro."

When he hung up, the phone rang immediately. At this rate, he'd never get anything else done.

"Bartholomew Quinn here, Jason."

"Bart? What's up? Is something wrong with my new house?"

"No, no. Everything's fine there. But you need to know about Lila, and I'm the one to tell you."

Jason's heart thudded. The old man wouldn't be calling unless something bad had happened. "What happened? Is she hurt? Where is she? I'm on my way. Talk to me."

"Heh, heh, heh," laughed Bart softly.

Huh? "What game are you playing, Bartholomew?"

"No game, my boy. You've been out of touch for a few days, so you don't know yet. The ring's gone from her finger."

Now Jason collapsed on the kitchen chair. "What happened?"

The Realtor's voice became thin. "She wouldn't share the details, lad. Just something about 'not being Eileen.' That was his wife's name, you know."

Jason wasn't surprised. "So, how's she...adjusting?" He groped for the right word.

"Well, lad, that's what I'm worried about. She's going into a deep freeze, my granddaughter is. She says she'll never be anyone's 'Eileen.' And that no one could ever be her 'Jason.'"

"But that's crazy. I'm right here and she knows it."

"And that's the sad part, my boy. She doesn't want you now. And she's stubborn. She wants the old you, but since that's impossible, she'll stay alone. Now, that's crazy. Too sad, isn't it? Makes my heart hurt."

"You're making my brain hurt," replied Jason, his thoughts twirling. Bart was talking a sad story, yet his voice vibrated with quiet excitement.

"So do something about it," said Bart. And for the third time that day, a buzzing dial tone was all Jason heard.

He glanced at his watch and dashed for the car. Definitely time to get away from the phone and get the kids. He was tempted to leave his cell on the table.

Perfect timing. He pulled up to school exactly as the children were being dismissed, and several minutes later, he spotted the third-grade class coming down the front steps. Katie and Casey waved at him, but only Casey ran over. He glanced at his daughter, and saw her talking to Sara.

"What's happening with the girls, Case?"

He shrugged. "I'm not sure. Sara's real sad. Katie, too. I guess they wanted to be sisters."

Oh, boy. The trickle-down effect.

"Uncle Jase—maybe they could be blood brothers."

"You think?" He ruffled Casey's hair. "Let's find out." He strolled to the girls, Casey alongside him. As soon as he was in earshot, Katie ran to him, spilling the entire situation about Lila and Adam not getting married and Sara and Katie couldn't be sisters anymore, but they wanted to be sisters, anyway. And who needs a dumb old wedding to have a sister?

"That's right," said Sara, looking at Jason with big round chocolate-brown eyes. Troubled and worried eyes. A sensitive child. "Who needs a dumb old wedding?"

"You don't need a wedding ceremony," said Jason. "You need a sister ceremony. A very special ceremony that will make you sisters of the heart forever and ever."

"Oh-h-h—good idea, Daddy. Can we call Dr. Fielding and see if Sara can come home with us?"

Jason pulled out his cell phone and handed it to Sara. In the end, Jason had to speak with Sara's father, assuring him he'd bring Sara home in time for dinner. It could have been an awkward conversation, but Jason had to give Fielding credit for not letting his pride stand in the way of the girls' friendship.

He drove the kids to the Shell Shop, which carried gift items made of seashells. It also carried arts-and-craft supplies. They walked out with three old-fashioned cigar boxes—Casey decided to make a gift for Laura—as well as plastic bags of shells, colored sand, glue, paper, markers. They would create beautiful boxes to hold secrets and gifts between sisters. A picture. A poem. A toy. A note. Whatever little girls wanted to share.

Jason marveled at their nonstop enthusiasm.

Their ever-flowing ideas. How they made selections in the store. He loved the sound of their giggling. It ebbed and flowed like the tides. He began to whistle alongside them. Casey cocked his head, then followed his lead. Katie took notice. Listened. Became a member of the whistling chorus.

Then Jason looked at Sara, who was staring at the other three in awe and confusion. "Your job is to giggle," he told the child. "You're the one who started the whole thing."

The girl's eyes shone with delight and off she went into delicate peals of laughter. She was moonlight to Katie's sunshine. The girls filled a need in each other, their personalities locking like puzzle pieces.

After they returned to Sea View House, the children worked on their projects until he had to take Sara home. He arrived at the veterinary clinic at six. Fielding emerged from the building and Sara ran to him. He stood with his hands on Sara's shoulders and looked at Jason, who was standing outside his car.

"Sara had a good time, so if it's okay with you, she's welcome to come back tomorrow to finish the project," said Jason, waving at Sara.

Adam stared at him as though he were a specimen under his microscope. "Have you seen her?"

Electricity filled the air. The back of Jason's neck tingled. He knew to whom Fielding referred.

"No," said Jason, beginning to climb back into the driver's seat.

"You killed something in her, Parker. She didn't deserve it. So I figure it's your responsibility to fix her up." He paused for a heartbeat. "For Lila's sake…good luck."

Jason had wanted to flatten the guy when he'd heard his first words, but the man spoke the truth. He nodded to the vet and got behind the wheel.

NEXT STOP, Bay Road. Lila's house.

Bart opened the door. "She's in the kitchen."

Jason looked at Katie and Casey. "Hang out with Papa Bart for a few minutes." It wasn't a question, but an order. They both nodded.

"Thanks, guys."

They grinned.

Lila didn't grin when she saw him in the doorway. "Another flying visit?"

He ignored her jibe and walked toward her at the sink where she was cutting vegetables. Her hands slowed as he approached. Her back straightened.

"How are you, Lila?" he asked softly.

"Does it matter?" She didn't turn around.

"What kind of question is that? Of course it matters!"

She turned then, her eyes glowing like a banked fire. "I'll survive, Jason. Like I've done until now."

"That's not enough. Not when you can have more."

"It's enough for me."

"Oh, no… No, it isn't." He leaned toward her, and she froze. His lips touched hers. Moved across them gently. As though he were breaking in a nervous colt, he was gentle when he stroked her cheek, when he caressed her shoulder. Light touches. Light kisses. He finally heard her sigh. And just when he was about to press his mouth a little more firmly, she stepped to the side.

This time the shine in her eyes looked like tears. "Why are you being so cruel?" she whispered. "We're not living in a movie where the girl falls into the hero's arms after one kiss. This is real life."

"And so is this—I love you, Lila. I've never stopped loving you."

But she was shaking her head. "No. No, you don't. You don't know me anymore, Jason. You love the girl you remember. But that girl is dead. As dead as Jared. As dead as the boy you once were." When she looked at him now, her eyes were clear and her soul shone through. She was speaking from her heart.

He couldn't ask for more than that.

But his voice cracked when he tried to respond. "Then let's start over, Lila. Since you think we're different people now, let's give ourselves a chance to know each other."

She turned away from him to stare through the window at the descending darkness. "I'm afraid," she whispered. And he wrapped his arms around her then. She fit so perfectly, he could have stayed as they were forever.

"Are you afraid of me?" he whispered. "Lila, honey. I'd protect you with my life. You are breaking my heart right now. What are you afraid of?"

She twisted in his arms and stared into his eyes. "I'm afraid of not surviving another round with you. And if I don't survive, Katie doesn't survive. She needs a strong mother. I can't risk folding."

Backward reasoning. "If your strength is rooted in fear, then you're not truly strong. And you can't be happy. But if your strength is based on confidence, then you'll not only survive, you'll thrive."

She broke away from him. "I'm doing the best I can," she said. "And I don't need any psychoanalysis from you!"

He held up his hands. "Sorry. I'll let you even the score. Come to the senior-class program next week at the high school. You might find it interesting."

And it might be a starting point for them. On the other hand, she might run as far and as fast as her long legs could carry her. He examined her tired face, the face he loved, and wished she'd let him help her.

"I'll be looking for another piece of property," he said, trying to distract her. "Commercial this time."

That got her attention. "Commercial? For what purpose?"

"A sound studio. Not only for recording demos, but also for recording the real thing. I don't think the basement in my new house will be big enough."

He'd gotten her attention. "Here? In Pilgrim Cove?" she asked.

He nodded. "I'm back, Lila. For good."

LILA FINISHED PREPARING the salad, retrieved the hamburgers from the broiler and called Katie and Bart in for supper. Her thoughts kept shifting to Jason. He wanted her and Katie to join him at Matt's house later, but wouldn't tell her why. Only that it had to do with some new recordings.

She didn't know what to think. What did Jason really have in mind? She wasn't a musician, but he'd invited her, anyway. She glanced at Bart. "Did Jason ever ask you to look for space to use as a recording studio?"

Bart's eyes gleamed. He put his utensils down with a clatter. "A studio! What a good idea. Our boy is thinking ahead. No need to go to L.A." His brow creased in thought. "Do we have anything on Main Street? How big a place does he need? And what about utilities?"

"I know nothing."

"This is so cool!" said Katie, jumping from her seat. "Maybe famous people will come here. Maybe even Luis Torres. Maybe Christina Aguilera. And Britney Spears. Ohh…maybe some cute boy bands!"

Lila's mouth opened and closed like a fish. "You're only eight years old! What do you know about boy bands, anyway?"

"Ma-a-a! Do you think I only know Grandpa Sam's songs? I know lots of other stuff!"

She looked at Bart. "What do I know?" he said with a shrug. "But I bet her dad knows a lot. Why don't you ask him?" He glanced at his watch. "We've got an extra card game at Lou's tonight. Don't want to be late." He reached for Lila and kissed her on the forehead. "I'm feeling mighty lucky today."

"You feel lucky every day," replied Lila, planting a kiss on his cheek in return. "How do you manage that?"

Bart laughed. "It's easy. I'm surrounded by four-leaf clovers!" He waved to her and left the room.

Lila stared after him and shook her head. Her Irish granddad and his glib responses. Four-leaf clovers, indeed! She was Irish, too, but along with her one perfect rose, her garden was overrun with thorns.

"Katie, let's go to Uncle Matt's house and see what's going on. Bring some pajamas."

She might as well learn what Jason was up to and what she had to do to protect Katie. Or to protect Pilgrim Cove, for that matter. She leaned against the fridge. Luis Torres in Pilgrim Cove? The town would go nuts! It would be a madhouse.

Ten minutes later, she knocked on Matt and Laura's back door. She heard footsteps approach, and then Laura was greeting her with delight.

"You two are just in time!" she said, waving them inside. "Everybody's in the music room." Katie ran off.

"Do you know what's going on?" Lila asked as they walked.

"Not a clue."

"Probably some harebrained idea," mumbled Lila.

Laura squeezed her hand in response. "We've got Matt and Sam in there, Lila. They're not harebrained at all."

Lila began to breathe more easily. When they approached the back of the house, however, and she heard the familiar music of Scott Joplin's "The Entertainer," she could barely breathe at all. She managed to steady herself. Until she saw the two men at the keyboard. Two brothers. Two look-alikes. Time collapsed and she froze on the threshold. "Oh, my God…" Her whisper was enough to catch Jason's attention.

"Lila! How nice…" He jumped from the seat and caught her as she swayed. "What's wrong?" he asked, leading her to the sofa.

"I'm fine, I'm fine." She pushed his arms away. She looked at Matt, still watching from the piano bench. At Sam, who was looking at her with concern. At Laura, whose blue eyes were wide open. "It's just that the two of you… When I walked in…"

"You thought it was Jared with me," Jason said.

She smiled in apology at Matt. "I'm sorry."

"It's okay. You weren't expecting to see us at the piano."

"The past will haunt you till you face it," said Jason. "Believe me, I know. You need to face it and move forward."

What did he think she'd been trying to do all these years? "Is that a convenient sound bite from the West Coast? 'Face the past. Move forward.'" Her hands on her hips, she moved into his space. "And after facing that past, what do I do with my memories?" she asked. "He killed himself because of me. I screamed at him to leave you alone! Leave *us* alone. 'Go to New York,' I said. 'Get out of here already. You're tearing Jason into tiny pieces.'" She couldn't stop the tears.

"My God," said Matt Parker. "There's enough guilt to go around for everyone."

But she hadn't finished. She took a step closer to Jason. Poked him with her finger. "And what did you do? You blamed me, too! He blamed me for keeping you back, and you blamed me for his recklessness that night. You took your grief, your guilt and your anger and you left. In the end, you chose a dead man over me."

If Jason was shocked, he didn't show it. He put his hands on her shoulders, shaking her gently until she looked at him. "You listen to me, Lila Sullivan.

You did not put him behind the wheel. You did not force-feed him a keg of beer. You did not tell him to smash into a telephone pole."

She heard his harsh breathing. His dark eyes blazed like a steel furnace, unbearably hot but controlled.

"He did it to himself, Lila. I didn't cause it. You didn't cause it. No one's to blame but Jared, himself." His eyes darkened as he stared at her. "My God, Lila. I never once thought to blame you."

No one moved. No one spoke. Not even Sam Parker who had lost a son. But Jason hadn't finished.

"You want to know where I was for nine years?" asked Jason. "I was figuring out what happened to us that night. That year. The three of us." He was silent, until finally, a slow grin crossed his face. "I sure as hell hope you learn faster than I do. Time's a-wasting."

Lila stepped back. "Don't rush me, Jason. Right now, it's my turn to put it to rest instead of hiding behind motherhood and career building." As soon as the words left her mouth, she knew they were true. All the painful threads of her past had tied her in knots too tangled to unravel by herself. So she'd focused on her daughter and building Quinn Real Estate and Property Management. She'd avoided looking inside until now. Until she wasn't alone. She'd needed Jason to put the memory of that night into focus. They were the only two on earth who'd been there.

She walked to Jason's dad, a man whom she'd known and loved her whole life. A man she trusted. "Sam. Do you believe what Jason said about Jared?"

"I do, honey." He patted her cheek. Such a sweet man. "People have to be responsible for themselves. My wife was not…herself. You remember that. She blamed Jason."

Lila nodded.

"The day I left," began Jason, "didn't I say my mom couldn't stand looking at me? Seeing my face?"

She nodded again. "But that's not the same as blaming you."

"She said I'd chosen you over Jared and made Jared miserable. Said I could have pulled him out of the car…."

But Lila shook her head. "You couldn't. That much I know. We tried. He was so strong…."

"My dear children," said Sam, "we cannot undo the past. We can only learn from it." He looked toward his older son. "Matthew! Get out some schnapps. The bottle we save for Bart. We're going to toast to new beginnings. And allow those who are no longer with us to rest in peace." He pointed at Jason. "But you—you'll get lemonade!"

That was the second time in Lila's presence that Jason chose not to imbibe. She looked at him.

"I had a problem some years back," he began. "Four years ago to be exact. I had become an alcoholic. I got help. So now I don't touch the hard stuff. And life is good again."

Four years ago. That's when she'd received that fateful message. "So you just say no?" she asked, pasting a smile on her face while she tried to absorb the new information.

"Something like that."

SHE'D CLOSED DOWN ON HIM again. Stepped back just when they were starting to warm up. Just when all the bits and pieces of their shared memories were finally out on the table to be examined and understood. Well, at least they'd accomplished that much. But it wasn't enough. Not in Jason's mind.

He'd felt her withdrawal as soon as he mentioned the word *alcoholic*. He sighed, glanced at his watch and walked back to the piano. Only fifteen minutes had passed since Lila and Katie had arrived. He was surprised. Illuminating the past had exhausted him, had seemed to take forever.

And what about the future? Lila might be right after all. They weren't the same people they used to be. Years of living had intervened, and they weren't eighteen anymore.

He hefted his binder of original music. The proof of time passing lay right there. After seating himself at the piano facing the room, he studied each person. The kids sat on the floor, curious. His brother and father, eager and impatient. Laura, eyes twinkling, encouraging. Only Lila sat alone. Quietly waiting.

"I made a decision today," Jason began, "that will affect all of us in a good way, I hope." He took a breath, still suffering from a bit of disbelief himself. "I'm going it alone from now on. Writing and recording." He crooked his head toward Lila. "I decided not to submit material to Disney. I turned down Luis's tour. I packed up my apartment. As I've told you before, I'm going to stay anchored right here."

No reaction from Lila. "If you're not happy," Jason said, "blame my agent."

He filled his family in on the conversation with Mitch. "It's not ego here. Mitch has been wanting me to go solo for a long time. And it seems, the time is now."

He looked at his brother and his dad, whose musical abilities were as good as his own. "Will you guys help me choose?"

A cacophony filled the room, from the men's cheers and excitement, to Katie's "What Disney movies?" She didn't look so happy. His older nephew, Brian, looked stunned at first, then wildly happy, then deep in thought. "Where are you going to record? Are you setting up a studio? What backup are you going to have? Can I audition?"

Jason felt his muscles relax, one by one, and only then did he realize he'd been holding his breath waiting for his family's reactions. They were all he could have hoped for.

He turned toward Lila, who hadn't said anything yet. She sat as though she were an audience of one trying to comprehend the play in front of her. "I've asked Lila to find a location for a studio."

All three children ran to her, offering their help. Finally, she came out of her stupor—had no choice with Katie and Casey all over her lap—and promised to let them know. "I need more information myself," she said, glancing at Jason.

"Uncle Jason," said Casey. "Are you going to be famous?"

Jason shrugged. "Maybe a little. If the folks like my music."

Lila's "Ah…" preceded her standing. "That's where this idea sticks in the craw."

Jason saw every head turn toward her in unison like a funny scene from a movie. "Explain."

Now her spirit caught fire. "If you become another Billy Joel, what will happen to Pilgrim Cove? To our town of five thousand, except 'higher in summer,'" she quoted. "We'll be overrun with too-eager fans, reporters, even Peeping Toms. We don't need that here." She studied him. "You don't need that, either, Jason," she added, her voice softening. *That had to count for something.*

"Long Island hasn't disappeared or blown up because Billy Joel lives there," replied Jason. "Neither has Manhattan which is filled with celebrities."

"But we're a small town. What will happen to us?"

Sam answered the question. "Have you forgotten the ROMEOs, my dear? There isn't anything we can't do when the you-know-what hits the fan. We'll put the chief in charge of this project when the time comes. Put your mind to rest."

"Or *if* the time comes," said Jason, picking up on his dad's comments. He searched Lila's face. "There's always the chance I'll fail."

Now, she was shocked. "You won't fail," she said. "That possibility never crossed my mind."

The strength of her words indicated a vote of confidence, but the underlying inflection begrudged it. He decided to concentrate on the positive.

"Thank you, Lila. I appreciate your faith in me."

The wrong thing to say. The pain in her eyes was reinforced when she shook her head. "I never doubted the *music.*"

She doubted the man. Still didn't trust him. Still hadn't forgiven him for not coming home when he'd promised. Maybe if she'd listen to some of his songs…but she was heading out the door.

"Would someone bring Katie home?" she asked the group in general. "I don't want to spoil her fun."

And she was gone in an instant.

"Seems to me," said Matthew, "you've got some work cut out ahead of you. And I don't mean on the keyboard."

Jason rolled his head to get out the knots. "No," he said. "I think I'll leave her alone for a while."

Suddenly, the sound of crying came to his ears. Katie! He scooped his daughter from the floor, and deposited featherlight kisses all over her cheek.

"No, Daddy. You can't."

"Can't kiss you?"

"Uh-unh," she replied shaking her head. "You can't leave Mommy alone. She's too sad all the time. And…and I don't know what to do." Her words ended in a wail and more sobs, and the pain in her voice ripped Jason's heart into tiny pieces.

He cuddled her closer. "You don't have to do anything, sweetheart. That's my job. And I'm not giving up. Not at all."

"Promise?"

"Promise." Kissing her again, he said, "Your mom's one stubborn woman. You know that?"

She laughed up at him, tears sparkling from her lashes like twinkling stars. "Yup. That's what Papa Bart calls her all the time."

Some vindication.

Katie wiggled down to the floor, her sunny self back in place. "So, when do we hear some music, Daddy?"

"Thought you'd never ask."

CHAPTER THIRTEEN

HE TAPPED ON LILA'S DOOR two hours later, Katie sound asleep in his arms. Lila tilted her head toward the back of the house and he followed her to the child's room, then gently lowered his daughter onto the bed. Tucking her in, he placed a last kiss on her cheek and enjoyed seeing a tiny smile emerge even as she slept.

Lila, too, smoothed the blanket around the little girl and pressed a kiss on her forehead. "Sleep well, sweetheart," she whispered.

For a moment, Jason stood beside the mother of his child watching over their most precious gift. There was no need for words. He belonged here. In silent communication, he and Lila exited the room at the same time a minute later, maintaining their silence until they returned to the kitchen.

"How did the music session go?" Lila asked.

Was she really interested or being polite? "It was…satisfactory."

Her eyes reached dinner-plate size. "What kind of insipid word is that?" she asked with a laugh. "It was probably fantastic."

"I wish you had stayed."

She avoided his glance, turned away. "Couldn't be helped. But you don't have to show off for me. I know—the whole town knows—about the Parker family and music."

Jason stepped around her, so that she had to look at him. "My music isn't about showing off. It's about truth. One man's truth. It's all there in the songs. What happened to us. What happened to me afterwards. I write about what's in here," he said, placing his hand over his heart. "The best songs ever written, whether they're joyous or poignant, come from in here. Truth resonates with listeners."

She stood quietly in front of him, listening, concentrating. Or so it seemed. "Wait a minute…wait a minute," she said. "Go back. Are you saying that all the bad stuff you went through is going to be public knowledge? Like an autobiography?"

He nodded. "Some of it. Depending on the song."

"But…but Jason! What about the alcohol part? All the drinking. Aren't you afraid for Katie to know?"

He hated the fear, the worry on her face, but he couldn't compromise his writing. Not for Lila. Not even for Katie. "Lila, honey. I don't want to hide anymore. And I can't live my life afraid of everything. Katie will judge me on her own terms. I'll try hard to be the best father I can. She'll know that."

He traced his fingertip along her jaw, her lips. She

didn't move away. He leaned toward her, and lightly rubbed his mouth against hers.

"Umm…"

His heart filled with hope. Maybe touch was the key to Lila. Maybe his familiarity reconnected them to a time of trust. All right! *Let yourself go with it, Lila.*

His nuzzling evolved into a kiss. A sweet kiss. Romantic. *Don't rush.* He wrapped her gently in his arms. Hummed a slow tune and danced with her. She laid her head on his shoulder, one arm looped around his neck. Her eyes closed. Her other arm tightened around his waist. *He'd live in the moment. The now.*

"I've always loved being held by you," she whispered. "So safe. So loved."

He almost tripped. Instead, he whispered, "And I've always loved holding you. We belong together, sweetheart. In each other's arms." Then and now. But he didn't voice the thought. He'd be as patient as Job this time around.

"My mother says you're a Svengali. You have some power over me."

Good God! Maggie Sullivan. He'd almost forgotten about the influence she could have over Lila.

"If that's true, sweetheart, then your dad's guilty, as well. Only a powerful guy could put a spell on your mom, and Maggie seems *very* happily married." *Keep it light, Jase. Keep it light.* But if he ever

had the chance, he'd tell Maggie Sullivan a thing
or two!

He heard a giggle from the region of his chest.
"That's just what I said to her, Jason." She stopped
dancing, her face alight with the memory. "I said
Dad must have hypnotized her, and she turned five
shades of red. Told me to mind my own business."

"And you said…" he prompted, hoping like hell
he knew the ending to this little story.

"Let's make that mutual, Mom."

He swung her around the room. "You are one
fantastic woman. Think of that. You stood up to your
mother!" He set her on her feet again. Gave her a
hard kiss on the mouth. "Sleep well, sweetheart." He
wouldn't be greedy for more. Instead, he'd end the
day on a happy note.

He walked toward the door, then turned. "Might
stop by The Lobster Pot one of these evenings. Don't
want Maggie to forget who I am."

"Ha!"

LILA DIDN'T KNOW what to expect at Katie's "Sisterhood" ceremony with Sara, but encountering
Adam and Jason in the same place was not ideal.
When Katie and Sara had invited her, she should
have anticipated both fathers showing up.

On Friday afternoon at five, however, when she
walked onto the beach behind Sea View House,
Adam was already there. The girls were setting their

stage halfway to the shore, and Jason was nowhere to be seen. Adam walked toward her, an inquisitive smile on his face. A brief hug. "How are you?"

"Fine," she replied. "Trying to find my way." She glanced behind her at the house just as Jason appeared on the porch.

He waved. "Glad you could both make it. I'm in charge of the refreshments, but you have nothing to fear. They were all store bought." He grinned and disappeared back into the kitchen.

"Smart guy," said Adam.

And that's when Lila felt awkward. She twisted her hands over one another until Adam's larger hand stilled her movements.

"Don't fret, Lila. It's okay."

"I know, Adam. I really do. It's just…everything's happening so fast. Changes."

"One thing's not changing," replied the vet, taking a step back.

Lila's arms dropped quietly to her sides. "And what's that?"

He looked at the two children who were arranging a variety of seashells in a large circle. "Sara and Katie's friendship."

"Of course not!" replied Lila, dismayed. Did he think she'd break the little ones apart because of Adam and herself?

"No, no," said Adam, quickly stepping toward her again. "You misunderstood. It's just that I like living here in Pilgrim Cove. Not only for Sara's sake, but for my own. I'm going to stay, Lila." His voice was steady, but his eyes held a question mark when he looked at Lila.

"I never thought you wouldn't." She paused. "We'll both get past this time, and hopefully remain friends." Now she started to laugh. "In a town like Pilgrim Cove, you have no choice!"

Adam chuckled. "So true." Then he become silent, staring at her. "You really are a lovely woman."

She met his gaze without flinching. "But not the right woman for you. I'm sorry, Adam."

"I'm sorry, too. I should have known." He shrugged, then looked toward the house. "Let's see if the boy wonder needs any help with those eats." He headed for the porch.

Lila followed at a slower pace. She reached the steps just as Adam called out toward the house, "Is everything under control in there?"

Jason opened the door with one hand, a tray in the other. He stepped outside and placed the goodies on the oval table. "That's just what I was going to ask you." He glanced at Adam, but his gaze rested on Lila.

"Yeah. We're fine."

He nodded briskly, then called to the girls. "Let's get started."

Lila was impressed with the entire event. Jason seemed to take it as seriously as the kids. First, the adults admired the large friendship circle where the ceremony took place. Then, the children exchanged the shell-decorated gift boxes they'd each made for the other. Katie got the better of that deal, thought Lila, Sara being more artistic and patient by nature.

Third came the recitations of why they wanted to be sisters. Lila was amazed at how much insight the youngsters had. Sara admired Katie's imagination. "You always come up with good ideas."

Katie admired Sara's loyalty. "You always take my side and understand me."

She glanced at the dads and couldn't tell who looked prouder. Jason certainly seemed more in awe. He was still getting used to little girls. And then came the sisterhood oath—bloodless—for which Lila was thankful:

"By the shores of the Atlantic
Under sunny skies above,
Kathleen and Sara are now sisters
Friends forever, filled with love."

Three times, they heard the oath. Once recited and twice sung. The third time through, Katie harmonized with Sara's basic melody.

"Unbelievable," whispered Adam, blinking hard.

"Gorgeous, girls," replied Lila.

"Wow." Jason's contribution. Then he said, "Don't move." He ran to the house and was back with a camera. "I've got to learn to carry this always. Opportunities abound with these kids." He glanced at the other man. "I'll put some on a CD for you."

Lila watched as he took candid shots of the girls finishing off their ceremony. Exchanging poems, notes, baby pictures. Baby pictures? Gosh, they'd thought of everything to put into their gift boxes.

But finally it was over. Everyone satisfied. The girls, however, were still wired. Jason indicated that Lila and Adam should step aside with him. "How about I keep them for an overnight? I'll order in a pizza, and then run on the beach with them until they're exhausted enough to sleep."

"Don't you have work to do?" asked Lila. "Songs to worry about?"

"They'll still be there." He stared at Katie and Sara. "The kids won't. Childhood goes by too quickly." Love shone from his eyes as he looked at his daughter, a blinding, mesmerizing love for a child he'd known for less than three weeks.

He might have been reading Lila's mind when he said, "It only takes a heartbeat, doesn't it?"

She looked around at the remnants of the ceremony, the piles of shells on his porch, the plate of leftover cookies and pitcher of lemonade. He'd come through for his child—without prompting. For Katie's sake, he'd rearranged his whole life to return to Pilgrim Cove.

Maybe Lila hadn't given him enough credit.

She raised her eyes to him again, just as he turned toward her. The love already burning there for his daughter blazed hotter when he looked at her, and Lila felt her own heart begin to soften.

JASON SURVIVED the girl's sleepover, took them to the Diner on the Dunes for breakfast the next morning, and watched the ROMEOs fall under their spell. Six grandpas seemed like a good number regardless that Katie had two real ones sitting there.

"I l-o-o-o-v-e Saturday mornings at the Diner," said Katie.

"You do?" asked Jason. "Are Saturday mornings a routine for you?" There was so much he was still learning about his daughter and her life.

"Yup. No school. And I get to be with my grand-pas at the same time—sometimes three of them. But Grandpa Tom mostly has to work at the restaurant."

Lila's father. "Speaking of the Lobster Pot," said Jason to his dad. "How about you and the family be my guests tonight."

Bart slapped the table. "Great idea! I'll be there, too. Ringside seat."

Sam rolled his eyes. "Maybe a quieter time…"

But Jason laughed. "Safety in numbers, Dad. What can Maggie do when the place is jam-packed? Throw a pot of chowder at me?"

"Better take an umbrella," said Bart with a wink. "You don't know my daughter!"

But it was Thea Cavelli, Maggie's sister, who greeted them that evening at the Lobster Pot. She led them to the main dining room and seated them. Although she sent a server to take their orders, she checked back with them from time to time.

"Maggie have the night off?" asked Jason on one of Thea's visits. "Or are you being punished by having to work the whole crowd by yourself?"

She chuckled, but gave him a steady look. "I can work twice this crowd with one hand behind my back. That is, if we had room for that many. But no, Maggie's supervising in the kitchen."

Bart approached from behind her and jumped into the conversation. "What Thea means is that Maggie's hiding in the kitchen."

"Dad! She is not."

He winked at the table. "Well, she won't be as soon as you go in there and tell her what I said." He pulled up a chair next to Sam.

"You're incorrigible!" Thea wended her way around the table until she reached Bart. Then she gave him a hug and a kiss on the cheek. "But I love you, anyway."

"I know." He sat back and preened.

Jason, Matt and Laura chuckled loudly. Sam grinned. And Jason realized how much the Quinn loved putting on a show. He loved playing to an audience. Jason sat back in his chair, totally relaxed, enjoying the company and appreciating his surroundings.

The Lobster Pot looked great. The nautical motif was perfect. So was the hometown atmosphere with the personalized artwork on the walls. Several posters caught his eye.

"We call that section the Sea View House display," said Thea, waving her arm to an arrangement of three large posters. All the couples in the pictures had lived at Sea View House this year. "Take a good look at the first one. You'll be most interested in that."

Jason glanced at it, then did a double take at the spitting-image caricatures of Matt and Laura. His brother wore an oversize tool belt—acknowledging Parker Plumbing and Hardware. One arm was raised high in the air, holding a huge wrench with Laura balanced on top. Matt's other hand was fisted at his hip and he was winking at the viewer. The caption read Matt Parker Loves His *Wench!*

"This is great stuff! Goofy but great," exclaimed Jason, feeling himself grin from ear to ear. He studied the other two posters and enjoyed the wordplay.

"Who did these?" Jason stared up at Thea. "They're perfect for the restaurant. For Pilgrim Cove. The wall is like a hometown diary—"

"That everybody reads!" said Matt.

Jason chuckled. "The love life in Pilgrim Cove is really an open book because everyone eats here sooner or later. After all, the Lobster Pot is the best seafood house in New England!"

"And my sister's an idiot," murmured Thea, patting Jason on the shoulder.

Jason heard her. "Come again?" he asked.

"Never mind," she replied. "My sister draws the posters—she's quite an artist—and I usually come up with the taglines. Boy, we surprised ourselves! We started creating the posters five or six years ago, so they're new to you. I'll tell her you like them. In the meantime, enjoy your meal, everybody. And, welcome home, Jason."

She disappeared in a hurry, but Jason felt he'd done a good night's work by showing up. He'd wear Maggie down the same way he was chipping away at Lila's defenses. Little by little.

He surveyed the restaurant, wondering where Lila was that evening, then dug into his lobster.

"COME ON, KATIE," said Lila. "Grandma will give us a meal at the restaurant. Strap yourself in." She waited while Katie complied before starting the car. She'd put in a long Saturday, and her hungry stomach was sending messages. Having a restaurant in the family was a fine idea.

"I had such a good day!" said Katie. "I had breakfast at the Diner this morning with Daddy, and now I'm having dinner with you at the Lobster Pot."

Lila chuckled. "Is it the food or the family that you like, Katie?"

"Both! It's fun to eat with everybody. Papa Bart

said I'm a member of the Clean Plate Club. Do you think I'm getting too fat, Mommy?"

Good God! Now what? Raising a healthy child kept a person on her toes. "Are you kidding? With all the running around you and Sara do? You're just perfect the way you are."

"Good. 'Cause I really like pancakes and bacon. And I really like clam chowder…and I'm really starv-ing right now!"

Whew! "And here we are, sweetie." Lila pulled into the first spot she found. A minute later she and Katie bypassed the outdoor eating area and pulled open the front door. Delicious aromas, clinking utensils, people chattering, staff waving at her. All so familiar. So good.

"Let's find Grandma," said Lila.

"But I don't want to eat in the kitchen. Too hot."

"We won't eat in the kitchen…but near the kitchen. If there's a table," said Lila, waving to the familiar staff while following Katie down the center corridor.

"Look, Mom! There's Daddy and Grandpa Sam and Uncle Matt and…and… Let's go!" She was off like a rocket. Lila hurried to keep up.

"We're here, everybody," sang out Katie as she headed toward Jason. "Hi, Daddy." She crawled onto his lap, kissed him, jumped down and then made her rounds while Lila greeted the table in general. Jason stood up and waved her over.

"Let's get a couple more chairs." He suited action to words and Lila found herself part of the Parker clan.

"Look! There's Grandma." Katie was off again. Lila also stood and walked toward her mother, as Maggie approached their table.

"How's the dinner, folks?"

Lila's eyes narrowed. Her mom's professional face was on. Then Bart spoke up. "I'm glad Thea was right after all. You're not hiding out in the kitchen."

If looks could kill, Bart would not be among the living. "Hide out? From what?" Maggie's voice squealed with incredulity.

Jason rose and extended his hand. "Hopefully, not from me. Hi, Maggie. Nice to see you again."

The woman whirled toward him. "The day I hide from a thoughtless boy…"

Lila stepped to the side and grasped the back of her chair. Now? Her hotheaded mother was going to make a scene now? In the middle of the crowded restaurant? "Oh, God," she murmured. "No."

She didn't know whether Jason heard her or not, but to her shock, Jason began to laugh. "Ah, Maggie. A boy? If only it were true!" He hoisted Katie in his arms. "Grandma says I'm a boy. So I'll have to play with my favorite girl. Who's that?"

"Me!"

Lila watched Katie giggle as Jason blew raspberries on her belly. She folded herself into her chair, relieved not to witness a Maggie theatrical. Jason glanced at her and winked, and Lila had to cover her own chuckles with her napkin. She'd have a heart-to-heart with her mom later. Although Maggie insisted on blaming Jason for everything that had happened in Lila's life, Jason was not responsible for controlling Maggie's behavior in public.

She tapped Jason's arm. "Thank you. I'll talk to her."

He leaned forward and whispered in her ear, "That's 'the boy's' job." Then he kissed the sensitive spot behind her lobe, and she shivered.

JASON LEANED against his rental car, waiting for the Saturday night crowd to disappear. He hadn't said a word to Lila about talking to Maggie that very evening when he'd escorted her and Katie to their vehicle almost two hours ago. He'd merely said good-night and that he'd see them the next day. Now only a few cars were left in the lot. He walked to the back door of the restaurant.

The outer storm door was wide open on this warm May evening, and through the screen door, Jason saw the late crew of kitchen help cleaning up. Thea and Maggie were both there, supervising. Their husbands, Charlie Cavelli and Tom Sullivan, were taking orders along with the employees.

No question that Lila came from a line of hardworking women. Women who took pleasure in their accomplishments. He watched how Thea stood, hands on her hips, surveying the area. She nodded, pointed, nodded again. Thumbs up!

He watched Maggie direct the staff to refill salt and pepper shakers, he watched how she sent them with clean tablecloths and silverware from the kitchen to the dining areas. He remembered the drill from years ago when the women were making their mark, and he and Lila would help out as needed. They'd set the tables in advance for the next day's customers. Man, as a kid, he was either in the plumbing and hardware store or in the restaurant. Family businesses always needed a few extra hands.

He sighed. That was then, and this was now. She'd throw him out if he offered to help—which would accomplish nothing. So he waited a bit more, until the hired employees approached the door. Jason stepped back, let them pass by, then knocked on the door and walked in.

"Good evening, everyone. Sorry to intrude."

"Jason!" said Tom Sullivan, walking over. "Car problems? Need a phone?"

Lila's dad was a cool guy. Had the reputation of being fair. Jason had been so focused on Lila's mother, he hadn't thought much about Tom Sullivan earlier. But now he changed his mind. Tom was a coach and now an athletic director for the high school. If anyone knew about fair play, he did.

"Thanks, Tom. My car's a rental, but nothing's wrong. I really came to see Maggie. But if you want to join us, that would be fine." He'd leave it to the Sullivans to figure it out. Maybe Maggie would prefer a private conversation.

Maggie walked toward the door. Toward Jason. "What are you doing here?" No small talk.

"Picking up where we left off." And sparing Lila from witnessing whatever happened next.

Maggie's eyes shone with the anticipation of an imminent conflict. The woman was not a wuss. But was she able to think beyond her own desires?

"Where we left off?" she asked. "Oh. That must be when I referred to you as 'a boy'?" She paused, looked at him. "I really hit a tender spot, didn't I?"

He said nothing yet, allowing her to vent. It took almost a full two minutes before he spoke.

"Maggie. I hear you. I understand how frustrated you feel."

"You—you understand nothing! You're not a mother. You're just a boy. A thoughtless boy with bad timing. And you call yourself a musician!"

"Look at me, Maggie!" It was a command. His voice whipped the words into the air, and the kitchen became silent. In the background, he knew that Charlie and Thea existed near the sinks. He knew that Tom stood beside his wife. But Jason kept his eyes on Maggie.

"Look at me," he said again, softer this time.

"What do you see, Maggie? Do I look like a boy? Sound like a boy?"

"A *man* would have come home!" Her voice shrilled, her eyes shone with tears.

"A man *did* come home," he replied, gently.

Silence filled the room. He'd made his point, and he left.

CHAPTER FOURTEEN

"HIS FEELINGS FOR YOU haven't changed, Lila. That was Jason's message to us last night," said Tom Sullivan. "Even Mom had to admit it—after he left, of course. Your aunt and uncle witnessed the whole shebang and they agree."

Her morning coffee forgotten, Lila—showered, dressed and ready for a busy Sunday morning at work—held the phone tightly against her ear and listened to her dad's recitation of the prior evening's events. Seemed that the Lobster Pot's kitchen had gotten hotter after closing.

"The big question is, princess," continued Tom slowly, "do you still love him, or have you cried too many tears because of him? You're the only one, sweetheart, who knows the answer to that question."

Lila respected her dad's insight into people, but she didn't need his confirmation about Jason's feelings toward her. Not when Jason treated her like fragile porcelain with his gentle kisses while his eyes shone hot with passion. He was showing her, not just telling her, that she controlled the pace, that what she wanted was more important than what he wanted. At least for now. She understood that. But…

"Oh, Daddy…you're right when you say it's a big question. Do I still love him?" she repeated. "When I see him, I want to run to him. My heart tells me, 'Go!' But then I remember…." She paused, her throat tightening, and had to regain control. "I remember the empty years, the loneliness…. I still don't know about or completely understand everything that happened to him. Although I do know that parts of his life were bad. Very bad. When I remind myself of that, my head tells me, 'Wait!' I don't know what I think.

"If only he'd kept in touch! If he'd visited once in a while…and shared with me…I'd wrap him in my arms right now and love him so hard, he'd never want to take off again. God, how I loved him! He's the only man I've ever… I've ever… Oh, you know what I mean!" She broke off *that* topic, but continued to let other words pour out.

Strange to be talking to her dad this way. Or not so strange. He'd always been a good listener, but it had been a long time since their last heart-to-heart. And now it felt so good to confide in someone she could trust to hear her out and not judge.

"What about Fielding?" asked Tom. "You never wanted to…ahh…you know what I mean!"

Lila remained silent.

"Then, sweetheart," said Tom, "in my opinion, Jason did you a favor by showing up now. But—that doesn't mean that I'm endorsing him as a son-in-law. Not yet or maybe not ever. That will be your call. And only yours."

Was she the luckiest girl to have Tom Sullivan as a father?

"And if you're not sure," Tom continued, "then do nothing. When in doubt, do nothing. This decision is too important. And this time, Lila, no one will be pushing you down the aisle."

"Mom sure won't!"

"You can count on that! Maggie May will be thinking before speaking…for a while at least." His chuckle came through the line. "But your granddad might start hinting. The Quinn's not above a little manipulation."

"You don't say!" Lila began to laugh.

"That's my girl," said Tom. "Jason's not going anywhere, and you're not going anywhere. If he's the right guy for you…you'll know. I love you, princess. Remember that. You and Katie come first."

"I know," she whispered. "And I love you, Dad. Thanks."

She replaced the phone gently, enjoying the unfamiliar serenity that filled her. A pleasant change. A needed change. For her own sake. Not for her mother. Not for her daughter. Not for her granddad. Not for Jason, either. But for herself. She needed a peaceful mind in order to move forward on her own terms.

She'd start by learning more about Jason's missing years.

ALTHOUGH JASON DROVE to the high school on Tuesday morning, ready to interact with the senior class, most of his thoughts centered on Lila. Would she show up? And if she did, would she understand or be totally disgusted with him? There was a part of him that didn't want her to know how low he'd fallen. Another part of him, however, knew relationships had to be based on truth.

He'd worked so hard to forgive himself for what had happened to Jared, to forgive himself despite his mother's accusations, which still rang in his ears, and despite his dad's inability to set his mother straight. And then he'd had to forgive himself for being weak. For reaching for the bottle to deaden the pain. Something he'd never done in the past.

He'd put all his feelings in a song called *Forgive Me,* and yesterday his dad and brother had voted for it as the first cut on his demo. Yesterday was one of the best days he'd had in too long. A full day of... male bonding! He smiled at the memory. They'd all had the same goal, but it was not a quiet day. Each one had sat at the keyboard, wanting to learn Jason's music. And each one had had opinions. Jason had even brought out the synthesizer, and Matt had had a ball with it. His nephew Brian had shown up after his morning baseball game—with his flute and trumpet—just in case the men needed some help. Jason knew Matt and Sam would join him again many times until they were satisfied with his selections. Never again would he be cut off from his own family.

But he was greedy! He wanted more. He wanted a life with Lila. A Lila who would drop her defenses and begin to trust him again. If he remained patient—maybe, just maybe—he'd wake up and see her face first thing in the morning for the rest of their days. She had no idea how difficult it was to kiss her good-night on Bay Road each evening before he returned to Sea View House. She had no idea how many miles of jogging he'd accumulated on Pilgrim Beach after he got home.

He turned into the school's large circular driveway and immediately saw the wrecked car in the grassy middle island, its nose folded in upon itself accordion style. The huge sign hanging from it said Drinking and Driving? Call a Friend.

Jason pulled into one of the few empty visitors' spots, his eyes narrowing as he looked at the familiar red-brick building with the big double doors. A lifetime had passed since he'd last walked through them.

Five minutes later, Rachel Goodman-Levine greeted him in the main office and led him to her own, all the while warmly thanking him for participating in the safety program.

"The bad news is that the other speaker had to cancel," she explained. "The good news is that you're here. So, Jason, it's your show. You can have as much time as you need. The sound system is on, we've got the special CD you wanted, and the twins are prepared." She was ticking each item on her fingertips as she spoke.

"The girls are great," he replied, "at least they were at our rehearsal yesterday."

"Not to worry. They'll come through for you."

"Shoot! Rachel. In the two years I've been doing these programs, improvisation has become my middle name. Something always seems to go wrong or differently than planned at the last minute when I visit the schools! At the very least, I can simply tell my story. The room is always quiet, so I guess the kids are listening. They know the subject's important. At least, I hope that's true."

She smiled. "Could it possibly be that you know how to tell a story and people believe you? You feel things deeply, Jason, and it comes across."

"Just listen to the shrink!"

"No, Jason. Listen to the songs!" She winked and said, "I bought the CD." Then she glanced at her watch. "Let's go. The kids should be filing in."

The program was set for ten o'clock. At ten minutes after the hour, Rachel began introducing him. From his seat onstage, Jason looked out at the sea of faces—young, excited, eager. Energy filled the big room.

As he scanned the audience, however, he focused

on the back of the room seeking one special person. She wasn't there. Lila hadn't shown up, and disappointment filled him.

DARN! IT WAS HARD ENOUGH leaving the office midmorning, and now she couldn't find a spot! Had the whole town come to the high school today? She saw Jason's rental. And Sam Parker's vehicle. By the time she found a place in the back lot and raced around to the front entrance, she had to pause to catch her breath, or she'd disturb the audience.

Finally, she made her way to the auditorium and carefully opened the door. Jason was walking toward the microphone center stage. A loden-green sport shirt with sleeves rolled to his elbows was tucked into a pair of belted tan chinos. His dark hair had grown so that she wanted to brush her fingers through it. He looked casually professional, confident and scrumptious enough to make her mouth water.

He reached the microphone and gazed out at the audience. She knew exactly when he spotted her. His head stilled, a grin appeared and he nodded.

"I'm glad you decided to come," he said, looking from Lila to the general audience. He waited a beat, then added, "You mean, like at all the other schools I visit, you didn't have a choice?"

Some of the students started to laugh as Lila slipped into an empty seat in the back row. She and the students knew the assembly was mandatory, but

Jason had already managed to get the group's attention as well as hers.

"My name is Jason Parker," he began, "and I graduated from this very high school nine years ago. In fact, so did my brother, Jared. Except he's not here to chat with you today."

Lila found herself at the edge of her seat, listening hard. How much was Jason going to tell about that night? And would he reveal more of himself?

"Jared and I were twins," he continued. "Do we have any sets of twins in the audience today?"

Lila, along with five hundred other people, looked around the room. Six youngsters stood up. Two boys, four girls, two of them Jane Fisher's daughters.

Jason kidded around with them for a minute, pretending not to know that twins could come in different genders. The audience was relaxed, and Jason looked like he was having a good time.

"We're going to narrow this down now," said Jason. "Will sister and brother teams remain in their seats and the identical twins come—on—down." His imitation of a game-show host was right on.

The Fisher girls were dressed exactly alike and sported identical hairstyles. From the distance, Lila couldn't tell Amy from April. She doubted anyone else in the audience could, either.

Jason soon proved her hypothesis. He had some fun with the group trying to tell the girls apart. No one could. Lila realized that his joking was simply his means of getting the youngsters totally focused on him and the girls on the stage. And he'd succeeded well.

"So, Amy and April, are you both going to the prom tomorrow night?"

They nodded.

"Are your dates in the audience?"

"Yes." A duet.

"Are they nice guys?"

Giggling, they said, "Yes," again.

Jason cocked his head. "Let's see about that." He asked the two boys to stand up. "The girls say you're a couple of good guys. I hope you can prove them right."

He paused and scanned every section of the auditorium. "We all know that the legal drinking age in this state is twenty-one, but let's get real—some of you won't observe the law." He eyed the two boys again. "My point is that good guys take responsibility. So who's the designated driver for the prom?"

Simultaneously, each boy pointed toward the other. "He is!"

Giggles sounded. Moans. Heads were shaking, including Jason's. "My, my, my," he said. "Pilgrim Cove, we have a problem!" After the boys sat down, Jason said, "Let's see what could happen on prom night to these two couples."

Suddenly, Lila's stomach felt jumpy. She

gripped her hands together, knowing Jason had finished with the fun stuff and was getting into the meat of the program. Prom night. And what could happen. Sharp memories stabbed her like heat lightning. Quick. Then gone. She wasn't sure she wanted to go back and relive the horror. She looked at Jason chatting with the kids as if it were the most natural thing in the world. And he put himself through his own memory album every time he did a presentation.

As Lila watched, the twins went to the side of the stage. A white curtain came down and the house lights darkened. A spotlight shone on the curtain. The two girls could be seen only in shadow behind it. They were seated facing the audience and the auditorium was silent.

Without warning, a loud roar of a car engine filled the room. Everybody jumped, including Lila. The twins began to scream. "Slow down! Watch the road! Watch!" Then shrieked, "Oh, my God. Omigod! No! We're...we're...! Ma-a-a! M-o-m!" A huge crash. The sound effects had Lila reeling. It happened too fast. Just like real life.

Silence. Darkness.

Then a spotlight shone on one twin standing at the side of the stage. Bandages covered her head. She limped forward holding on to a cane and looked at the audience.

A familiar melody filled the room and the in

jured girl began to sing in a clear soprano that conveyed the message:

> "Two girls glance in the mirror,
> One face is all they see,
> Along the shore, they are no more,
> What's left of them is me."

Lila felt tears run down her face, her heart in a million pieces for the boy twins she had known. She'd buried the details of this part of the story for so long that now she sobbed into her hands. It took a young girl with a voice. It took Jason's words. She reached for a tissue… Oh, God, there was more.

The spotlight had moved across stage to the second twin who sported identical injuries and bandages. She sang:

> "In my dreams, I'm in school again,
> With my sister by my side,
> In my dreams, we're just starting out…"

Her voice broke. She spoke to the audience: "We had everything ahead of us…plans for college…falling in love…a life…." She shook her head, then finished the verse.

"We had the whole world big and wide."

Lila's eyes never left the stage. She barely blinked.

The melody on the piano accompanied the sisters as they limped toward each other. When they met, they turned toward the audience and joined the piano to repeat the last verse. Now, they held hands, they looked at each other, and when the final notes lingered, they wrapped themselves in each other's arms and held on.

The piano faded, leaving a hushed silence. And then came the applause. Huge applause. The house lights were turned up, and once again Jason took the stage, keeping the girls at his side.

He looked at the audience. "Now, where are those supposedly 'good guys' accompanying these young ladies tomorrow night?"

The same two boys stood up.

"Who's the designated driver?" asked Jason, cupping his hand behind his ear.

"I am," said each one in a loud voice, both pointing at themselves this time.

Spontaneous applause mixed with laughter again before the boys sat down. The two girls left the stage and found their own seats.

Once more, Jason looked out at the audience. "My brother died on the night of our senior prom. He drank too much and crashed himself headlong into a telephone pole. And he was gone. Just like that!" He snapped his fingers. "Man, that ticked me off! Because I loved him, and I miss him every single day of my life."

"And so do I!" came a deep voice from across the room. Sam Parker stood up and walked down the aisle like a man on a mission.

"Dad!"

This part wasn't planned. Jason looked too surprised and more than a little concerned. Even Rachel stood up and watched Sam as he came forward. Again, Lila sat on the edge of her seat.

Sam climbed the steps to the stage and took the mike right out of Jason's hands. Jason's gaze rested on Lila, and he put his palms out in question. She shook her head.

"Most of you know me or have been in my store at one time or another," began the older man. "But in case your father shops somewhere else, my name is Sam Parker, and this is my son, Jason Parker. He worked hard for us today, and I'm very proud of him. So proud, in fact, that I think the sun came up this morning just to hear me crow!"

Sam? Was that the peaceful Sam Parker Lila knew so well? Or thought she knew. Man, the ROMEOs were going to be mad they missed this. Lila studied Jason's dad. He was just as comfortable in front of an audience as Jason. But who was his real target? The kids or his son? Then it clicked for Lila. The kids didn't care about Sam's pride in Jason. But Sam wanted Jason to know and had grabbed his chance. In public.

"Nine years ago," continued Sam, "Jared died

and Jason disappeared. Maybe you remember your parents talking about it. I lost two children that season. One on prom night, and one a month later. Can you imagine losing two children?

"We don't want to lose any more young ones in Pilgrim Cove, so here's what we'll do. You'll call me!" Sam walked up and down the stage looking at every part of the audience. "I'm the one to phone if you can't call your parents. Not only on prom night, but on any night that you're in trouble. I don't gossip, and I don't preach. But I'll be there for you because…well, the truth is, that I wasn't there for my son when he needed me. Somehow, this boy of mine—" he slapped Jason on the back "—figured all this out by himself. Pretty darn smart if you ask me. So, I'm crowing."

Jason faced the kids, leaned over and spoke into the mike. "And you thought *your* parents were the only ones in the world who enjoyed embarrassing their kids!"

The youngsters were eating it up, thought Lila. They were eavesdropping with Sam's permission on someone else's drama.

"I always leave time for questions," said Jason, reaching for the microphone. "And because my dad decided to join us, he'll take some, too."

Someone asked why he left town. Jason spoke about his own feelings of guilt, his mother's grief and reaction to seeing him. Sam spoke about being so concerned about his wife, he hadn't paid attention to his son. Where did he go? How had he lived? Jason told them the facts.

The next round of questions focused on music. Lila wasn't surprised. Teenagers and music went hand in hand. Was Luis Torres going to come to Pilgrim Cove? What was he like? Was Jason really going to live here and write more songs? Did he need any backup musicians? That question caused a stir! Lila imagined a dozen boy bands popping up all over the peninsula.

She admired how he fielded the questions without insulting anyone. No one, however, was asking the questions *she* wanted answered. It wasn't until she heard her name being called that she realized her own hand was in the air.

"When did you start drinking?"

"I'm glad you asked. I started…when the loneliness finally destroyed something inside me…my spirit… my soul. It took a couple of years after I left town."

She wasn't finished. "What made you stop?"

"I drank heavily for two years. And then early one morning, I woke up in my car in front of my apartment building, and I couldn't remember how I got there. Had I killed someone the night before? The thought scared me to sanity. That's when I knew I was an alcoholic. That's when I called for help. And when I sent you the message to forget about me."

HE KNEW HE'D SHOCKED HER when two minutes after answering her question, her seat was empty. She wasn't standing in the back of the room, she was simply gone. But he'd had to respond to her question honestly, the way he always did at these programs. At a social event, he could joke about his ginger ale if necessary. But not here. Not when the whole point was education, and when "been-there, done-that" testimonies had the most effect on youngsters.

Doubts riddled him. Would Lila ever learn to trust him again?

He thanked the audience, thanked the twins and walked with Rachel and Sam to the front exit of the building. At least *they* were ecstatic about the program.

"Looks like Jason's got a new partner," said Rachel, giving Sam a hug at the door. "And the kids have another adult they might trust."

"I'm game," replied Sam, his questioning glance, however, focusing on Jason.

"You were great, Pop! Just great. And we do not need to rehash that time in our lives over and over again between ourselves. Everything's square. I'm glad to be home."

Rachel left them with a last thanks, and the two men walked out into the morning sunshine. And there was Lila, standing next to Jason's car.

"She waited," whispered Jason. "I can't believe it."

"She's a smart girl, our Lila. And now I'll be going. Good luck, son."

His dad was sounding more like Bart every day, but Jason was too intent on Lila to mention it. He walked toward her, looked into her concerned blue eyes and brushed his finger across her brow. "There. That's better," he said when the furrow smoothed itself out. "My heart stopped when I couldn't find you."

"You knocked me on my keister, Jase. I needed to catch my breath."

"Sorry. But I can't help being glad you asked the question. I've already told you I don't drink hard liquor anymore. It's the truth. Period. And I wanted the kids to know it."

But she remained silent.

"Uh, you have anything else on your mind?" he said, encouraging her. "Any more questions?"

"Yes," she whispered. "But I'm afraid of the answer."

"Why?"

"Because too much is at stake. I'm willing to walk into the shallow end of the pool with you, Jason, and I know you want it, too—but if you lie to me, I won't swim to the deep end, and I really will never forgive you."

Lie? She thought he'd lie to her? Disappointment surged through him like a wave flowing from head to toe, but he forced his voice to sound calm, with no inflection, no indication of his feelings.

"I've never lied to you, Lila, except for the original broken promise so many years ago. I've always been up-front, and I'm not changing my personality now." He waited a moment, then felt his heart soften because she looked worried again. If only she'd trust him, trust herself. "I don't lie, sweetheart, and I especially don't lie to the people I love."

She stepped back. Her eyes flashed and her hands fisted on her hips. "So are you telling me that when you're with Luis Torres and Mitch Berman and all those…those Hollywood stars at all those wild parties that go on out there, you've never had a drink with them? A beer? A vodka? Anything?"

"Oh, Lila! I'm just a lowly hardworking songwriter. I've never tipped a glass with anyone in Hollywood or anywhere else for the last four years. And I don't intend to."

Her eyes were clear. Sparkling now. She gave him a quick kiss on the mouth. "Good. I believe you."

He licked his lips. "You're not worried anymore?"

"Should I be?" she countered.

"Actually, no. I'm a recovering alcoholic, Lila," he said softly. "My experience scared me, and I checked myself into a clinic. That was my low point.

I learned that sometimes you have to reach bottom before you can get to the top. Now I abstain from all forms of alcohol. I'm afraid to take a chance."

The smile she gave him reached her eyes. "Good choice. I'd be scared, too, if I didn't know how I'd gotten home."

She was so cool about the question that had concerned him most. He didn't understand why. "So, you don't have a problem with this? You believe me?"

"No problem. And, yes, I believe you."

She hadn't hesitated, but he still must have looked confused because she reached up and gently cupped his face with her hands. "You really haven't changed, Jason. You always shouldered more responsibility than was expected. You always seemed older than your years. Older than Jared, too. You've probably had awful dreams about what *could* have happened during the night you can't remember. So of course, you're abstaining. It's so—you!" She brushed a kiss across his mouth.

If he weren't kissing her delicious mouth, he would have wept with relief. She believed him and believed *in* him. He'd thank her later, but right now he'd rather make love to her somewhere other than a school parking lot!

"How about some lunch at Sea View House?" he whispered as he trailed a series of kisses toward her ear.

Her delight at the suggestion sent his spirits soaring.

"Granddad's watching the office," she said. "Let's go."

HE'D WAITED TO MAKE LOVE with her for so long, he could wait a little longer. That's what Jason told himself as he produced a couple of tuna sandwiches and brought them outside to the back porch. On the way to Sea View House, Lila's stomach had rumbled loudly, causing them both to laugh, and their tension had dissolved for the moment. Now Lila poured them both some iced tea. A breeze blew off the Atlantic, but the sun managed to warm the air enough for them to enjoy an alfresco meal.

"I've rarely been back here," said Lila as she gazed out at the ocean.

"Back here as in on the porch? Or back here as in Sea View House itself?" asked Jason, interested in how she'd coped with all the reminders of their youth.

"Sea View House. After you left, I didn't want to come here," she replied. "It was our place. Remember?"

"Sure, I do. Convenient, you having access to Bart's keys."

She shook her head. "I'm sort of ashamed of that now, but at seventeen you do all kinds of stuff."

"At any age, you rationalize all kinds of stuff to be with the person you love."

Her head jerked up and she stared at him. "Like uprooting yourself three thousand miles against your agent's advice?" she asked softly.

He smiled. "Exactly. Except I see it more like re-planting those roots, Lila."

She studied him carefully for a moment, took a sip of her tea and then replied, "Before those roots take firm hold, Jason, I'd really like to hear about the whole time you were away. The missing years."

Could this day get any better? It was the first time she'd asked him about his past in a supportive way, because she really wanted to know, because she cared. "I'll do better than that, sweetheart, I'll show you. Come on inside."

He brought her to the living room, sat her on the couch and gave her the first of his five binders. He knelt in front of her to give her a guided tour. "This one's got the early days in it," he said as he turned the pages. "Songs about leaving home, about trains and planes and 'Running away—to work in a kitchen for cash-only pay.'"

He shot her a glance. Her bottom lip was caught between her teeth, but she kept turning the pages.

"There's one about gambling on the riverboat," Jason continued. "I dealt cards. I'd go down to the lounge and play the piano. Here's one about being 'on my own and almost grown.' About being lost and 'woven in the shadows of other people's lives.' I started playing in clubs, writing and drinking. I wrote about everything—about children playing, about working people and homeless people—but you were always in my mind. In my dreams.

"You might think that no one would care about street people, but Phil Collins had—" He stopped midsentence. A drop of water had fallen to the page, then another drop splashed, this one landing on his finger. He tilted his head back and saw a river of tears flow down Lila's face. Then she started to sob.

"I can't bear it," she whispered. "I can't bear it that you went through all of this. So alone."

She shifted the book to the sofa and reached toward him. "You were just a boy…with no one. Anything could have happened to you." She stroked his cheek. "And the songs—the songs are who you really are. They're what's in your heart. This is the person I remember. Sweet and kind. And smart and strong. And caring about others." Her arms twined tightly around his neck, and his heart overflowed with love for her.

He levered them both up and held her close in his arms, nuzzled her. "You were with me every night," he whispered, "but this is better than any dream."

He captured her lips. She opened to him and he explored her mouth, their tongues in duet with each other. He wanted to inhale her, all of her. Closer and closer. He kissed the spot behind her ear and felt her shiver. Oh…he remembered…when Lila shivered…

"Your call, sweetie," he gasped, his reaction to

her now obvious to them both. "Before I forget my own promise to go slowly. Yes or no?"

She pulled off her blouse in one quick motion. "Does that answer your question?"

SHE LET HER BLOUSE REMAIN on the living room floor. Shoes lay in the hall. By the time they reached the master bedroom, Lila had left a trail of clothing behind her. And so had Jason.

She tingled everywhere, and he hadn't really touched her yet…except for those kisses. And holding her hand. And telling her how absolutely beautiful she was.

But he was wrong. It was he who looked like a Greek god of old. "Wait, wait," she said when they reached the bed. "I want to look at you. I want to see…"

And she saw shoulders broader than she remembered. She stroked them. Chest tapering down to a narrow waist with abs that rippled. Her fingers followed the center path. Arms with muscles firmly developed, and, goodness…he was taller. No high-heeled shoes on her feet now. Barefoot to barefoot, they faced each other. Now, she stroked his face and felt the slight roughness of incipient whiskers. No more bare areas.

She stared at him inch by inch, and her body temp ricocheted off the charts. "My God, Jase," she whispered, brushing her hand across his chest again, loving how the rough texture of the curling hair felt against her fingertips. "You're so different. You're… you're…so big…."

"And getting bigger by the second…." he replied, his voice hoarse.

Oh! He was right. She grinned up at him. "Let's see if you remember…"

And then he caught her up, lifted her high, and they fell on the bed together, Lila nestled in his arms. Lila, in another world. Jason's world.

"I've waited nine years for this, love," Jason gasped. "I can't wait a minute longer."

She rolled toward him. "You don't have to." And they flew. Hard. Hot. Fast. Done!

They stared at each other, eyes wide. "What was that?" Lila panted, her voice squeaky.

When Jason laughed, happiness resonated in his tone. "That was, shall we say, blowing the froth off the beer…or taking the edge off the appetite…or playing a short prelude to a symphony…."

"Enough! Enough explanations! I get the point."

He became quiet. Very quiet. "Do you, Lila? Do you understand the real point?"

Serious and intent when he spoke, his question crashed against her heart. She felt her lips tremble as she replied. "Of course, I understand, Jason. But I need to take it slowly for a while. One day at a time."

"Slowly? All right, sweetheart. We can do that.

We can start again—slowly." He hoisted himself to one elbow and looked down at her on the bed. "But I want to see your beautiful body, these beautiful breasts…." He stroked them as he spoke, brushing across one nipple, then the other.

She knew he was misunderstanding her on purpose, but didn't care as she lost herself in his actions and started quivering inside.

"And don't forget my beautiful stretch marks while you're at it," she joked between gasps. The stirrings inside her intensified and began twirling like a growing tornado.

"Lila, honey, those stretch marks are the most beautiful part of all," he said, "at least, to me."

At those words she fell totally in love with him all over again. Without reservation.

CHAPTER FIFTEEN

BART QUINN would have celebrated his granddaughter's wedding with as much hoopla as she wanted. Tom and Maggie would have gone along, too. But Lila preferred an intimate party at Sea View House. After a nine year interlude, neither she nor Jason wanted to wait.

Bart's thoughts drifted from Lila to his daughter. Maggie had only needed one look at Lila's and Jason's happy faces and interlocked hands at the Lobster Pot on the night of the school safety program to ask, "When's the wedding?"

Jason had met Maggie's gaze straight on. "As soon as your daughter says yes."

He'd pivoted toward Lila, his expression so hopeful and eager. And Lila had given him his answer before he'd even asked.

Bart Quinn had witnessed the whole thing. Including the kiss that followed. He grinned at the memory. There should have been fireworks.

So here he was on the last Saturday evening in June, standing in the living room of the Captain's

Quarters, a glass of single-malt scotch in his hand. Intimate was a relative term, he mused. In this case, a lot of relatives. Plus lifelong friends. He glanced at the assortment of ROMEOs, every one of them taking as much pleasure in this union as he did. He shook his head. Where does a man get friends like that?

He had new friends, too. The young couples were as loyal to the town as the retired old men. And as loyal to Sea View House as Bart was. He truly had a wonderful life in Pilgrim Cove.

"Attention, everyone. Attention!" Bart took himself and his scotch to the center of the room. "We've raised a glass to the bride and groom, and we've toasted little Katie who is, as she says, 'happy, happy, happy.'

"And now a salute to the spirit of Sea View House, a place where hearts can heal, a place where love can be found, where love can grow."

The guests nodded, smiled and sipped.

"Hear, hear!" called out Daniel Stone, a Harvard law professor who'd come to town looking for peace and quiet and had found Shelley Anderson and two kids instead.

"To Sea View House!" said Matt Parker, his free hand intertwined with Laura's.

"To romance!" Rachel Goodman's eyes were on her husband, Jack Levine.

"To life! *L'chayim!*" Lou Goodman's addition boomed across the room.

Lila walked up to Bart then, so beautiful in her simple wedding dress, the least fancy of all the brides who'd come before. But that's what she'd wanted. Classic straight lines and a short veil. "The vows are the important part," she'd said. And here she was, ready to speak her own heart.

"I propose a toast to Sea View House," she said, "and to Bartholomew Quinn." She lifted her glass to the room. "In this house, anything can happen to anyone at any time at all." She twirled toward Bart. "Even to you, Granddad!"

"To me?" She'd caught him by surprise. A rare event, indeed.

"And why not? You're a handsome devil, you are, boyo," she teased, imitating his Irish brogue. "And single, to boot! Why, Granddad, you're a great catch!" Lila raised her glass high. "To Bartholomew Quinn. Long may he reign, prosper and fill Sea View House with worthy tenants."

She kissed him on the cheek and whispered, "I love you, Granddad. Thank you, thank you, so very much."

He blinked hard. "Saints above!" he blustered. "You're still my lassie."

"Always," she replied.

But she twirled away to her Jason, which was as it should be, he thought. Each couple, each family. Together. So many links among those in the room.

Sam Parker came over, his hand outstretched, his eyes shining. "There's nothing more for me to wish for, my friend," he said, shaking Bart's hand. "Every dream has come true. And you did it, Bart. When I wanted to leave well enough alone with these two, you dove right in."

Bart patted his stomach. "It's the instinct, Sam. You should know that everybody's got a talent. Mine's matchmaking! But I don't say it out loud—bad luck, you know."

"Well, thank God for…" Sam paused. "Listen to the music," he said. "Jason's added a new verse to the story."

The entire room became quiet. Only Jason's true tenor rang through:

"She stands beside the water's edge,
Eyes burn with unshed tears,
A pledge of old,
Her hand I hold,
Love shining through the years."

Bart blinked and looked slowly around the room. He was surrounded by miracles, gifts he'd learned never to take for granted. Family. Friends. And Pilgrim Cove, the town he'd loved since boyhood and continued to love.

More miracles were bound to happen here at any time. He rubbed his hands together in anticipation. Why, his phone might ring tomorrow with someone needing a special place! And the Quinn would be on the job. Yes, indeed. He certainly would.

HARLEQUIN®

AMERICAN *Romance*®

The McCabes of Texas are back!

Watch for three new books
by bestselling author
Cathy Gillen Thacker

The McCabes: Next Generation

THE ULTIMATE TEXAS BACHELOR

(HAR# 1080)
On sale August 2005

After his made-for-TV romance goes bust, Brad McCabe
hightails it back home to Laramie, Texas, and the Lazy M
Ranch. He's sworn off women—and the press. What he
doesn't know is that Lainey Carrington, a reporter posing
as a housekeeper, is waiting for him—and she's looking
for the "real" story on Brad!

And watch for:

SANTA'S TEXAS LULLABY (HAR# 1096)
On sale December 2005

A TEXAS WEDDING VOW (HAR# 1112)
On sale April 2006

HARLEQUIN®

AMERICAN *Romance*®

is happy to bring you
a new 3-book series by

Dianne Castell

Forty & Fabulous

Here are three very funny books
about three women who have grown up
together in Whistler's Bend, Montana.
These friends are turning forty and are
struggling to deal with it. But who said
you can't be forty and fabulous?

A FABULOUS WIFE
(#1077, August 2005)

A FABULOUS HUSBAND
(#1088, October 2005)

A FABULOUS WEDDING
(#1095, December 2005)

Available wherever Harlequin books are sold.

HARFF0705

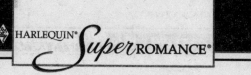

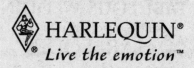

ANOTHER WOMAN'S SON

by Anna Adams

Harlequin Superromance #1294

The truth should set you free.
Sometimes it just tightens the trap.

Three months ago Isabel Barker's life came crashing down after her husband confessed he loved another woman—Isabel's sister—and that they'd had a son together. No one else, including her sister's husband, Ben, knows the truth about the baby. When her sister and her husband are killed, Tony is left with Ben, and Isabel wonders whether she should tell the truth. She knows Ben will never forgive her if her honesty costs him his son.

Available in August 2005
wherever Harlequin books are sold.

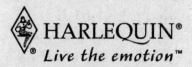

HARLEQUIN®
Live the emotion™

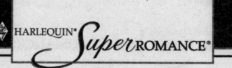

HARLEQUIN *Super*ROMANCE®

HOMETOWN
★ U.S.A. ★

DEAR CORDELIA
by Pamela Ford

Harlequin Superromance #1291

"Dear Cordelia" is Liza Dunnigan's ticket out of the food section. If she can score an interview with the reclusive columnist, she'll land an investigative reporter job and change her boring, predictable life. She just has to get past Cordelia's publicist, Jack Graham, hiding her true intentions to get what she needs. But Jack is hiding something, too....

Available in August 2005
wherever Harlequin books are sold.

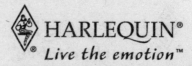

HARLEQUIN®
Live the emotion™